THE CONFESSION

M. A. HUNTER

Boldwood

First published in Great Britain in 2025 by Boldwood Books Ltd.

Copyright © M. A. Hunter, 2025

Cover Design by Lisa Horton

Cover Images: Shutterstock

A CIP catalogue record for this book is available from the British Library.

Paperback ISBN 978-1-83561-752-6

Large Print ISBN 978-1-83561-751-9

Hardback ISBN 978-1-83561-750-2

Trade Paperback ISBN 978-1-80625-723-2

Ebook ISBN 978-1-83561-753-3

Kindle ISBN 978-1-83561-754-0

Audio CD ISBN 978-1-83561-745-8

MP3 CD ISBN 978-1-83561-746-5

Digital audio download ISBN 978-1-83561-747-2

This book is printed on certified sustainable paper. Boldwood Books is dedicated to putting sustainability at the heart of our business. For more information please visit https://www.boldwoodbooks.com/about-us/sustainability/

Boldwood Books Ltd, 23 Bowerdean Street, London, SW6 3TN

www.boldwoodbooks.com

Dedicated to all the staff in the Coronary Care Unit (CCU) at Southampton General Hospital.

1

THURSDAY

The court is so quiet that all I can hear is my racing heart. We've waited three days for the panel of five to deliberate and reach consensus, but Damian has been waiting seven years for justice to finally be delivered. I dare not glance over at him behind the large wall of glass, because if I see his reaction to bad news, I won't be able to stop myself from breaking down.

It's going to be okay. It's plain as day that he didn't kill Rodrigo.

The five judges at the front of the court are the most senior in the UK, and their only job is to ensure the criminal justice system is working correctly. Yet I can't escape the uneasy feeling in the pit of my stomach. That the panel is made up of four men in their late sixties and early seventies – plus one token woman who is the oldest of the lot – doesn't fill me with confidence. In a country as diverse as ours, how are there no persons of colour qualified to hear appeals such as Damian's? And I don't believe a single one of them knows what it's like for two men to be so in love that murder is the least likely outcome.

The senior judge shuffles the papers before him, before clearing his throat. The clerk asks Damian to stand, and I hear his seat creak as he complies. I hold my breath and cross the fingers on both hands, sending all the positive thoughts I can muster to Damian.

'Having considered the judgements of the lower courts, and the new evidence introduced at this late stage, it is the judgement of this court that Mr Damian Johnson's conviction for the unlawful killing of Mr Rodrigo Johnson should be immediately overturned.'

My head snaps around to the dock and I see the look of shock and relief on Damian's face. There is a small cheer from the handful of friends who've been here with Damian since the case started two weeks ago. But then I also hear the cries of anguish reverberating from the opposite side of the viewing gallery where Rodrigo's brother and sister, and the team of detectives who promised them justice, are seated. As relieved as I am for Damian, I can't begin to understand how double-edged the verdict is for them. It's almost eight years since Rodrigo was snatched away from them, and yet all today proves is that the person who ended his life is still at large; still breathing the same air as them. I want to offer them words of condolence, but they've already made their views of me and my work abundantly clear.

I look back over to Damian, who mouths his thanks, before burying his head in his hands. For him, the verdict is also bitter-sweet. Tonight, he will be able to sleep in his own bed for the first time in nearly a decade, but I'd bet he'd give it all up for one more moment with Rodrigo.

The senior judge concludes his judgement, citing the reasons they don't believe statutory and case law were properly followed previously, and even though he specifically cites the report I provided to the court, I'm not here for plaudits or acclaim. The clerk invites everyone to stand while the five pensioners in red robes shuffle back to the small room behind the court, and the clamour inside rises. Over my shoulder someone – I think it's Rodrigo's sister – is wailing. Damian's barrister and solicitor are hugging and patting one another on the back, while the prosecuting barrister congratulates them before beating a hasty retreat.

I remain seated, taking it all in. I glance over to the dock again where I can see Damian is talking to his mum through the panel. She can barely stand, so bad is her arthritis, but I can see the tears of joy streaming down her face. When she first approached me earlier this year, begging me to look into her son's case, I was instantly drawn in by her passionate assertion that he couldn't have inflicted the severe and sustained beating that ended Rodrigo's life. I've met enough parents who swear blind that their child is innocent, but it was her description of the actions of the investigative team that piqued my interest. She looks over and offers a little wave and I reciprocate.

'She's done it again!' barrister Robert Timmons-Drake's voice booms, and I see the man in black heading towards me. He pulls off the white wig and slaps it against his hand, a huge smile breaking across his face. 'I was just saying to Eddie that as soon as I heard you were involved, I just knew we were going to win. This makes it ten in a row, doesn't it?'

I notice Damian's solicitor, Eddie Douglas, skulking away, an unlit cigarette already between his dry lips. I didn't expect him to show any gratitude, as had he done his job properly in the first place, Damian would have walked free a lot sooner. Why he stuck with Eddie as his solicitor for all this time is beyond me, as I can think of dozens of better-qualified solicitors who would have stepped into the breach.

'How you worked out that the barman was lying about what time Damian left the club that night is beyond me,' Timmons-Drake continues.

'We all have tells when we're being deceitful,' I say, underplaying just how well my mind is somehow able to cut through most people's bullshit. 'It was just fortunate that his statement was video recorded by the police. I don't think I'd have so easily spotted the dishonesty otherwise.'

'Well, we are truly indebted to you. Are you coming out to celebrate?'

I look at my watch and shake my head.

'It's a little early, isn't it?'

'You know what they say: it's always five o'clock somewhere. Come on, you've earned it. And in fact, I will make sure you don't have to pay for a drink all night. It's the least we can do for the woman of the hour.'

Whilst Damian's acquittal is cause for celebration after all he's been put through, any joy is tainted with the fact that Rodrigo is still dead. I look back over at Rodrigo's sister, who is being comforted by one of the detectives.

'We'll be in The Seven Stars in Holborn when you're ready to join us,' Robert continues, now heading over to the dock to presumably advise Damian about his next steps and to get him processed out.

I collect my handbag, and pull out my phone, immediately seeing a missed call from my business partner, Sasha. She knew I was going to be here all morning and that my phone would be on silent, but she hasn't left a message. I'll call her back when I eventually get outside, though I'd prefer to wait for the throng of gathered journalists to unblock the main entrance to the courthouse.

I stand and turn to head out, when a portly man with a shaved head and grey handlebar moustache steps out and blocks my way.

'I really don't know how you can sleep at night, knowing you've colluded to set a convicted killer free.'

I try to sidestep him, but he mirrors my move.

'If you don't mind, Detective Roach, I have places to be.'

'I imagine you'll be heading to The Seven Stars with the rest of your cronies, whilst an innocent man's family drown their sorrows at home.'

I grind my teeth, determined not to let him get to me.

'You still can't see that there were two victims in this case: Rodrigo Johnson, who was beaten to death in the safety of his own home, and his husband, who you pinned all your best hopes on for a quick conviction.'

He scoffs.

'You're so quick to forget that your pal Damian twice put the victim in hospital in the months prior to his passing. Leopards don't change their spots, Miss Veritas.'

According to Damian, it was Rodrigo who instigated the two fights he's alluding to, but both had been in counselling to overcome their anger management issues. Damian never denied their dark history, but it was his word against that of Rodrigo's disapproving family.

'Remind me, Detective Roach, did you ever consider any other suspects in your investigation? Oh, no, that's right, you decided Damian was guilty from the first moment you met him.'

He scoffs again.

'You know as well as I do that ninety-nine times out of a hundred, the victim's spouse or partner is the most likely perpetrator of a murder.'

'Exactly! But what happens in the 1 per cent of cases where that isn't true?'

'You need to check your attitude, love.'

'I need to check my attitude? What about yours? You found a grief-stricken, homosexual person of colour who didn't meet your narrow parameters of *normal*, and you targeted him for a quick resolution, rather than focusing on finding out the truth.'

'Don't bring this down to race and sexuality; it had nothing to do with that! He has a history of drug taking and alcoholism and on the night in question he was seen snorting coke off one of the toilet cisterns in the club. Rodrigo was also heard arguing with someone in their flat less than an hour before he died.'

'But we now know that Damian was still in the club when Rodrigo was attacked. Had you and your team investigated properly, you would have discovered it was impossible for Damian to be guilty.'

'Semantics! We both know there is nobody who can actually corroborate where Damian was at the time of the attack; we only know the barman lied about seeing Damian leave when he said he did. Of course, it would help if your client could recall any of what happened that night.'

I know he's just trying to get a rise out of me, because that's how men like him behave; putting others down in an effort to feel superior.

'Verdicts like today must be great for business, though, right?' he continues. 'I bet you love seeing your name up in lights as the hero who saved the day again. I bet you live for it. And all the better that your client is from a minority group as well.'

He doesn't wait for me to correct him, turning and shuffling, whistling under his breath. I'm about to hurry after him and give him a piece of my mind when I see Sasha is calling again.

'Yes,' I answer, struggling to keep my petulance in check.

'Hey, I thought it was good news today. You don't sound happy.'

I take a deep breath and slowly let it out.

'I'll be fine. And yes, Damian has been acquitted.'

'Oh, that's great news! It really is. You must be thrilled.'

I don't tell her how I'm really feeling.

'I thought it best to remind you that you have that interview with Peter Graves this afternoon, in case you were thinking of joining Damian to celebrate.'

I clamp my eyes shut in frustration. I had forgotten all about Graves's request to meet today.

'Oh, can't you do it instead?' I ask, adopting my child voice. 'Please? We both know you're the real brains of this little operation. It's you who should be in the spotlight, not me.'

'Ha, nice try, but flattery will get you nowhere. And this little operation will fold if we don't generate some more clients.'

'What are you talking about? We've got a huge list of referrals.'

'I'm talking about *paying* clients, Abbey. I admire your dedication to these pro bono crusades of yours, but they don't pay the rent. The interview will be featured in the weekend pullout of the newspaper. It's a great opportunity to showcase what you do and your incredible success rate. It's free advertising. You know I wouldn't ask unless I thought it was vital to our survival.'

I know she's right, and that is why we work so well together: she is the stick I need to stay on the straight and narrow. I confirm I'll return to the office to meet Graves, and as I exit the courtroom I see that Damian has just stepped out into the cold grey air. Cameras flash as he drops to his knees and breaks down in tears.

2

Despite promising Sasha I'd immediately return to the office, I don't rush, taking a more secluded route back, buying myself time to compose my thoughts. I pull my coat tight around my waist, but it does little to fend off the bitter wintry wind. London always feels so magical at this time of year, with shop windows bright and glittery, and the large neon decorations that hang above the road waiting to be lit.

My eyes are glued to the screen in my hand as I search for any information I can learn about Peter Graves before I encounter him. I can't say I recognise his name, but when I see he works for *The Daily Bore* newspaper, I'm not surprised his name and face don't ring any bells.

I must remember not to refer to it as The Daily Bore *when we meet.*

It's impossible to tell how tall he is from the professional headshot that accompanies his profile page on the newspaper website, but he has piercing blue eyes and a mop of chestnut-brown hair, and if I had to guess I'd say he's not long since graduated from journalism school or wherever he trained. I skim the highlights of the CV that accompanies the headshot. Born and raised in Dorset, he graduated from Cambridge and worked at several online periodicals before taking over the features section with his current employers. The titles of his last few pieces all read as barely human-interest stories. I've yet to meet him, but already I have a feeling of dread about our impending encounter.

I hear Sasha's voice reminding me I just need to focus on stories about the cases I've worked on. If he starts probing into my background, I simply need to tell him it's far less interesting than some of the miscarriages of justice I've helped overturn. I'm relieved the interview is taking place in our offices, rather than at his. My chest is already tightening, but at least I'll have my things around me. And if his questions become too much, I'll just have to tell him something urgent has come up and rearrange the interview for another day; I'll also insist it's via telephone rather than face to face.

I can see our offices up ahead. I say our offices, when really, it's just a two-bedroom flat above a fancy wine bar where we've installed desks instead of beds. I have the largest room to accommodate the library of criminology and behavioural science books I've accumulated over the years. Sasha always jokes that I should write my own book, sharing aspects of how I'm seemingly able to see the details that others miss, but I don't even know how to explain this *gift* bestowed upon me. It isn't something I can switch on at will; if I could, God knows my love life would be a lot more active than it is. In a courtroom I can instantly sense when someone is hiding the truth, but when a handsome man approaches in a bar or restaurant, it abandons me. This is why I've now entrusted Sasha with all decisions affecting potential relationships; I can't be trusted.

I cross the road and take a deep breath before punching in the code on the panel beside the door at the rear exit of the wine bar, quickly pulling the door closed behind me to shut out the icy air. I ascend the stairs slowly, but the soles of my boots slap the old wooden steps, making it sound as though I'm playing castanets.

Sasha emerges from the door at the top of the staircase and flaps her hand in an effort to hurry me up.

'He's here,' she says in a loud whisper.

She air kisses both my cheeks as she always does, her face covered in a skin-tone foundation and with bright red lipstick clinging to every pore of her smile. She's in a tight miniskirt and tights and a crop top despite the freezing temperatures outside, and it just serves to remind me of the ten-year age gap between us. Sasha is desperate to cling to her youth, whereas I've accepted I've crossed the threshold into my forties and refuse to make an effort for anyone but myself. Despite our contrasting styles, I know how reliant I am on Sasha's street smarts and organisational skills. She always makes sure I am where I should be at any time of day and is a firm hand when invoicing clients.

'You don't need to worry,' she says now. 'He told me his interview will be focused on the connections your mind makes when tackling a new case, and how this has made you a powerhouse in the appeals courts in recent years. I thought it might spur a few ideas for that book we're always talking about.'

I don't mention that my writing a book is very much her idea, rather than mine. I wouldn't know where to start such a mammoth challenge. Interpreting information is where I excel, not dispensing it.

'And Abbey? Remember to be polite. This is not one of those arsehole barristers claiming their years of practising law are more paramount than your ability to read between the lines.'

'It's a fluff piece,' I conclude, and she considers this for a moment.

'Yes, okay, it is a fluff piece, but what's wrong with that? You're big news right now, and we need to cash in on that while we can. You know what Andy Warhol said about the perilous nature of fame.'

Fame is the last thing I want. I know what it is to be in the public eye, with every aspect of my life under scrutiny, and it isn't something I ever want to experience again.

'Just show him that big, beautiful smile of yours and show him why you're my favourite person in the whole world. And in case you still need convincing, if all goes well, I promise to take you out to dinner tonight as a thank you. Anywhere you like; my treat.'

I raise a single eyebrow.

'All right,' she sighs, rolling her eyes, 'anywhere you like within a twenty-pound-a-head limit.'

I give her a tight squeeze and then open the creaky door and enter. The door to my office is ajar and I see the mop of brown hair in a pale grey blazer and trousers sitting with his back to me. I take a deep breath and head through, swinging off my bag and throwing it into its usual spot in the corner of the room, beneath the window.

'Peter,' I say with false enthusiasm, thrusting out my hand across the desk piled high with books and papers.

He stands, clutching the ginger tabby who moved in not long after we did. He shakes my hand and lowers the cat to the floor. He's much taller than I was expecting, a little over six feet at best guess. And he looks at least ten years older than the professional headshot I saw on my phone a moment ago, but maybe five or so years younger than me. He's certainly more handsome than I was expecting.

'Cute cat,' he says, retaking his seat across the desk from me. 'What's his name?'

'Freud,' I say, unravelling my scarf and hanging my coat on the back of my chair before sitting.

'No way,' he smiles in disbelief.

'Well, that's what we call him. He wandered in off the street one day and never left. We took him to the local vet who scanned the microchip in his neck, and it turned out he used to live here with the previous tenant. But she died, and so we unofficially adopted him.'

I don't add that I now consume a daily regimen of antihistamines to overcome my allergy.

'I wasn't sure what to do when he hopped up on my lap, but he seemed to settle quite quickly, so I let him stay there. I hoped you'd see it as a sign that I'm trustworthy; cats are good judges of character.'

I don't correct him, forcing a smile instead.

'Your secretary told me it would be okay to wait in here,' he says now, resting his hands on his knees in an open manner.

I resist the urge to laugh at his description of Sasha, though she'd get a kick out of it too.

'Sasha is my business partner, actually. If anything, she's the brains of the operation; keeps the accounts in the black. Would you like me to call her back in, so you can—'

'No, it's you I came to meet, Abbey. Congratulations on the Damian Johnson acquittal, by the way. I just heard through the grapevine that the verdict was quashed. You must be over the moon.'

I grind my teeth, thinking about Sasha's words, and trying to keep my responses short and polite.

'It's always good to see justice delivered.'

'And that's ten victories in the last three years, right? That's some record.'

Somehow, it never feels like a win.

'Had the police and CPS done their jobs properly in the first place, there'd be no wrong to correct,' I say sternly, meaning every word. 'Fixing the truth isn't winning.'

Graves considers my response and narrows his eyes.

'Damian Johnson told reporters outside the court that it's all down to you; he personally thanked the one person who believed him from the outset. That's a direct quote. It's you he's talking about there, isn't it?'

I picture Damian breaking down in front of the journalists, but I snuck out of the rear exit, so I didn't actually hear what he said when addressing them.

'I honestly don't know. If it is, then I can't shoulder all the responsibility. The whole defence team worked their socks off to secure his release.'

He considers this, before extracting a recording device and placing it on the desk between us.

'Do you mind? Recording the interview means I can spend my time focusing on your answers, rather than scribbling them down or trying to commit them to memory. I don't want you to think of this as an interview or a Q&A. I find the best interviews are conversational in nature and bring out more of the subject than just the standard, corporate responses. That's why I didn't send over my questions in advance as you requested.'

I don't think it was an unreasonable request, and had he sent them over I'd feel better prepared right now.

'Okay. Shall we begin?' I ask, gripping the arms of my desk chair.

'We already have,' he counters, smiling again.

I'm finding it impossible to read him. He looks so at ease, but I've known plenty of people – men and women – able to mask their true intentions better than the average person.

You're being paranoid, I tell myself.

Just because he's more handsome than I expected, and difficult to assess, doesn't mean he has malevolent plans.

'Why don't we start with something simple,' he continues. 'Something to break the ice and help settle you. Why don't you tell me how all of this began?'

'All of the appeals I've supported are public record. You can read what was used to support each appeal.'

'And I have. No, what my readers want to know is: who is Abbey Veritas really?'

'You want to know where and when I was born?'

'If you want to go that deep, then that's fine, but what I meant was how and why you decided to pursue criminology as a career, and how you wound up becoming an expert in wrongful conviction cases.'

'I don't know what to say... I suppose I've always had an interest in trying to understand how others think, and why they choose certain courses of action over others.'

'Can you give me any early examples of where you did this?'

For the briefest moment I picture Faye with her blonde ponytail running off in tears, but I quickly force the memory away.

'I'm sorry, what was the question?' I ask, dragging myself back to the present.

'I asked whether you have any early examples of reading others. What I'm asking is: was this something you were able to do in school, or did it develop later than that?'

I puff out my cheeks.

'I've never really thought about when it started. It's been there for as long as I can remember, though I suppose I didn't realise how unique it was until I was studying psychology at college and was able to see patterns in behaviour quicker than my peers.'

'What was that like?'

'College?'

'Sure.'

I remember having to reinvent myself and how I embellished my history, making it fit the character my new friends expected me to be. But I don't want to share any of this. Sasha promised it would be less personal and purely focused on our recent cases.

It suddenly feels too warm in the office, and I stand, crossing to and opening the window a fraction, welcoming the icy breeze cooling my chest.

'Hey, Abbey, can I make a suggestion? I'm sensing you're maybe not feeling particularly comfortable, and the last thing I want is for you to clam up. I've found subjects are usually less guarded and it can be easier to generate conversation once the blood is pumping. Why don't we go for a walk somewhere less stuffy?'

The whole point of conducting the interview in my office was so I'd feel safe, but it isn't helping like I thought it would.

'I promise that not everything we discuss will wind up in the article, and I will share the draft with you before it goes to print. Maybe I can buy us a coffee somewhere. What do you say?'

I can't think of a reasonable excuse to say no, so I reluctantly agree, grabbing my coat and scarf and following him out.

3

The streets are getting busier as the throng of office workers in nearby buildings hunt for lunch. I skipped breakfast this morning as I had no appetite; my nerves about the verdict taking over. But even now, I have no desire to eat. Leaving the courtroom and returning for this interview is like I leapt out of the frying pan into the fire.

I know these roads like the back of my hand, but Graves hasn't told me where he wants to walk to, and it isn't immediately clear which of us is in charge of the route.

'Have you worked in this area for long?' he asks as we meander along, the clouds creating a dull grey backdrop to our journey.

'A few years, yes,' I reply.

'And before you were here, where were you?'

'Why is that relevant?'

'It isn't necessarily; I was just attempting to break the ice.' He stops, and turns to face me. 'I'm sensing resistance at the moment, and I want to try and ease any concern you might have. This isn't a witch-hunt. There's genuine public interest in you, and I just want to show your human side.'

'If you're looking to interview a colourful character, then I think you should go back and talk to Sasha. There really isn't anything interesting about me.'

'I beg to differ, Abbey. There is a place and a time for self-deprecation, but not when your name is being mentioned by every legitimate source of news.'

'I'm really nothing special.'

'I beg to differ,' he says so quickly that it's almost like he knew how I would respond. 'I tell you what, can we do an experiment?'

'What kind of experiment?'

He raises a finger and asks me to wait, before darting into a small newsagent's, with a torn canopy over the narrow door. I wrap my arms around myself. The temperature has definitely dropped from earlier, and I don't know how long I can stay out here before my teeth start chattering. Graves returns a moment later with a huge beaming smile, tucking something into his pocket.

'Shall we go and get a cup of something hot to fight off this chill?'

He doesn't wait for me to respond, marching off, leaving me to hurry after him.

'Where are we going?' I ask, almost breathless.

'I know a place that produces the best hot chocolate in London. It's a bit off the beaten track, but those of us who know about it know better than to reveal its secret. I'll take you there, but you must swear not to tell anyone about it.'

I roll my eyes, but follow along, relieved that he's stopped asking questions for now. There's an assured confidence to him that I'm finding particularly unsettling. Instinct tells me he knows more than he's letting on, and I don't like it when that happens.

He turns sharply, cutting in to one of London's many smaller cemeteries. The large black gates are open, but the sense of death waiting nearby is impossible to ignore. The tarmac path is dark and twisty, and it feels dangerous following this virtual stranger into a dark hole where overgrown evergreen trees and bushes almost seem to block out the sky.

'I'm not sure I want...' I begin to say, but he quickly cuts me off.

'I promise you; it is the best hot chocolate you'll ever taste. Trust me.'

Against my better judgement, I do follow, quickly firing off a message to Sasha to let her know where I am. I'm half-expecting her to reply and tell me to get out of there, but instead she tells me how pleased she is that the interview is going well.

Sasha, ever the optimist!

The path bends around and through the trees, until I can no longer see the bustling street behind me. And then suddenly the trees part, and I see we're in an enclosed space. Identical weathered gravestones line the grass area in the centre of the enclosure, each lined up carefully in a grid-like formation. There are seven rows and seven columns, with seven benches evenly placed around the tarmac path, forming a perfect circle around the site. You'd never know we are a stone's throw away from one of the busiest cities in the world.

He directs me to a bench, and heads off in the direction of a small hut between two of the benches across the grass from us. There is an older woman on one of the benches beside the hut, wrapped in a thick woollen overcoat and with a headscarf pulled tightly around her white, straw-like hair. At first glance, she looks like a statue, but then I see the paper cup in her hand slowly rise to her mouth and then return to her lap.

What are we doing here? He said he wanted to put me at ease, but has brought me somewhere so morbid, and I feel like we are intruding on others' grief.

Graves returns and offers me one of the paper cups he's holding, before joining me on the bench.

'Give this a try,' he says, 'and tell me if you've tasted better.'

'Won't it be too hot?'

He shakes his head.

'It is the perfect temperature; that's one of the reasons it tastes so good. The guy who runs the shack melts the chocolate in warm milk, but keeps the temperature at an even fifty degrees. Go ahead, try it.'

I remove the plastic lid and the sweet smell of chocolate hits me in an instant, reminding me of Easter. I delicately place my lips on the edge of the cup and take a sip, quickly followed by a larger swallow. It is just like drinking liquid chocolate, and I'm not going to lie, it is the best hot chocolate I've ever tasted.

'See, I told you it's the best.'

'How did you find this place?'

'Do you know what this place is?'

'A graveyard.'

He smiles.

'Yes, it is, but it's more than that. This cemetery is home to the forty-nine nurses who died when their hospital was struck by a German V2 rocket during the Blitz in 1941. Their bodies were recovered from the wreckage, and a local philanthropist donated this section of land for them to be buried in as a mark of respect. I did a piece on it eighteen months ago, which I'm guessing you didn't read.'

He chuckles.

'I'm sorry, I don't tend to read newspapers any more.'

'To be sustainable?'

'No, to avoid the agendas of those who own them and their views of what is newsworthy.'

I instantly hear Sasha's voice in my head: *Remember to be polite.* 'Touché.'

He smiles again, but then frowns as he remembers something. He places his cup on the floor before reaching into his pocket and extracts a packet of playing cards. He removes the plastic seal and then shuffles them.

'Are you going to do a magic trick?' I ask.

'No, you are.' He pulls out three cards at random, and fans them out, but doesn't show me what they are. 'In my hand, I am holding a king of hearts, a seven of diamonds, and a three of spades.'

'And?'

'And, am I telling the truth?'

'I've no idea.'

He stares at me in silence.

'I'm not a mind reader if that's what you think.'

He continues to stare at me, the cards just below his eyeline.

'Humour me. Based on our brief conversation this morning, and what I'm guessing you probably googled about me before we met, am I telling the truth about the cards I'm holding?'

I look into his eyes, searching for the usual tics and tells I've seen from so many others. I don't understand what he's trying to prove one way or another. It's a fifty-fifty decision, and I could get lucky with my guess, but if I do that doesn't prove anything. Or if I guess wrong, does that suddenly mean I'm fallible? I can't tell in whose best interests this game is.

'Do you want me to be right?'

He considers this for a moment.

'I want you to tell me the truth.'

'Fine. You're lying about the cards.' He's about to speak again, when a second thought strikes me. 'Actually, I do believe you're holding a king, a seven, and a three, but not in the suits you said.'

A large smile breaks across his face as he flips the cards around to face me, and I see a king of spades, a seven of hearts and a three of diamonds.

'That is incredible,' he says. 'How did you know?'

I don't know which of us is more shocked. I genuinely have no explanation for how I sensed he was telling a half-truth.

'The best lies are partially based on fact. You were trying to suppress your natural tells, so you gave me half the information, but manipulated the rest.'

'Is that how you knew the bartender was lying about the time Damian Johnson left the nightclub?'

'I guess.'

'And what motivated you to help Damian?'

'It was a no-brainer; anybody in my position would have done the same to help someone in need.'

'I think you give humanity too much credit.' He pauses. 'Is your desire for justice driven by what happened to your sister thirty years ago?'

Again, an image of Faye with her blonde ponytail crashes into my mind, but this time it's not so easy to disregard.

'I thought you wanted to know about the appeals I've supported.'

'Absolutely, but I want to get to the crux of what motivates you to take on these – often – helpless cases. You were the prosecution's star witness when Faye's killer was on trial, and I just wondered if that's where you got your taste for it.'

'I'm not here to talk about my sister.'

'But you've said before that she was your best friend, and that's what drove you to help the police secure the conviction of Terry Anderson.'

'I never gave permission for that story to be printed. I didn't know the guy I was talking to was a tabloid journalist posing as a student. And I didn't appreciate being front-page news.'

He tightens his lips and raises his hands in a passive gesture.

'Alas, there are some real snakes in this profession; you won't hear a word from me justifying that kind of behaviour. It's those kind of ambulance chasers that give the rest of us a bad name. Now, I've been very open with you about what we want to achieve through this article, and your sec— I mean your business partner was keen for us to meet and proceed.'

I don't want to cause a scene, but if he's planning to pursue this line of questioning, then I'm not going to hang around.

'I believe my readers will have nothing but sympathy for what you and your family had to endure, and my only reference to your sister's murder is to show just how far you've come; that trial and your role in it shaped your future, whether you realised it at the time or not.'

'I don't want people thinking I've benefited from my sister's death in some way. He took her from us, and not a day has gone by when I haven't thought about where she would be now or what she'd be doing if she hadn't been in those woods that day.'

'It would make a great angle for the feature: The criminologist who's never overcome losing her sister to a known sex offender and is now on a crusade to overturn miscarriages of justice.' He pauses momentarily. 'And I've no doubt there will be many of Terry Anderson's victims' families who will understand exactly how you feel. But including it helps give a voice to those who aren't in a position to talk about what he did.'

I can sense he doesn't necessarily believe what he is saying but is trying to butter me up nonetheless.

'Has the television production company contacted you to appear?' he asks next.

I frown at the question.

'What are you talking about?'

His cheeks redden instantly.

'Oh, shit, I assumed you knew.'

'Knew what exactly?'

'That Terry Anderson is appealing his conviction.'

My eyes widen. I had no idea and would have thought someone would have been in touch to notify me.

'On what grounds?' I just about manage to stammer.

'New evidence of some sort, I believe. One of the streaming services has offered him big money to allow them to film his campaign and hear from him directly.'

I had no idea Anderson was in talks about a documentary, and I can't understand who in their right mind would want to watch such a programme. I don't watch a lot of television, and I will never understand the general public's morbid fascination with such shows.

'I take it from the look of shock and anger they've not been in touch. Doesn't it bother you that he's attempting to profit from your sister's death?'

I picture Terry Anderson's mugshot that the police showed me all those years ago, and I feel my blood freezing over.

Graves moves closer, and places a comforting arm around my shoulders.

'Let me tell the story from your point of view. What Anderson did to Faye, how you saw him in the woods and were able to positively identify him, and ensure he was tried not just for Faye's murder, but those of his other six victims too. It would be a great side piece to how you've now helped the likes of Damian Johnson to receive justice.'

After that tabloid hack published his story about me, I vowed I would never use my sister's name to help me get ahead. I hate that the compensation I received from the newspaper is what paid off my student loan and helped Sasha and me set up the business.

'Don't let Anderson win,' Graves continues, but I shrug off his arm.

This was the exact reason I didn't want to be interviewed by *The Daily Bore*.

I march through the tunnel of evergreen, and out of the gothic gates, not even thinking about where I'm going. I eventually stop when I see The Seven Stars pub ahead, and deviate in through the door, ordering a large glass of Chablis. And I don't know if it's just my imagination, but I can't shake the sense that I'm being watched.

4

FRIDAY

The clomp-clomp-clomp of Sasha's clogs on the wooden staircase wakes me, though they seem louder than usual; almost as if she's slamming each foot down as she slowly ascends; like nails being hammered into a coffin.

I stir, only now realising I am slumped on my desk, with no memory of how I got here, nor how long I've been asleep. I instantly regret moving my head as a herd of tapdancing elephants perform an encore inside my skull. They're even louder than Sasha's stomps. Something is wet at the corner of my mouth, and I quickly wipe the drool away with the back of my hand, just as Sasha marches in.

'Morning,' she coos, as she passes the ajar door and heads through to her office space. 'I can't believe you beat me in this morning,' she calls out from the other room.

I scour the fog in my brain, but don't remember why I would have raced into the office this morning, and when I look down and see I'm still wearing yesterday's clothes I suddenly understand.

Memories of singing and dancing in The Seven Stars flash

through my mind's eye. I see my reflection in the large mirror behind the bar as I raise a large glass of wine in toast to myself. I see glimpses of Damian with his arm draped around my shoulders, insisting on buying my drinks for the rest of the night. Then a flash of us all downing shots of something transparent and wincing at the bitter aftertaste.

Whose idea was it to do shots?

I entered The Seven Stars with the intention of enjoying one glass of wine and then I'd planned to come back here and tell Sasha that the feature interview for *The Daily Bore* was now off, as Peter Graves asked too many personal questions. But then Damian spotted me at the bar and insisted I come over and celebrate with barrister Robert Timmons-Drake and his team. I initially resisted, but then he dragged me over, ordering me a second glass. It felt rude to say no, and then I don't know much about what happened after that.

'Tut-tut,' I hear Sasha say from the doorway. 'Do my eyes deceive me, or have you not been home yet?' She glides into the room and sits down across from me. 'I want all the details. Who is he? Was he any good in bed? Are you seeing him again?'

'What? No, I didn't...'

But I stop myself, now searching my memories for anything I might have missed. No, I definitely have no recollection of sleeping with anyone last night.

'Oh my God, was it Peter Graves? Did you let him interrogate you and then seduce him?'

'No,' I say, glaring at her.

She raises her hands into the air.

'No judgement here. He's handsome, and if I was your age, I definitely would have had a go.'

'Sasha,' I chastise under my breath.

'Sorry. Speaking of Peter Graves, how did the interview go?'

This doesn't feel like the right time to break the news. My head is spinning, and I suddenly feel very dehydrated. I could try and phone Graves later and see if I can salvage the article. Maybe if I give him clear instructions that I don't wish to discuss anything about my sister and Terry Anderson, then he'll know to stay well clear of the subject.

'Fine,' I lie, avoiding eye contact.

'Good. You look like you could do with a coffee, so whilst I go and make you one, why don't you freshen up? You probably have just enough time to go home and change before your first meeting if you want...'

I'm sure she wouldn't be suggesting I change unless I look a state, so I wait until she's headed to the waiting room, before I drag myself away from the desk and head into the bathroom we share, which is essentially a windowless box room with a shower, toilet and basin. I run the tap until it's warm, and then splash water on my face, before finally allowing my eyes to settle on my reflection. Maybe it's the lack of natural light, but my skin looks grey and stretched, like something out of a fifties horror movie. This is why I don't drink on a work night, if ever these days.

I splash more water on my face, and then take a slug of cold water from the tap, swilling it around and then spitting it out. The inside of my mouth tastes like stale coffee and cigarette smoke, and I would give anything for my toothbrush and a hot shower, but both will have to wait until later.

'You shouldn't do the crime if you can't do the time,' my dad said the first time he found me vomiting into the toilet after a night out with the girls. I was fifteen, and swore off alcohol with my first hangover, but like most adolescents, the promise didn't last.

He was right, of course, and surviving today will be my punishment for last night's ill choices.

I switch off the light as I leave the bathroom, but my eyes are instantly drawn to the open filing cabinet across the room. I can hear Sasha singing away to herself as the kettle boils in her office.

Did I leave the cabinet open? Is that why I came back here last night instead of returning home? Was I looking for something?

I approach the filing cabinet, hoping it will trigger another memory from last night and offer some kind of explanation as to what made me come here instead of catching a taxi home when I finally emerged from the pub. But I have no recollection of why I would have opened the filing cabinet.

I run my fingers across the plastic separators, again hoping that it might trigger something, and then I spot Damian Johnson's name, and realise his file is missing. I don't remember taking it to yesterday's acquittal but can't think of any reason why I would have wanted to read through it last night. I close the drawer of the cabinet and head to my desk, searching for the file. I check under each of the stacks of paperwork that need filing, and in each of my three desk drawers, but there's no sign of it.

I head out and knock on Sasha's door as the kettle reaches its crescendo and ask if she still needs the file.

'What file?'

'Damian Johnson's case file.'

'It should be in the usual folder on the network.'

'No, I mean the paper copy.'

She frowns.

'It's you who insists we keep a paper backup of everything. I only ever use the digital files.'

'So, you don't have the paper copy of Damian's file?'

'No, why would I?'

'Then where the hell is it?'

My mind is creating images of a masked figure following me back here and sneaking about inside whilst I was passed out behind the desk. But I can't imagine who would want to steal Damian's file, let alone why.

'I'm sure it will turn up,' Sasha says, shrugging. 'Have you checked your desk? It's probably there somewhere amongst all the other paperwork you're yet to file.'

Now isn't the time to get into our regular argument about my lack of organisation.

'Do you want me to print off another copy for the filing cabinet?' she offers, and I quickly nod, though it troubles me that it's missing.

I slide the drawer closed and return to my chair, grabbing what little makeup I can find in my handbag, and do my best to cover the cracks. Sasha returns a few minutes later, carrying a steaming mug of black coffee, and a packet of Jaffa Cakes.

'I know we said we'd save these for an emergency, but this feels like it might be the time to crack them open.'

She tears the cellophane and holds the packet out for me. I take one and consume it in two mouthfuls. The sweetness of the marmalade contrasts with the bitterness of the chocolate, but the combination is the first speck of light in the dark tunnel of my vision.

'Did you leave the filing cabinet unlocked last night?' I ask her once I've swallowed and the ache behind my eyes lifts slightly.

'No, I locked everything up when I left at six last night. I phoned you and you said you wouldn't be back, so I shut up shop and went home. What did bring you back here anyway?'

'I have no idea,' I answer honestly.

'Well, take a swig of coffee and then we can run through your diary for the rest of the week.'

I do as she instructs, wincing at the bitter aftertaste.

'These might help,' she says, sliding a foil packet of parac- etamol and a packet of gum across the desk. I pop out and swallow two of the pills with another swig of the coffee, before popping the gum into my mouth, chewing to release the spearmint flavour and take away the stale taste.

'With Damian's acquittal yesterday, you don't have any further open cases at the moment.'

'What are you talking about?' I ask, waving my hand towards the two stacks of paper on the corner of my desk.

'I meant *paying* cases.'

'Oh,' I mouth.

'I know you don't want to, but I really think it's time to ask whether any of the pro bono cases you're reviewing have any way of paying for your services.'

'The whole point of them being pro bono is that the service doesn't cost them anything.'

'I know that, of course I do, but *any* contribution would help.'

She's right, and I know she wouldn't be raising this topic if things weren't as desperate as they are, though I still think she's shielding me from the truth.

'I don't mind asking them to contribute,' Sasha says. 'If you don't feel comfortable about asking, I can do it instead—'

'No, it's fine,' I quickly say.

I love Sasha to bits, and I meant what I said when I told Graves that she is the keystone in this business, but I don't want her frightening away the clients who are in desperate need of our help. She can be aggressive when it comes to money, and the last thing we need is to earn a reputation for putting remuneration ahead of justice.

'I don't mind,' she persists.

'No, it's fine, Sasha. You have enough on your plate already. I'll make contact with a couple of the solicitors to see what I can get.'

'You should start with Eddie Douglas. I know we took on Damian's case on a pro bono basis, but I imagine Eddie is already planning a civil suit for wrongful arrest and detention. It wouldn't be unreasonable to ask for a cut of whatever he secures for Damian.'

I nod, and watch Sasha leave, praying the painkillers kick in sooner rather than later. The thought of going cap in hand to Damian's defence team fills me with dread; as does offering an olive branch to Peter Graves.

5

I use the Tube to make my way from Holborn to Ruislip but an hour spent on the Piccadilly line is the last thing my developing hangover needs. It smells like stale body odour and dead fish; almost as if the city's pollution problem is riding with us. I eventually find a seat once we've passed Earl's Court, but it's too warm and the motion of the carriage is making me feel nauseous. I wish I'd brought my headphones with me, as music would be a welcome distraction. All I have is my phone and my satchel, but staring at the screen will only make me feel worse.

It's a relief to escape the carriage at Ruislip Manor, and I follow the handful of passengers who are also disembarking up the stairs, through the barrier and out onto the main road. It's much cooler out here, and I can feel drops of rain in the icy wind, forcing me to pull my overcoat around me. It's almost ten o'clock, so the school run traffic has dispersed. I head south along Victoria Road, the small high street littered with local businesses: a couple of estate agents, several Turkish barbers, a chemist, a bakery and three pubs. The creeping sense of being watched returns, and I stop and spin full circle, looking for anybody out of place, but I can't see anyone giving me undue attention. I shudder and continue walking.

I eventually make it to the home of Woodley and Douglas solicitors, an enterprise that looks more like it houses funeral directors, with black signage and darkened windows. I head inside, but it's almost as cold as the outside. I keep my overcoat on, and cross to Kayla's desk to ask if Eddie is free for a five-minute chat. She's Eddie's sister, but is also responsible for the administration of three solicitors who work alongside Eddie and his business partner Jake Woodley.

'He's in a consultation at the moment,' Kayla says empathetically, 'but you're welcome to wait, and I might be able to squeeze you in before his next meeting.'

I smile and nod, claiming one of the seats beside the darkened windows in the makeshift waiting area. The shadow of the glass is welcome for my head, and I even close my eyes, whilst I try to internally rehearse what I'm going to say to Eddie when I see him. He's probably one of my least favourite solicitors to have worked with, so I'm less concerned about hurting his feelings. I know how slippery he seemed when we first met, never accepting accountability for failing to keep Damian out of prison. I know I should have tried to negotiate a fee when he first engaged me, but I don't do what I do for financial reward, though Sasha wishes I would be more selfish.

Eddie said he was working on a no-win-no-fee basis with Damian, who had been denied access to Rodrigo's estate following his conviction. And once I'd met Damian in prison I sensed that he was telling me the truth and it was no longer a question *if* I would help him. I couldn't be certain I would manage to get him free, nor how long it might take. The subject of remuneration never entered my head.

Now that Damian has been acquitted, and is free, I don't think it's unreasonable to ask for a little redress for all the time spent studying the evidence against him, reinterviewing witnesses, and reading the court transcripts. I wish Sasha had come with me this morning. She is so much better with these kinds of awkward conversations, but it's also time that I put on my big-girl pants and fight for my future; I can't keep relying on Sasha to keep our heads above water.

The bell on the door pings, as someone else enters the office.

'Abbey?'

My eyes snap open, and I'm shocked to see Damian looking down at me.

'I didn't realise you'd be joining us today,' he says. 'Eddie never mentioned it, but it's lovely to see you again.'

He waves over to Kayla, and then sits beside me.

'I know I told you last night at the pub, but I am eternally grateful for everything you did for me over the last few months. I was at my wits' end, and you pulled me back from the abyss.'

I'm thrown, and have totally lost my train of thought.

'You can go through, Mr Johnson,' Kayla announces.

'Great, thanks,' he replies, standing. 'Are you coming too, Abbey?'

Kayla said Eddie was in consultation, but if he's supposed to be meeting Damian, then it must relate to the case, so I also stand and follow him through to the back, and into Eddie's office. I shouldn't be surprised that Robert Timmons-Drake, Damian's barrister, is also in the room, though it is surprising that neither of them mentioned this morning's meeting when I saw them in The Seven Stars last night.

Eddie looks shell-shocked to see me alongside Damian, but I offer no explanation.

'You take the free chair,' Damian says. 'I'm happy to stand.'

I sit, and remove my overcoat, reaching into my bag and

extracting a notebook. I feel like a spy infiltrating a top meeting, but remain tight-lipped.

'Um, what are you doing here, Abbey?' Eddie eventually asks.

'Well, I presumed you were just finalising all the details following yesterday's success, um, and thought my insight would be valuable.'

'Actually, this has nothing to do with Damian's appeal, so I'm going to have to ask you to step outside.'

I try to keep my tone as even as possible, almost playful.

'Why? If you're not meeting to discuss Damian's appeal, why are the three of you here?'

I see Eddie and Robert exchange nervous glances, with Robert offering an almost imperceptible shake of his head.

'With all due respect, that's none of your business. Please, Abbey, just step out and I'll speak with you once we're finished here.'

'What's going on?' Damian now pipes up. 'I thought we were going to talk about my civil suit for damages. Is that not the case?'

I give Eddie a knowing look, but don't speak. He looks as though he's just swallowed a wasp.

'What we're here to discuss is no concern of Abbey's,' Robert speaks up, with a smile so false my stomach turns. 'In the interests of client confidentiality, Abbey, please do leave the room.'

Damian is looking over at me, unable to keep the confusion from his face.

'But Abbey was key to my release, why wouldn't she be part of the next stage?'

I'm about to tell him that his greedy legal team are trying to exclude me from any cut of damages, when Eddie crosses the room and places a hand on Damian's shoulder.

'Can you give us a couple of minutes?' he says rhetorically, leading Damian to the door, opening it, and then guiding him outside. 'I'll explain everything when we're done here.'

Damian still looks confused as the door is closed on him, and Eddie moves back behind his desk, squeezing his paunch into the chair.

'I don't understand what you're doing here,' he says, glaring in my direction, and I see Robert is now also leaning over me. It suddenly feels as though the room has shrunk; the sharks have come out of hiding.

'I'm here to ask for my cut,' I say simply, trying to channel Sasha as much as I can.

'You're not entitled to anything.'

I figured this would be his response, and I had prepared a response in the waiting room, but now my mind is blank.

'I've received no payment for my services,' I say sharply.

'You never requested payment,' Robert says factually.

'That's because you said Damian couldn't afford to pay me. Well, that situation is about to be reversed, and so, yes, I do think I'm entitled to payment.'

'You really should have negotiated that at the outset,' he replies, and I feel the heat rise to my cheeks.

'That's exactly what Robert and I did,' Eddie says smugly, but seems less confident when I give him a hard stare.

'Damian wouldn't be free now if it wasn't for what I found.'

'Well, I think you're exaggerating matters a tad.' Robert's tone is condescending, verging on rude. 'Sure, it helped Damian's case, but it was only one cog in a much larger machine.'

I should have brought Sasha with me. She wouldn't stand for such manipulation of the facts.

'That's bullshit!' I fire back, frustrated to lose my cool so quickly.

'You may have identified an inconsistency in the barman's

statement, but it required me to get him to admit as much on the stand. No mean feat.'

'You wouldn't have even known to do that if it wasn't for me, so don't belittle my involvement.'

Robert puts his hands together, pressing his index fingers to his lips, an action I've witnessed him perform in court to make it look as though he has thought long and hard about the gravitas of what he's about to say. It's a cheap lawyer trick.

'You're right that you definitely played an important part, and I've openly acknowledged that in my statements to the press. If anything, you should be thanking me for all the free publicity I've sent to your little business.'

I want to leap out of my chair and slap him hard across the face, but I'm better than that. I can see what he's trying to do – what they're both trying to do. I just need to take a breath and compose my thoughts.

'I can understand that you now realise the magnitude of Damian's situation,' Robert continues, his hands still pressed together, 'and you can probably estimate the redress he will receive. But he deserves every penny of that for the hardship *he* has suffered, don't you agree? He lost the love of his life, was wrongly charged and convicted, and his reputation was dragged through the mud. He's been vilified and victimised. He's grateful – we all are – that you found the key to his freedom, but it's beneath you to be scrabbling for any breadcrumbs that fall from the table. I really did think more of you, Abbey.'

I glance at Eddie, who looks relieved that Robert is taking the lead in belittling me.

'Wow,' I retort. 'Is that what years of legal study taught you? How to flex your muscles and decree lies as truth? You almost make it sound like God bestowing The Ten Commandments on

Moses. What do you do as a follow-up trick? Are you going to speak from a burning bush?'

I pause and see Robert's lips curl up at the sides ever so slightly.

'And I assume that neither you, nor Eddie here, will be receiving a portion of Damian's windfall?'

'We are in the employ of Damian Johnson, and will receive recompense for that, but you were never working for Damian; you were working for us, and you never discussed payment for your services when we engaged you. I can see this is distressing news for you, Abbey, but legally speaking, you don't have a leg to stand on.'

'That's as may be, but I bet if I called Damian back into the room and informed him what his cheapskate lawyers are trying to do, he'd think twice about continuing to employ you. Tell me, Eddie, has Damian actually instructed you to seek punitive damages on his behalf yet? Have you made him sign a contract? Because I think if I go and have a private word with him, I could convince him to seek alternative representation.'

Neither answers, and so I stand and move towards the closed doors.

'Wait,' Eddie calls out.

I remain facing the door, trying to hide my growing smile.

'We may be able to offer you a payment from any settlement we receive,' Eddie continues.

I take a deep breath and turn back to look at them, stony-faced.

'How much?'

'We can recoup your standard fees.'

I consider this, and whilst Sasha would be relieved to bring something in, I don't think she'd settle for their first offer.

'No, I'm sorry, that's no longer going to work for me. I think I'll just go and have a chat with Damian instead.'

'Okay, what is it you want?'

I hear Robert sigh to my left.

'I don't want a share of Damian's proceeds. As you said, he deserves every penny. Instead, I want a third of each of your shares. You employed me to work on Damian's case, and I see this as a three-way partnership. So, whatever the two of you have negotiated, I think it only fair to receive my share.'

Eddie's face is so red that it looks as though his head will explode.

'I'll expect you to email me a contract by close of play today, and if I don't receive it, I won't hesitate to speak with Damian and warn him away from you both. Understood?'

I don't wait for them to respond, turning on my heel and heading out of the door, linking my arm through Damian's.

'Wait, what's going on?' he asks, as I lead him back out to the waiting area.

'Your lawyers have more pressing matters to attend to this morning, and they've asked for you to return tomorrow instead. So, I'm going to take you for a cup of tea.'

I hear the rumble of Robert's voice chastising Eddie behind us, and I finally allow my pride to shine through my smile.

6

We find a small café a stone's throw from the Tube station, and Damian locates a table whilst I go to the counter and order drinks.

'Thank you,' Damian says, when I place the cups on the table between us.

I remove my overcoat and drape it over the back of my chair, before sitting.

'Is everything okay?' he asks, catching me off-guard. 'I sensed some tension back in Eddie's office.'

Part of me is pleased that he noticed, should I need to follow through with my threat and persuade him to instruct new counsel, but I don't want to add to his already full plate.

'No, everything is fine now. We were just ironing out a few creases. More importantly, how are you?'

He takes a sip of his tea, his eyes sinking beneath his frown.

'Honestly, this all feels like a dream I'm about to wake from. I keep waiting to hear the sound of my cell door being unlocked to wake me up to the reality that I'm still going to spend the rest of my life in prison.'

I reach across the table and give his hand a gentle squeeze.

'I promise this is not a dream, but I can appreciate it's a change that's going to take some time to get used to. Have Rodrigo's family made contact yet?'

He shakes his head sadly.

'When Rodrigo and I first got together, they were like a second family to me. His mum virtually adopted me and treated me like a son of her own. I never told them about the drunken fights he would start when he became overwhelmed with work. So, when it came out in the trial that he'd ended up in hospital on two occasions, they instantly assumed I was guilty. I know that detective was speaking to them regularly, telling them they'd found the right person and would get justice for Rodrigo. He poisoned them against me, and despite my protestations to the contrary, they've spent the last seven years believing they got justice. And now the stitches have been mercilessly torn.'

My heart aches for him.

'It's going to take some time, but I'm an optimist and I hope for both of your sakes they begin to come around. Hopefully, your acquittal encourages the Met to reopen the case and for fresh eyes to detect what really happened that night.'

'I don't know how to thank you for getting me out.'

'You don't need to. I'm just glad it was worth the effort.'

'Eddie reckons we can sue for millions, but I would swap it all to have Rodrigo back, even for a few seconds. That probably sounds stupid.'

In my head, the memory of Mum wailing as Faye's small coffin was lowered into the ground plays out.

'No, it doesn't sound stupid,' I say. 'I understand better than you know.'

* * *

The Tube ride back to the office is sombre, and I sit all the way, not even noticing as the carriage fills, and I'm back at Holborn before I know it.

Is your desire for justice driven by what happened to your sister thirty years ago?

Graves's question at the cemetery yesterday has stirred up memories I've long tried to suppress, but now every time I close my eyes, I can't help thinking about Faye and everything that happened in the build-up to that day. I suppose it is true that it has shaped the course of my life, but I've never really thought about it in that way. There must be a reason my brain works in the way that it does, like I was put here to help those who've been failed by the justice system in this country. It isn't heroic but serves a need that isn't otherwise being fulfilled.

These are the thoughts that follow me like a shadow as I walk slowly back to the office, the wind even more bitter than first thing. The joy I was feeling when I nonchalantly left Eddie's office has since passed. At least Sasha should be happy at the prospect of payment in the not-too-distant future, assuming Eddie and Robert don't try to double-cross me again.

Sasha leaps from behind her desk as I head inside my office and hang my coat on the stand behind the door.

'I've got news,' she says, almost bouncing into the room.

'So do I, but you go first.'

'We had a call while you were out. A new case for you to work your magic on.'

I think about the two pro bono cases I've barely started because I've been so focused on Damian's appeal.

'Seriously? It's so close to Christmas. I don't think I have capacity to start something new.'

'No, no, listen to me. This one should be your priority. The solicitor said he saw you talked about on the news last night and he believes you are the only person who can help his client.'

I head over and sit behind my desk, with Sasha settling in one of the chairs across from me. I unlock my computer and open my email account, searching for anything new from Eddie, but he hasn't responded yet.

'Who's the client?' I ask Sasha, opening a fresh Word document, ready to scribble notes, which is what I always do when considering new opportunities.

'To be honest, I don't know. He only gave sparse details. It's a murder appeal; maybe something like Damian's case. I'm really not sure though. He said it's sensitive, but he is utterly convinced that you will be able to help overturn the conviction.'

I can't understand why Sasha is so excited about a case with so few details. Usually, there is a spark of something that piques my interest, but so far she's not hooked me. When Eddie approached and told us how the police had homed in on Damian because of the homosexual, interracial marriage, I felt a yearning to help. It's probably why I never even contemplated seeking a cut of any subsequent civil suit.

'The solicitor said he would courier over the files for you to take a look at,' she continues. 'On the back of yesterday's success, and the feature in the weekend newspaper, another quick success would all but crown you the Queen of Appeals. It could be enough to secure funding for the next twelve to eighteen months.'

I fix her with a hard stare.

'What aren't you telling me?'

She smiles back at me, her eyes practically on stalks.

'He's offering a substantial fee if we agree to take it on.'

I sigh. Of course, money had to be behind her motivation for pushing this.

'You've already signed terms with him, haven't you?'

'No... Not exactly.'

'Sasha, please don't treat me like a child.'

She sits forward in her chair.

'Okay, okay, listen, I said we weren't taking on any new clients this month, but he said you would want to work on this case. He said he would pay an initial twenty thousand as a downpayment, just for you to look at the files. That's why he's sending them over as we speak. Twenty grand, Abbey! All you have to do is give them the once-over, and if you don't think it's worth pursuing, we walk away. Twenty thousand for a few days' work. It's a no-brainer.'

'And that's it? If I decide there are no grounds to continue, he still pays?'

'Yes. But, if you do decide that it's worth your time, the initial fee rises to one hundred thousand.'

That's the largest single fee we've been offered since starting this business. Given how dire our finances currently are, I can now understand her excitement, and why she's pushing so hard. What troubles me is if his client is so well-off, why would they seek us out, when they could afford the most prestigious law firms in the country?

'How did you get on with Damian's defence team?' Sasha asks next, and I refresh the internet page, but there's still no email from Eddie.

'Good, I think. You'd have been so proud of me.'

Her eyes widen.

'You managed to get him to cough up?'

'Well, not exactly. Damian is still as broke as he was when we took the case, but apparently Eddie and Robert are seeking compensation in a major civil suit.'

'Well, of course they are. They'd be mad not to.'

'Exactly! Anyway, Eddie and Robert refused to offer me a cut, until I gave them an ultimatum, and they should be sending over confirmation of our cut by close today.'

Sasha frowns.

'So, they're not paying us now?'

'No, but when the civil suit succeeds, we will receive a cut of it.'

She rolls her eyes, far less impressed than I thought she would be.

'And how long is that going to take?'

'I don't know, but Damian reckoned they're seeking millions, so it should be a big payday for us.'

She still doesn't look impressed.

'That's assuming they are successful. Civil suits for wrongful conviction can take years to go through, and then there are various appeal stages before a final figure is agreed. They might be seeking millions, but I'd be shocked if that's what they actually receive.'

I feel crushed by her denouement.

'I know it's not an instant payday,' I say, uncertain why I need to embellish what felt like a real achievement this morning, 'but it could be huge when it happens.'

'*If* it happens,' she corrects. 'And I don't mean to be brutal, but we may not even have a business by then.'

When she said we were struggling, I didn't think we were in danger of actually folding.

The intercom buzzer breaks my train of thought, and Sasha leaves the room to answer it. She waves me over, saying the courier has the files, and we both head down, Sasha's clogs once again echoing off the narrow staircase. A man in bike leathers and a helmet confirms our identities, and unstraps two large plastic boxes from the back of his motorbike, and passes one to each of us. They weigh significantly more than I'm expecting, and it's a struggle for both of us to carry them back up to my office.

'I'll make us a drink while you start looking at the detail,' Sasha offers, the spring back in her step. 'The fee has already hit our account,' she calls out, 'so we can be certain the second offer is real. Imagine what it will do for us to be linked to a case as newsworthy as this. Once the documentary hits the screens, it will be all anyone is talking about.'

The breath catches in my throat.

I hear Graves's voice in my head: *One of the streaming services has offered him big money to allow them to film his campaign and hear from him directly.*

No, it can't be.

He has been locked away for too long to have the kind of money Sasha is talking about. And he'd know better than to seek my help after what he did.

My fingers tremble as I lift the lid of the first box and freeze when I see Terry Anderson's mugshot staring back at me.

7

I slowly lift the A4-sized image out of the box, desperately hoping it's just my imagination playing tricks on me. I blink several times, turning the image over, but the face of the monster who has haunted my darkest nights continues to stare back at me.

The image slips from my hands and floats back into the box, but I don't move; frozen in time as the door I've kept barricaded for so many years in my mind is ripped open. And then I'm no longer in my office above the wine bar.

I see the confusion in my dad's eyes change to anger and then panic.

What do you mean you don't know where Faye is? his voice echoes.

When I couldn't find her in the playground, I naively assumed she'd gone home. And for the briefest of moments, I felt hatred towards her, because in returning home without her, I'd inadvertently hung myself with my own noose.

My parents locked me inside the house whilst they both went out to scour the park and local roads for Faye. I couldn't understand why they were panicking so much. She was thirteen and old enough to find her own way home. I remember thinking she must have gone to one of her friends' houses and would eventually saunter in, smirking with the trouble she'd caused me. I'd probably be grounded indefinitely, and that would put an end to my relationship with John-Paul. Anger towards Faye flowed through my veins like venom; it never crossed my mind that I wouldn't see her again.

It wasn't until they returned without her that I began to understand the gravity of the situation. I can still feel Dad's tight grip on my arms as he interrogated me.

Where was she when you last saw her? What were you doing?

I kept thinking it was just a nightmare I would wake from. I remember pinching thick chunks of skin on my arms and legs, trying to break the spell. But nothing would work.

I was fifteen years old, and instead of tucking in to the traditional Sunday roast – my favourite – I was being interviewed by the uniformed police officers now taking up residence in my home.

I was forced to go out with them, as the evening sky darkened.

Show us where you last saw her. Can you think of anywhere she might be hiding? Did you see any unfamiliar faces in the park at the time? Was anybody watching you?

I step forward and slam the lid down on the box file, hoping that out of sight will mean out of mind, but the door in my head remains wide open, the flood of memories painfully over-whelming.

Are you sure this is the man you saw in the woods? Did you see him abduct Faye?

I crash to the floor, unable to breathe.

I hear my mother wailing as the family liaison officer broke the news. I was sitting at the top of the stairs and although I didn't hear the words I knew what she'd told them both. I stomped up to Faye's room, and fell onto her bed, pressing my face into her pillow, breathing in her scent, as warm tears flowed.

Please, I'll do anything if you bring her back, I prayed. *Take me instead. She doesn't deserve to die. Bring her back and take me.*

My prayers went unanswered, and despite their protestations to the contrary, I knew my parents both blamed me for Faye's murder. Everything changed in that one brief second. Had I made a different decision – the *right* decision – everything would have been different. Faye would still be alive; Mum and Dad wouldn't have divorced; Dad wouldn't have drunk himself into an early grave; and Mum wouldn't have taken an overdose on the day I graduated university.

'Oh my God, are you okay?' I barely hear Sasha say, as she places the two steaming mugs on top of the filing cabinet and hurries to where I remain in a frozen heap on the floor. 'What happened? Do you feel faint?'

I don't respond; I *can't* respond.

She takes my hand in hers, and presses a warm palm against my forehead.

'Did you bash your head? Do you feel sick? Have you eaten today? Should I phone for an ambulance?'

'No,' I manage to mouth, but it takes all of my effort.

She hurries back out of the room and returns with the half-eaten packet of Jaffa Cakes, and forces one between my dry lips. I reluctantly bite down, the feeling slowly returning to my legs, as my cheeks flush with embarrassment. Sasha helps me to my feet and into my desk chair, before fetching the mugs and placing them in front of me.

'Are you sure you're all right? What happened?'

I should tell her the truth; she's probably the one person I trust more than anyone in the world, but I'm not ready to admit what I did.

'Drink some tea,' she suggests, pulling one of the other chairs closer and sitting down, our knees inches apart.

I don't move, desperately trying to will the memories back into Pandora's box, before I taint the future with my curse.

'If you're sickening with something, maybe you should go home. Shall I order you an Uber?'

The thought of being trapped alone in my small flat with the weight of these memories has me quickly shaking my head. I need to pull myself together before Sasha starts picking at the scab and I tell her everything.

'No, I'm fine,' I say, only now realising how much I'm panting.

She raises her eyebrows.

'Well, we both know that isn't true. You might be the human lie detector, but you have a terrible poker face.' She smiles warmly. 'This is what happens when you burn the candle at both ends. How drunk did you get last night?'

Ordinarily, I'd be mortified to have Sasha thinking I'd lost control, but this is a better alternative than the truth, so I simply shrug, looking away.

She gently rubs my shoulder.

'I have some painkillers if your head is hurting,' she says.

The truth is, my head feels as though it might explode, but painkillers won't touch it.

'No, I'm okay,' I say.

'What you need is a distraction,' she says, dragging one of the boxes across the desk and starting to lift the lid, but my hand lashes out and slams down on it.

'No,' I say firmly. 'Not this case. Phone the solicitor and tell him we can't help.'

Her brow creases.

'What? I don't understand. I thought we'd agreed you'd review them before making a decision. He's already paid us to look at them, so the least we can do is give them the once-over. It's the decent thing to do.'

'No,' I say again, louder this time.

She crosses her arms.

'Tell me why.'

'Because the man those files describe is a monster. I recognise his name, and he's a child killer.'

'Yes, I know that, and he was convicted for multiple crimes, but he's adamant that he didn't kill one of them.'

'It doesn't matter. He's a monster and he's where he should be.'

'But if he didn't kill the child as he claims, that means the real killer is still out there. Think about that child's family: don't they deserve to know the truth about how their daughter or sibling died?'

I sigh heavily.

'Have you thought that he could be lying? You said yourself there's a production company talking to him about a documentary series. This claim is probably just a money-spinner his lawyer has dreamed up to cash in on the trend for true-crime fans.'

'You've made that judgement very quickly. Without even looking at the files. That must be a record for you.'

I don't know how to convince her without revealing *I'm* the reason he's behind bars.

'I'm sorry, Sasha, I know you just want to balance the books, but we shouldn't be anywhere near this one. We don't want to be associated with a man like Terry Anderson.'

'You're the one who always says the innocent deserve true

justice.'

'He got the justice he deserved. He's a child rapist and killer. Have you read up on him? He is one of this country's worst serial killers, and now he's trying to profit from the misery and grief he caused so many. It's wrong, Sasha.'

'So, you're happy that this child's real killer could still be out there somewhere? What if they've killed again because the police stopped searching for them? What if he's still out there killing innocent children? Don't you think we have a duty to find out who they are and bring them to justice?'

I hear the detective's voice echoing in the back of my mind again: *Are you sure this is the man you saw in the woods? Did you see him abduct Faye?*

'Well,' Sasha says, standing and lifting the lid off the box, 'if you won't look at the files, I will.'

She pulls out Anderson's mugshot, and I see her nose wrinkle.

'Admittedly, he's a creepy-looking man, but we shouldn't judge a book by its cover.'

She places the image on the desk, and I lock eyes with him again. To be honest, if I didn't know what he'd done in the past, I wouldn't sense creepiness in that face. He looks like any normal man. If I'd seen this face outside of school, I'd have dismissed it as just another dad collecting his child. That's what I find so frightening about him; hiding in plain sight.

Sasha gasps suddenly, and I look up to see her holding one of the files open. Her eyes dart from the file to me.

'It's you,' she whispers. 'You were the eyewitness who placed Anderson at the scene of the crime. It was your testimony that secured his conviction.'

I snatch the file away from her in shock. My name was supposed to be redacted in all the court documents. I skim the page and see my name in black and white.

This isn't right. I was never supposed to be named.

Sasha looks devastated that I didn't tell her, but I need her to understand the truth.

'It was my sister he murdered,' I say evenly.

But even as I utter the words, I can't ignore the voice niggling at the back of my mind: what if he wasn't the one who killed her?

8

I'm in tears as I reveal the abridged version of the last day I saw my sister. Over time, my imagination has inevitably embellished certain details and redacted others, but it doesn't make it any less painful to relive. Sasha listens intently; her skin drained of colour by the time I finish.

'It was thirty years ago,' I conclude, blowing my nose. 'If he was only guilty of killing Faye, he would probably be out by now. But she was one of seven that he either abducted, tortured, or murdered. I don't understand why any production company would go anywhere near him.'

'Are you kidding me? One of the most horrifying monsters to have existed in this country claiming innocence is the kind of gold these streaming services *love*. I imagine they'll spend the first episode building up his notoriety; the background to the cases against him. They'll paint him with the same brush as the Yorkshire Ripper and Ian Brady. Then they'll put him on camera so the audience can look into the eyes of this sadist, and they'll end the episode with the cliffhanger of him claiming to be guilty of all but one of his convictions. It'll be the number one watched episode within days. It'll be advertised through word-of-mouth, conversations around the coffee machine in offices, and streamed on handheld devices as normal people travel to and from work.'

I'm wide-eyed at Sasha's conjecture. If she's right, then my sister's name is going to be everywhere, and with her unable to respond, all eyes will be on me. And as the key witness in his trial, my version of events will be scrutinised.

I need to warn John-Paul.

'Are you okay?' Sasha asks.

It's a question I don't know how to begin answering. My fight-or-flight response is telling me to book a flight to the middle of nowhere, and not return until the dust has settled. But my bank balance is almost as dry as the company's.

The intercom sounds, and Sasha says she will see who it is, whilst I try to push Terry Anderson from my mind. There is a part of me that wanted to lay *everything* on the table for Sasha, but I fear how she would react to the truth.

Two pairs of feet are clomping up the stairs. I don't recall Sasha mentioning any appointments today, but then I'm not even sure if it's still morning or now late in the afternoon.

I use a fresh tissue to dry my eyes, and seeing yesterday's clothes makes me want to just go home, shower and change. I don't think my mind can cope with any more plates to spin.

Sasha gently knocks on my open door.

'Abbey, this is Rhys Morgan... he's Terry Anderson's solicitor.'

I slowly focus my gaze on the man in the grey suit standing just behind her. His dark hair is unbrushed, his glasses square in shape, with thick stubble covering his cheeks and chin. He's stick thin and several inches taller than Sasha, and not the face of someone I'd expect to see representing Anderson.

'I'm sorry to come over unannounced,' he says, with a noticeable Welsh accent, 'but I can see you've received the files I sent, and I'm keen to talk to you about my client's wishes, and time is not on our side.'

I wish Sasha hadn't allowed him to come upstairs. She should have checked with me first, especially after what we just discussed. I feel emotionally drained and I don't even have the energy to tell him to leave. I look to Sasha for help, but she's already turning to leave.

Rhys doesn't wait to be invited in, placing his tan leather briefcase on one of the chairs, and sitting down in the other. I see now he isn't wearing a tie, and that his trousers are a darker shade of grey to his blazer. The top two buttons of his plain white shirt are unfastened. I wonder how much Anderson has offered to pay him to torment me like this.

'Have you looked at the documents I sent over?' he asks, and I feel as though he is studying my reaction to the question.

I'm suddenly conscious of how much Rhys may know of the truth. Presumably, Anderson has spun him a line about what happened that day, but he may know more than I've shared with Sasha, and I don't want her overhearing whatever he's come here to say. I push my chair back from the desk, and make my way slowly to my door, without answering his question.

'Sasha, would you be able to grab me a wrap and an energy drink, please?'

She appears from her office and looks at her watch.

'Sure, no worries. Anything specific you want?'

Just for you not to overhear anything that's said, I think, but don't say.

'No, you know what I like.'

She mouths, 'Are you okay?'

I want to cry, but simply nod instead, and force a thin smile, and watch as she heads out and clomps down the stairs. I wait until I hear the front door click shut, before closing the door to my office and returning to my chair.

'I can't help you,' I say evenly.

'But your assistant said you would look over the case,' he replies quickly, a sense of panic and urgency in his tone. 'I've paid the fee.'

'My business partner didn't realise what this case was about, and it isn't something I feel comfortable reviewing. We will of course refund the fee you've paid.'

I picture Sasha's reaction to this promise, but hope she will be more understanding, given what I've shared.

'But I've seen you represent wrongful murder convictions before—'

'This is different,' I say, cutting him off, hoping a direct approach will have him eagerly heading for the door in frustration.

'My client believes he was wrongfully convicted of a crime, and is seeking justice. That is the service you provide, is it not? And as a key witness in his trial, nobody is better placed than you to truly understand the case.'

'With all due respect, Mr Morgan, I only help those that I believe have suffered a miscarriage of justice.'

'Terry Anderson *has* suffered a miscarriage. He acknowledges the crimes he's committed, but is adamant that one of the convictions is unsound.'

My head feels so heavy, and the irony isn't lost on me that I got drunk last night to block out thoughts of Anderson, and now it's all I can think about.

'There are other miscarriage advocates out there that you can try. I can even recommend a couple who are just as good, if not better than me.'

'I doubt that. I've seen your track record, and on the back of yesterday's acquittal, I can't think of anyone who would serve my client better. It was Terry who insisted we employ you to help. He says the police fabricated testimony against him and that there was no physical evidence putting him at the scene of your sister's murder.'

I push one of the boxes towards him, and stand, turning to face the window behind me.

'He was found guilty by a jury of his peers in a court of law,' I say between gritted teeth. 'His previous appeal was considered and rejected.'

'That doesn't mean he isn't innocent of the crime.'

My skin crawls at the word *innocent*.

'Look at the cases of the Guildford Four and the Birmingham Six. Their initial appeals were dismissed, but they were eventually overturned when new evidence was presented.'

I spin on my heel.

'You have new evidence?'

'That's what we're hoping you'll be able to find for us. The lead detective in your sister's case coerced witnesses. He was investigated for misconduct a decade after my client's initial appeal was dismissed.'

I frown at this statement.

'Was he?'

Rhys nods, lifting the lid of one of the boxes, and searching through the papers within.

'Multiple times. It's all in here. Several misconduct notices were served against him.'

He continues rummaging.

'So, that's your plan? A smear campaign against the police. I will have no part of that.'

'Oh, so you think it's okay for the police to send innocent men to prison, do you?'

'Terry Anderson is not innocent.'

'He is of your sister's murder. I can't believe you're so willing to allow her real killer to walk free.'

I'm winded by the jibe, but I've no doubt he's using parlour tricks to try and force me to question my own integrity.

'Because if you don't help us that's what you'll be doing,' he continues. 'Is that what you want? Your sister's real killer to get away with what he did to her; what he did to you all?'

'Terry Anderson killed Faye. That's all I know.'

'I'm sorry, Abbey, but you're wrong. I beg of you to come and see Terry and—'

'No way. You couldn't drag me to that monster's cage.'

'He's willing to pay substantially for your help, Abbey. All you have to do is give him ten minutes of your time, and I am certain you'll realise how wrong the police got it.'

'Get out,' I say, pointing at the door.

He stops rummaging and returns the lid to the box, and stares at me.

'I can see you're upset. And I totally get it. But ask yourself one question: what if he is telling the truth? Could you really live with the fact that you'll never know who really killed your sister that day?'

My vision blurs as tears fill my eyes.

'Get out,' I say in a loud whisper.

He collects his briefcase and moves towards the door, before stopping and looking back over his shoulder.

'He's dying, you know. That's why he's doing all of this. He wants to go to his grave with his conscience clear. He wants to help you and your family get the justice you deserve for Faye. That's his only motivation. He'll be gone in less than a year, and so will the answers you desperately crave. The police won't consider any other suspects unless Terry's conviction is over-turned. You're the only person who can help him, Abbey.'

I wait until he's gone before I collapse back into my chair and the years of grief and remorse bubble to the surface. I allow the tears to flow, but what's stinging most is the guilt that I should have kept her safe.

9

I watch Rhys through the blinds of my window as he crosses the street, phone to his ear. I hope he's phoning Anderson to tell him of my revulsion at their request. I wait until he has turned the corner, before grabbing my coat and hurrying out of the door, making sure to turn in the opposite direction when I hit the street. I need to clear my head.

I've put so many steps in place to shut out that traumatic part of my life. Moving away and developing a fictional, abridged version of my upbringing, so people wouldn't realise who I really was. And I'd even begun to believe it myself. What happened between Anderson and my sister became just a childhood nightmare I can still recall.

And now Anderson is back to tear up my life all over again.

Why can't he just die?

It is starting to spit, but I don't care, putting my face down and marching onwards. Deep down, I know that what's annoying me most is that Anderson's appeal and documentary is going to put everything that happened under the microscope. And there are secrets that I can't have exposed.

I chase the thought away, but when I look up, I don't know where I am to begin with. And then I spot *The Daily Bore*'s gleaming sign in the distance.

Did I intend to walk here?

Certainly not on any conscious level. But then I picture how Sasha will probably react when I tell her we need to return Rhys's fee. I need good news to offset the bad. The thought of grovelling to a tabloid journalist sends a wave of nausea cascading through my body, but I have little other choice if we are to keep the wolves from our doors.

I am surprised I've made it as far as Marylebone though. I have no real memory of walking a couple of miles, but I guess that just shows how much of a disarray Anderson's claims have left me in.

I have to face the fact that my history with Anderson is going to come out. My only option is to try and control the narrative somehow. The last thing I want is to appear on camera talking about my sister's murder, and that's assuming the production company would even be interested in hearing my side of things.

If I can convince Graves not to drop the feature, but to postpone it by a week, then maybe I can undermine Anderson's appeal without having to go anywhere near him; paint him as the villain that he is, and indirectly convince the production company to cut ties with him. For the first time all morning, I feel more upbeat about the future.

I arrive at the automated rotating doors and am greeted by a tall man dressed head to toe in black. He offers a cursory glance before returning his gaze to the passing footfall on the pavement ahead of him. I head on through where a second security guard in black blazer, shirt, trousers and tie directs me towards the queue at the reception desk. Others pass by and move to the turnstiles, scanning passes on lanyards around their necks and head on through without a second glance.

I check my inbox, but there's still no email from Damian's defence team offering terms. If nothing arrives by six o'clock, I will phone Damian and tell him what they're up to.

The person in front collects their visitor's pass and moves to the end of the counter. I step into his position and am greeted by the wide red smile of the woman behind the desk.

'How can I help?' she beams, and I spot what looks like a bite-sized sliver of kale between her teeth. She can't be much older than me, but she's in much better shape. The pencil skirt is smaller than any I've ever owned.

'I'm here to see Peter Graves.'

She stares back blankly at me.

'Which company does he work for?'

I'm about to say when I notice an image of his face in a sea of many in a large rectangular frame hanging behind the desk.

'That's him,' I quickly say, pointing. 'He's a journalist.'

She nods as she reads the publication's name.

'Oh, yes, they're based on the top two floors. What time is your appointment?'

'Oh, I don't have one,' I say, pulling an awkward smile. 'He doesn't actually know I'm coming.'

She seems confused by this statement.

'He's writing a feature about me for this weekend's paper.'

She stares at me for a long time and then her eyes widen.

'Are you that lawyer who keeps overturning miscarriages of justice?'

I feel the heat rise to my cheeks. I've never been recognised by a stranger before, and I don't like that there are now people out there who know more about me than I'll ever know about them.

'I'm not a lawyer,' I correct, 'but yes, I do help those who've been wrongfully convicted.'

I have to stop myself speaking, as nerves are getting the better of me, and I'm likely to start telling this poor woman my life story.

'Can you phone Peter and tell him I'm down here?'

She slides the visitors' book across the desk to me.

'I've already messaged him. He's on his way down.'

I sign the book but hesitate at the column that asks for the purpose of my visit, unsure what to write.

'You can just put interview,' she says. 'I don't think anyone ever reads the book anyway.'

She collects the book and slides a visitor's lanyard towards me, before greeting the next person in the queue. I take the pass, unsure that I'll need it as Graves could just as easily be coming down to kick me out of the building after the way I left things yesterday.

I look up when I hear him calling my name. He scans himself through the turnstile and stands beside me.

'Sorry, do we have a meeting I've forgotten about?' he asks, his tone playful.

'Um, no,' I say, lowering my voice because I don't want the red-lipped lady to hear me. 'I didn't like how we left things yesterday, and I came to apologise.'

He tilts his head.

'There's no need to apologise. I should have told you how I envisioned the story before we met.' He smiles again, and I catch myself smiling back, relieved that he's not making things difficult for me.

'Let me take you upstairs and I can show you what I've got so far in terms of copy, and proposed layout.'

I nod gratefully, though I can't believe there is much to read so far, based on the brief time we spent together yesterday. We head through the turnstiles and head to the bank of six lifts to the right.

'How is your head this morning?' he asks, and I frown at the question.

How does he know I woke with a hangover?

I picture the open filing cabinet and Damian's missing file, but quickly dismiss the idea that he could have stolen it.

'How do you...?' I begin, but my words trail off, remembering I'm still wearing yesterday's clothes.

'Oh, my, you don't remember, do you?'

'Remember what?'

He covers his mouth to try and suppress his laughter.

'I met up with a friend at The Seven Stars after work, and I saw you in there celebrating with what I assume was Damian Johnson and his defence team.'

My cheeks redden.

'I approached you at the bar to check you were okay after our encounter, and you defiantly told me you were, and I should leave you alone.' He snickers. 'I sensed maybe you'd had a couple and might be feeling it this morning.'

The lift pings as the doors open and we step inside. We ascend in silence, much to my relief, and when the doors open, he leads me through rows of desks, each with monitors and laptop docking stations. More of the desks are empty than occupied, and I wonder how many of the staff are either out chasing stories, or simply working from home.

'It's probably best if we look at it in one of the larger rooms,' he says, collecting his laptop and an A4 notepad from a desk and leading me towards a conference room with darkened windows.

The room is much cooler than the rest of the office, but it's welcome relief, and I slip off my overcoat and hang it on the back of one of the chairs. He invites me to sit down and pulls out the chair closest to the cables and control box that presumably allows computers to connect to the large screen at the head of the table. He pauses as he's about to plug the USB-C lead into his computer and releases it instead.

'Listen, before I show you this, you should know I had a long, in-depth conversation with my editor yesterday evening, and it was her idea to present the feature in this way.'

It's a half apology, but I've no idea what he's so keen to apologise for. He's noticeably trying to avoid direct eye contact, and it immediately puts me on the back foot. Suddenly, I'm regretting my decision to come inside and offer an olive branch.

'What is that supposed to mean?' I say, when he isn't more forthcoming.

'I know you've now said you don't want the feature to mention Terry Anderson, nor your sister for that matter, but the thing is... you can't keep running from the past. The truth is going to come out as soon as the docuseries hits the streaming platform.'

He is definitely avoiding looking at me as he connects his laptop to a cable in the centre of the desk and projects a newspaper layout onto the screen. There are no pictures, but spaces in the layout where images will be added before going to print. But the headline is the first thing that catches my attention.

CRUSADER FOR JUSTICE HAUNTED BY SISTER SHE
COULDN'T SAVE

10

She has built a reputation as a crusader for justice, righting the wrongs of the British justice system single-handedly. But behind the bravado lies a grieving woman, unable to forgive herself for not being there when her slain sister needed her most.

Speaking in public for the first time about that horrific day thirty years ago, when the body of Faye Turnbull, 13, was discovered at the foot of a disused quarry, Abbey Veritas (née Abigail Turnbull) played a key role in the prosecution of the man accused of the murder. With that same man now claiming a miscarriage of justice in a documentary due to hit streaming services early next year, Abbey is here to set the record straight.

Abbey's face will be familiar to many who have seen her hailed as the Queen of Appeals after multiple interventions that secured the freedom of inmates wrongfully convicted of crimes. Most recently, it was Abbey's eagle-eyed expertise that led to the acquittal of Damian Johnson, a man who has spent the last seven years incarcerated for a crime he could not have committed. The police were so certain of Johnson's guilt that they stopped looking for other potential suspects, meaning the real killer of Rodrigo Johnson, Damian's husband, is still at large. We won't talk about the prejudices that might have played a key part in the police investigation, as the Metropolitan Police are set to launch an investigation into that themselves.

When I asked Abbey about her role in Damian's acquittal, she was self-deprecating, as I sense she often is, and hailed the hard work of the whole legal team who successfully argued for Damian's conviction to be overturned.

'I'm nothing special,' she told me when we met for hot chocolate earlier this week. But when you dig deeper, Abbey has a unique skill for reading people, predicting what they're thinking by reading their actions. I experienced this firsthand whilst we were talking when she accurately predicted my intentions in a card game. And I was keen to understand what drives someone to use that skill to the benefit of others.

Known sex offender, Terry Anderson, now 70 years of age, was the man police identified as Faye's killer, and when Abbey picked him out as the man she saw chasing after her sister, the police were able to include the crime as part of the multi-case trial that the Criminal Prosecution Service (CPS) was bringing against him. Abbey's testimony, played at the trial from a private room for her safety, was the final nail in the coffin for Anderson who was sentenced to multiple life sentences, with no chance of parole. To all intents and purposes, the justice system served the Turnbull family well that day. So, what drives Abbey to now pick at it like a trouble-some scab?

'I suppose I've always had an interest in trying to understand how others think, and why they choose certain courses of action over others.'

Damian Johnson's acquittal is just one in a long line of appeals that Abbey has contributed to, with each adding to her blossoming reputation. But with Terry Anderson now seeking to have his conviction overturned, the question is whether Abbey will be willing to look at her own role in his incarceration.

'What is this?' I demand.

He stares back apologetically.

'As I said, this is how my editor thinks we should frame the feature. It shows your human side and highlights what motivates you to keep helping those who've been failed by the British judicial system.'

'You've written this like I'm planning to support Anderson's appeal.'

He frowns at this.

'You are, aren't you?'

'Who told you that?'

'I was called by Anderson's solicitor this morning...' He pauses and studies some notes on the pad of paper beside his laptop. 'Rhys Morgan, that's his name. He said his client had instructed him to retain your services and you'd agreed.'

'I did no such thing!' I shout.

Again, Graves frowns before scribbling something on the pad.

'So, you're denying Rhys Morgan has paid a twenty-thousand-pound fee to you?'

I close my eyes and sigh in frustration.

'No, he did pay us to look at the case, but that was before we knew what we were being asked to look at. I intend to return that payment to him. We don't want Anderson's blood money.'

Graves taps the end of the pen against his teeth.

'Are you happy for me to quote you on that?'

'Absolutely, and you can also quote me when I say Terry Anderson is a manipulative sociopath who put his own depraved urges ahead of others' lives. My sister was one of seven he killed in a campaign that lasted almost a decade. He is exactly where he should be.'

I see my words appear in black and white on the large screen as he types.

'Anything else you want me to add?'

If this does go to print, such a statement could be considered libel, so I tell him to delete it.

'Have you ever considered whether there could be some truth in Anderson's claims?' he asks next when the text has gone.

I don't tell him that I've thought of nothing else all morning.

'There's no reason for me to do so,' I say instead. 'He was found guilty by an impartial jury of his peers.'

'It wasn't a unanimous verdict though, at least not in your sister's case. Split seven to five in favour of a guilty verdict.'

I do my best to hide my surprise at this admission, as I wasn't aware. I don't recall anyone ever sharing that detail with me, or if they did I didn't understand it. I'd always assumed all twelve jurors were convinced.

'That doesn't mean he didn't do it,' I say defiantly, but I don't know if that's more for my benefit than his.

'Have you spoken to him at any point in the last thirty years?'

'No, I have no reason to.'

'You should know that I have spoken with him.'

I blink several times, uncertain if I misheard.

'When? Why?'

He tilts his head to one side.

'Because that is part of the feature we're running. We're telling our readers both sides of the story. That's why we're so keen to hear what he put you through and why you're so certain that the justice system you've battled for so many years got it right in this case.'

He presses a button on his laptop and the image on the large screen flicks to a fresh headline.

FAILED BY A CORRUPT SYSTEM

By his own admission, 70-year-old Terry Anderson has committed some truly awful acts in his life. Convicted of seven murders and assaults in the mid-nineties, he has spent the last thirty years incarcerated in the High Security Unit of HMP Belmarsh, a Category A prison. He is segregated from other prisoners out of fear for his safety due to the crimes he was convicted of. His only contact with other people is his solicitor, and the prison officers who oversee his day-to-day routine.

I meet Anderson in a room no larger than a standard garage. The room is surrounded by reinforced glass and uniformed prison officers stand guard at the two exits. I've been given a panic button to use if I feel my safety is at risk, and I keep this enclosed in my left hand as he is escorted into the room in handcuffs, which are subsequently attached to a heavy chain that is concreted into the ground between his feet. A transparent plastic sports bottle is placed on the table within reach of his right hand.

'Sorry for all the formality,' are the first words he says to me. 'They know deep down that I'm not a threat, but procedure is procedure.'

It's not what I'm expecting to hear, following the small exchange of emails between me and Anderson's solicitor.

'Before we get started,' he says next, 'I'm not making

excuses for my behaviour. My time in isolation has allowed me to reflect on my life and my crimes, and I have no complaint about why I am here.'

He goes on to tell me how he has developed a real interest in psychology and that through reading almost every book available in the prison library, he now understands what makes him tick better than he ever did.

'I have a sickness, you see,' he continues, his hands resting gently on his legs. 'I was born different, and a challenging upbringing only moulded the impulses I feel. I know there is lots of debate about nature and nurture shaping human behaviour, but I firmly believe that both play an equal part; at least in my situation they do.'

Anderson is serving seven successive life sentences with no chance of parole, meaning he will never leave this prison, so I'm curious to understand why he would go to the effort to try and have only one of the seven convictions overturned.

'Because I didn't do it,' he says matter-of-factly, and I sense he would cross his arms if the cuffs would allow. 'I know what I did is unforgiveable, but it isn't fair on this child's family that the real killer is still at large. He could be alive or dead for all I know, but the closure they think they have because I'm in here is misplaced. They've been lied to, and they deserve to know the truth.'

The crime he is alluding to here is that of Faye Turnbull, the 13-year-old girl with blonde hair whose body was recovered at the foot of a disused quarry after a frantic search when she went missing in a park a stone's throw from where her parents were awaiting her return. It took the police less than forty-eight hours to flag Anderson as their prime suspect, and despite his protestations to the contrary, this charge was added to his arrest sheet when he was apprehended at a home not far from where Faye was last seen.

His arrest was the culmination of an eighteen-month investigation where a specially formed team had been building a case against him, involving the other six crimes he's willing to admit to now.

'I'm many things but I'm not the person who pushed that little girl into the quarry.'

'You can't print this,' I say, gasping.

'We can and we are,' he replies simply. 'There are two sides to every story, and Anderson's claims are compelling.'

'You believe him?'

Graves shakes his head.

'It isn't my place to believe one way or another. I'm just here to present both sides of the story in an impartial manner.'

'But you've now heard both sides, which do you think is true?'

He pauses for a moment before responding.

'I honestly don't know what to believe. You said yourself that the best lies are partially based on fact. He isn't wrong about the police focusing all their attention on linking him to Faye's murder. Read the case files and he is the only person of interest they focus on after they rule your parents out as potential suspects. A properly run investigation rules out nothing until the evidence is overwhelming, and all the evidence in the case against him for Faye's murder is circumstantial.'

'I saw him there.'

He smiles thinly.

'Your testimony was the only tangible evidence in the case. But Anderson claims the police coached you in how to answer the questions and actively encouraged you to say he was there.'

'This is bullshit, and you know it,' I erupt when my patience can no longer be sustained. 'You're running this story because you want to cash in on his notoriety as much as he and his solicitor do.'

'We're not receiving any payment from Anderson or his legal team.'

'Maybe not, but you're betting that this story will boost your sales numbers, especially with this forthcoming documentary.'

He doesn't respond, but I can read the guilt in his eyes.

'What if I rescind my permission for you to print our interview?'

He puffs out his cheeks, but doesn't look as worried by the ultimatum as I'm expecting him to.

'You're well within your rights to do that. Personally, we'd – *I'd* – prefer if you didn't. We can publish Anderson's story and include a line that says you declined the opportunity to comment. But I would counsel you against such a rash decision, because of how it will come across to readers.'

'What do you mean?'

'Well, think about it. Anderson makes an audacious claim that he was wrongfully convicted, and that you lied on the stand. Your refusal to deny the accusation and set the record straight makes it look as though you are hiding something or running from the truth. I meant what I said yesterday, I want to tell your story and stop him from muddying your name and reputation.'

I feel ambushed. He should have been open about the true nature of the feature they're planning to run. Anderson's interview makes him look like a victim of a prejudiced investigation, when Faye is the real victim in this story.

'This is your opportunity to frame how the public will view his appeal and the series,' Graves continues, but I've heard enough.

My already full mind can't handle this additional information, and I stand and move towards the door without another word.

'Abbey, please wait,' I hear him calling after me. 'The story is going to publish on Saturday whether you're part of it or not. Let me take you to dinner tonight and I can better explain why I think your view is so important.'

But I don't respond, desperate to get back outside as the walls feel as though they're closing in around me.

11

I am angry that I didn't see through Peter Graves's lies sooner. His personable nature, buying me a hot chocolate and pampering my ego were all hiding his true motives, and my usual sixth sense failed me when I needed it most. And the whole time he was telling me how special my ability is, deep down he must have been laughing that I couldn't see what was right under my nose.

I stalk through the city, darting in and out of tourists and office workers who are dawdling.

Get out of my way, I want to yell at them, but I just don't have the energy.

I feel emotionally drained. What started as a good day, with my success over Eddie's and Robert's attempts to swindle me, has dramatically gone downhill. My whole world has been turned upside down, and once again, Terry Anderson is at the eye of the storm.

Clearly, he's decided his dying wish is to ruin my life. I shouldn't be so surprised; I always knew he was a monster.

Actually, I think that's what annoys me most about Graves's betrayal. The way he has painted Anderson in the article doesn't show his true, evil nature. Why can't Graves see that Anderson is misleading him? Why can't his solicitor and the production company see it as well? Can the promise of financial recompense really make people turn a blind eye to his crimes?

A fresh wave of nausea passes over me as I cross the road, willing the distance to the office to shorten. It probably would have been quicker to jump on the Tube, but the thought of being trapped underground in a carriage full of strangers doesn't appeal. I need to walk, to breathe, and to figure out how I'm going to dig myself out of this situation.

Running away and starting over again has never felt more appealing. A new identity in a foreign country that doesn't import copies of *The Daily Bore*. I could be whoever I want to be, and do whatever I want to do.

But I know I can't abandon Sasha like that. Her whole future is invested in our business, and if I left, she'd be high and dry. She'd probably have to give up the lease on her flat as well as the office, and with no parents for her to fall back on, I dread to think what would become of her.

I could call Eddie Douglas and see whether there's any way to file a court injunction to stop *The Daily Bore* from publishing the feature, but he would want to know why, and I'm not sure I have a legal leg to stand on. And as Graves said, rescinding my interview will lead people to assume I have something to hide, and additional scrutiny is the last thing I need. Plus, after this morning's encounter, Eddie is probably the last person willing to do me a favour.

I'm relieved to see the wine bar up ahead, but I freeze as the feeling of being watched returns. I turn and look but the only two people I see are a couple across the street, holding hands, and they're more interested in each other than me. I slowly cross the road, but stop outside the wine bar, looking for who's watching me, but see nobody.

I pull open our door, and slowly ascend the stairs. I think I'm going to tell Sasha that I'm in no state to work and will head back to my flat instead. I need to give my subconscious time to develop a strategy.

The last thing I'm expecting as I open the door to the office is for Sasha to thrust a flute of something fizzy into my hand.

'Thank God you're back,' she says excitedly. 'I have news.'

She grabs my hand and pulls me over to the two seats in the makeshift waiting area, and pushes me into one.

'So, I know today has been a bit crazy,' she says, her eyes wide and bright, 'but what we were discussing earlier got me thinking.'

I have no idea what she's talking about as the only thing I can remember us discussing is what Anderson did to Faye.

'And before you say anything, hear me out,' she continues. 'I know what you're like, and your reaction will probably be outright refusal, but let me explain why this idea could be the answer to all of our problems.'

She takes a deep breath and sips from her glass, encouraging me to take a drink. The liquid smells like baby vomit and the taste is overly sweet.

'The television production company called here whilst you were out, and they are very keen to get you on board with their new series.'

I can't hide my revulsion, and I'm frustrated that she seems to be overlooking the fact I said I want nothing to do with Anderson and his appeal.

I pass the flute back to her and push myself out of the chair.

'No, Sasha. I already told you why I can't do that; why I *won't* do that.'

Her brow furrows, and she hurries after me into my office, as I peel off my overcoat and throw it onto the desk.

'No, this isn't what you think. You don't understand.'

I pause and fix her with a hard stare.

'I know you're worried about our finances, and that this could be the golden bullet to save the company, but you really don't understand why I can't—'

'Please, just hear me out. The production company weren't phoning about Anderson. They want *you*, Abbey. The producer I spoke to wants to develop a series based around you and your ability to read between the lines.'

'What are you talking about?'

She places the two glasses on the edge of my desk and takes my hands in hers.

'They've seen all the great press you've been receiving, and they want that to be the focus of the show. This is how they outlined it to me. Each episode will focus on a different case. They'll present the facts and you'll talk through what you see and feel about it; where your instinct sees possible deceit or inaccuracy, and then as a viewer, we get to see how your mind works and solve the puzzle along with you. It means you can take on as many of the pro bono cases as you want, because the production company will be footing the bill.'

The room is spinning around me.

'They pitched it as like a true-crime *Murder, She Wrote*, with you as the Jessica Fletcher character, but all the stories are real.'

In all our years of supporting appeals, nobody has ever approached like this. It can't just be coincidence that it's happening as Anderson decides to appeal and Graves is writing his feature. I can almost see the strings that some faceless puppeteer is pulling.

My gut grumbles and then I'm tearing across the office and

into the bathroom, barely making it before I painfully retch up bile.

I've spent years trying to hide my past, running from the name Abigail Turnbull because of the horror it brought, and no matter how hard I keep running, the past is catching up with me.

I use tissue to wipe my face and blow my nose, before crawling out of the bathroom. Sasha is standing in the doorway to my office, holding out a wrap and the energy drink she got for me.

'Please don't shut me out,' she says, quietly.

I accept both items and return to my office, slumping down in my chair, my stomach still uneasy. I drop the wrap to the desk and open the can, taking a long drink to try and vanquish the bad taste in my mouth. Sasha remains in the doorway until I signal for her to come in.

'I'm sorry,' I say. 'I know you've said things are a bit tight at the moment, but new work will come in. We'll survive.'

Something crosses Sasha's face and I see her mask drop.

'I've been trying to protect you,' she says, wrangling her hands in her lap, 'but things are a lot worse than I told you. We're three months behind on the rent for this place, and the agency is threatening us with eviction if we don't settle the bill by the end of the year.'

She is visibly shaking and when she meets my stare, I can see her eyes are watering.

'The fee Rhys sent over should cover that though, right? I could say I've reviewed the files but can't find anything and then we just walk away.'

A tear escapes as she gently shakes her head.

'I made that part up. I was hoping that you'd look at the files and decide to proceed with the case. I didn't know you were directly involved in it, and I only said what I did to try and convince you to take it on. If we pass on the case, we'll have to refund the money, but we don't have enough in the business account to do that. We were already over our overdraft limit, and so I can't access the full payment. I'm so sorry.' She buries her face in her hands and I hear her sobbing.

I close my eyes, willing my mind to find a solution to our predicament, but the only option we have is one I don't want to go anywhere near.

'So, I don't really have a choice,' I eventually say.

'I'm so sorry, Abbey. I know I should have said something sooner, but this side of the business is my responsibility and I didn't want to burden you with how bad a job I've done with it.'

'It isn't your fault, Sasha. I shouldn't have been so willing to work for free. We should have the contract terms from Damian's defence team soon, which means the future is brighter.'

'I don't want to piss on your fire, Abbey, but we both know a civil suit could take years to reach court, so God knows if and when Damian will win a claim. It could be at least a year before we see any return.'

I know she's right.

'What else did the production company say?'

There's a momentary glimmer of hope in her eyes.

'They said they'd need to film a pilot to start with, but assuming it gets picked up by one of the streaming services, they'd look for a further five episodes for a first series. You'd still approach each case in the same way as you do at the moment, and they'll take some background shots of you reviewing paper-work, meeting witnesses, and then you'd narrate your actions and offer insight to camera in a studio. And what they're offering per episode is twice the usual fee we bill paying clients. We'd double our annual income within six months. It means we could move to somewhere more permanent and certainly more elegant than this.'

'Would the fee for the pilot get us back into the black before year end?'

She nods.

'It would tide us over, even if the series doesn't get picked up for syndication.' She pauses and lowers her eyes. 'There's something else you should know... they want the pilot to be based on Terry Anderson's case.'

My heart sinks.

'Why? He hasn't even formally submitted an appeal yet.'

I'd assumed they'd base the pilot on one of the appeals we'd helped win, like Damian's.

'Because they've already agreed to use Anderson, and what they're offering you diverges from their original plan, but they think it will work better. I understand you not wanting to be involved, and I won't blame you if we walk away.'

I picture Anderson's smirking face and it sickens me to the stomach. On my walk over to see Graves, I told myself that I wanted to control the narrative, and what better way than to step into the eye of the storm and wrestle control back? Whilst he might be hoping reviewing the case will find evidence supporting his appeal, maybe there's a chance I can find something that proves him wrong once and for all.

With trembling fingers, I reach for the phone on the edge of the desk, and dial Rhys's phone number. He answers on the second ring.

'I'll meet your client,' I say through gritted teeth.

12

'We're nearly there,' Sasha says as we pass another brown sign indicating HMP Belmarsh. 'Are you ready for this?'

I bite my lip. In all honesty I've spent the entire journey trying not to think about how much of a mistake it is coming here. My parents would be turning in their graves if they knew I was here.

Rhys told me on the phone that he was due to visit with Anderson this afternoon, and a quick phone call with the prison governor was all it took for him to have me added to the visitor roster. He sounded overjoyed to receive my call, and I'm not sure which of us was most surprised I made it.

'Do you want me to come in with you?' Sasha asks, and I don't know if she's saying it because she knows it's too late to add her to the roster.

'I'll be fine,' I croak, my throat suddenly dry.

I see her glance over in my periphery; her hair is so big and curly that it's impossible not to notice.

'You don't look fine. It isn't too late for me to turn around. You could phone Rhys and tell him you've changed your mind.'

I keep my eyes fixed on the road ahead, willing the passing residential streets to slow down.

'We can't afford for me not to be here,' I say flatly, though I don't mean it to sound so blunt.

'I meant you could just delay the visit for a few days. Allow yourself to adjust to the idea. He's not going anywhere, and will still be here next week. There's a lot to be said for the impact of being mentally prepared for something like this.'

I don't think she understands that I'm out of time. Graves has made it clear that the feature will run tomorrow, whether I like it or not. I need to get ahead of the story, and decide whether I allow Graves to print my side or rescind it.

'I'll be fine,' I repeat, but not even I'm convinced by the lie.

'Well, if it gets too much, there's no shame in leaving early. This will be the first time you've seen him face to face since you saw him in the park chasing after Faye, won't it?'

I swallow my guilt and nod my head briefly.

'If you feel like it's too much, you're within your rights to end the meeting early and leave. I feel awful that you're having to go through with this.'

I know she's looking for me to reassure her, and whilst I don't hold her accountable, it does feel like I'm having to put more into the game to rectify our position.

The view outside the window is more desolate now. There is grass separating us from oncoming traffic, but it looks old and drowned by downpours in the last week. The trees that line the road to our left are leafless and resemble bony hands clawing at the overcast sky, and doing an awful job of hiding the prison building beyond. The sign ahead indicates that we need to take the next left and we'll have arrived. The knot in my stomach tightens.

Belmarsh Prison in South West London is home to 130 Cate-

gory A prisoners, some of the most dangerous and feared criminals in the UK. It also houses a further 750 regular and remand
prisoners in separate blocks of the massive complex.

Sasha follows the road and a man in a prison officer's uniform
greets us at the closed barrier. I lower my window and explain
who I am. He asks for identification, which he then compares to
the list of names on his clipboard. He finally hands it back and
tells us to go to the left where we can park and then to follow the
sign for the visitors' centre. The barrier rises; the point of no
return.

Sasha squeezes into a parking space, and kills the engine,
before turning in her seat to face me.

'You've got this,' she says. 'You're the strongest woman I know.'

I feel the sting of tears at the corner of my eyes, but hold it in
place.

'Are you sure you don't want me to wait? I don't mind.'

'No, it's fine. Rhys said he could give me a lift back when we're
done.'

She leans across and gives me a tight squeeze, and I realise
how lucky I am to have her in my life. I open the door and take a
deep breath as I exit, desperate for her not to see how close I am
to bawling.

The site beyond the car park is enormous, and surrounded by
a high wall that would be impossible to climb. It's like something
medieval in the way the walls are designed to prevent any
unwanted visitors from getting in, and the only break in the wall
is the bricked visitors' centre. I find Rhys waiting just outside the
door for me.

He opens it and ushers me in, explaining to the prison guard
on reception why we're here and that the governor is expecting
us. Rhys shows her his driving licence, and she searches for him
on her computer screen, before looking at me.

I smile at her as she examines my photo card driving licence, but she doesn't smile back. Instead, she asks me to remove any valuables and place them in one of the designated lockers. I do as instructed, swiftly realising there is no place for pleasantries here.

'You're allowed ten quid in change,' Rhys whispers to me, 'but that's all. No phones, no cigarettes, no jewellery. It's in case you try and pass it to Terry.'

My skin crawls at mention of his name. In my head he's always just been Anderson. Using his first name makes him sound more human; less of a threat.

With everything placed inside the locker, I pocket the key and return to the reception desk with Rhys.

I'm directed to a white wall, where my photograph is taken, the flash leaving stars in my field of vision. And then my fingerprints are scanned at a small portal on the wall.

'What happens to my data?' I ask.

'We hold it on record here for the next time you visit,' she advises. 'Don't worry. It's not shared with any third parties.'

I desperately hope there won't be a next time I visit here.

Moving to the first door, a prison officer with a paunch and rapidly thinning crown waves his wand over the front and back of me, and it squeals in protest as it searches and fails to locate contraband. This isn't my first time coming to a prison, but it's the first time I've come in a personal capacity.

There is a small canteen where two pensioners are busy nattering as they boil kettles, but otherwise we are alone in the area.

'You can take drinks, but no food in with you,' Rhys warns, when he sees me watching them. 'There aren't any facilities inside where we're going, so if you need something to eat or drink, get it now. I would also advise you go to the toilet out here though, as there isn't one in the main building.'

'You're kidding! What happens if I need to go?'

'One of the guards will escort you back here, and wait while you go, before escorting you back. If one of the occupants needs to go, they're taken back into holding.'

I head straight through to the toilets, grateful nobody else is in here. I stand at the basin, gripping the sides for support and stare at myself in the mirror. My face is so pale that I resemble a recently deceased corpse.

'Where are all the other visitors?' I ask Rhys when I'm sitting beside him in the waiting area.

'Been and gone. There are no afternoon visits on a Friday, even for legal counsel. Luckily for us, the prison governor is a reasonable man and he has allowed temporary dispensation for Terry as a result of the series.'

I shudder as I hear Sasha's voice in my head: *like a true-crime* Murder, She Wrote, *with you as the Jessica Fletcher character, but all the stories are real.*

'Rhys Morgan and Abbey Veritas,' the woman behind the reception desk calls out, and we stand. 'My colleague will now lead you to the private room to await the arrival of the prisoner. You will have exactly one hour to conclude your business. The meeting will be recorded using the prison's security cameras, but nothing disclosed will be admissible in court.'

She points us towards a secured door where a man is standing, restraining an alert German Shepherd at his feet. The dog sniffs us as we pass, presumably searching for hidden contraband, but we pass the test, and are allowed to pass to the next secured door and then into a corridor, where I immediately see the barred gate ahead. A sound buzzes somewhere overhead and the gate grinds open before slamming closed behind us, the sound reverberating off every wall, reminding me we're now also trapped inside.

My pulse is racing by the time we're escorted into a hexagonal room with three chairs and a table in the middle. I don't know what I was expecting, but I thought there would be some kind of barrier between us and Anderson. It seems we will all be in the same room, breathing the same air. The narrow, horizontal windows near the ceiling are reinforced glass, and let little light through.

It's only now that I'm acutely aware of just how out of my depth I am here. What if Anderson takes issue with something I say and reacts violently? Maybe he's been waiting years for his chance to get revenge on me for putting him here, and now I've offered myself up voluntarily.

It's too late to change my mind, however, as a moment later, the door at the opposite side of the room is unlocked and the large figure enters in grey jogging bottoms and a sweatshirt.

13

It's only when I finally blink that I see the figure in grey who is now being led to the table isn't the hulking monster that appears in my nightmares. This man is frail, the jogging bottoms and sweatshirt hanging from his frame, and the prison officer isn't so much manhandling him as supporting him. He has a scraggly white goatee, but then I see those dark brown eyes, and I know that it's him.

The prison officer helps him into the chair, and secures him to the thick chain in the ground.

The prison officer places a beaker of water with a paper straw on the table within reach of Anderson.

'Thanks, Pat, much appreciated,' Anderson says, his voice gravelly.

'No worries, Terry. Give me a shout if you need anything else.'

I watch as the prison officer heads back to the secured door they entered through, unable to understand why the two of them are on first-name terms. Does he not realise who this monster is?

My toes are making fists inside my shoes, but above the table I remain statuesque, still staring into those big, hateful eyes. I have pictured the moment when I might once again come face to face with him, and every time I lash out, scratching at his face and those eyes, beating my hands against his chest and demanding to know why he was allowed to live when Faye wasn't. But all I can think about is how much I want to get out of this room, but I'm so frozen in fear that I can't move.

Anderson places his hands on the table, fingers splayed and continues to watch me, as if he's trying to read my mind.

'I must admit I'm surprised to see you here, Miss Turnbull, oh, sorry, it's Veritas now, isn't it? Forgive me.'

I will never forgive you for what you did, I scream internally, but remain mute.

'It's interesting that you chose Veritas as your new surname. Did you know it comes from the Latin word *verus*, which means *true*? And in Roman mythology, Veritas was the goddess of truth, the daughter of Saturn and Virtue.' He turns and looks at Rhys beside me. 'Seems somewhat ironic, wouldn't you say?'

Rhys doesn't respond, but I see him nod.

'So, is that what you're here to do, Miss Veritas? Do you come in search of the truth?'

The question throws me for a moment. I suppose that is why I'm here, but I doubt our expectations of what that looks like are the same.

'I'm here because your solicitor is paying me to be here.'

He seems unmoved by the jab, but I want him to realise he's going to have to work a lot harder to convince me he's changed. The brief interaction with the prison officer could have been a show just for my benefit, and I'm not convinced he's as frail and helpless as he'd like the world to believe. If his plan is to try and pull the wool over my eyes, he picked the wrong woman to mess with.

'Well, either way, I appreciate that you have come to see me,' he says, covering his mouth as he coughs, before placing the straw to his dry, cracked lips, and taking a small drink.

My mouth suddenly feels so dry, and I wish I'd taken Rhys's advice and brought a drink in with me. I don't know how long we've been in here, but it already feels too long. I glance up and see two small cameras either side of the ceiling behind Anderson, angled down at the table. I imagine there are probably two more behind us.

I hear the voice of the woman at reception in my head: *The meeting will be recorded using the prison's security cameras, but nothing disclosed will be admissible in court.*

'I assume Rhys has told you I intend to appeal the conviction for murdering your sister?' Anderson says next, drawing my attention back to this airless room. 'I want you to know I had nothing to do with your sister's death. Hand on heart.'

'The jury would beg to differ,' I croak back.

'The jury reached a decision based on manufactured evidence, and I don't blame them for reaching that conclusion. My barrister and solicitor at the time should have fought harder for me, but the police and CPS did a great job of stitching me up.'

I'm watching him, listening to the words, and I don't believe a single one of them.

'You don't believe me, do you? You're not speaking, but I can read your face like a book.' He pauses for another sip of drink. 'I read up about you, y'know? I mean it's been hard not to when your face appears in the papers every few weeks. They describe you as a human lie detector, able to see through the bullshit. I know what that's like, Abbey, because I'm pretty good at it myself.'

I shiver hearing my name on his lips.

'It's a gift; it truly is. If you're able to read what someone else is thinking, it allows you to adapt your approach; manipulate your-self to win them to your way of thinking.'

'Is that what you're doing here?' I snap.

'Yeah, in a way, I suppose I am. I'm trying to figure out how to convince you that I'm telling the truth about your sister. Look where I am. There's no reason for me to lie about it. Doctor reckons I'll be dead within the year. I have nothing to gain.'

'So why bother with the appeal? It's a waste of taxpayers' money; a waste of your solicitor's time; a waste of my time.'

'You're the reason I'm appealing, Abbey. You deserve to find the person who really pushed your sister into that quarry.'

The crime scene photograph of Faye's broken body amongst the stones flashes into my mind, and I have to chase it away.

'I'm sorry if that's difficult for you to hear, but we both know deep down that I didn't do it. And I forgive you for what you said in court that day. The police manipulated you as much as the rest of the so-say evidence against me. You were just a pawn in their game. They wronged us both that day.'

I don't know how much more of this bullshit I can put up with. I don't believe that this unassuming, quietly spoken man before me is the real Terry Anderson. He admitted as much when he said he knows how to project different versions of himself to influence a situation.

'I can see you're not convinced, but let me share something with you. I *was* in that park that day. The police were right about that, but I wasn't there to try and abduct another child, like the police claimed. They said I tried to take your sister and she fought back and I pushed her into the quarry to cover my tracks, but I was nowhere near that quarry. And that's why I know you lied about seeing me there.'

The breath catches in my throat, forcing me to cough.

Are you sure this is the man you saw in the woods? Did you see him abduct Faye?

'I know what I saw,' I counter, but I don't think either of us is convinced.

'What was I wearing?'

The question throws me.

'What?'

He sips from the straw.

'It's a simple enough question. If you saw me in the park that day, what was I wearing?'

'You were in jeans and a flannel shirt.'

'Ah, but what colour was the shirt? I was often dressed in jeans and a flannel shirt – hell, that's what I was wearing when the police took me into custody – but I remember exactly what colour it was because I wore it for a very specific reason that day.'

I try to picture him in my mind, but I have no idea what colour his shirt was.

'It was thirty years ago, how the hell do you expect me to remember something like that?'

'You seemed so certain in your court testimony that I assumed it would be ingrained in your memory. I'll tell you what, I'll give you a clue, see if we can't jolt your long-term memory.' He pauses. 'Was the shirt red-and-black checked, green-and-white checked, or blue-and-white checked?'

I picture the three shirts, but I genuinely have no idea. I sense he is playing a game, and testing how good I am at detecting deceit. I watch him carefully. When people play two truths and a lie, they usually state the lie at the beginning as it's the first thing the listener is likely to forget or dismiss. So, that could mean it was the red and black pattern. But then, he isn't an average player. He probably knows I'll assume it's the first option, so that could be a bluff, and if it was me I would probably put the correct answer in the middle. But, if he's as good at reading people as he claims, then he may have predicted I would dismiss the first and focus my attention on the second.

'Blue and white,' I say, watching on in horror as a wide smile breaks across his face, revealing teeth stained by years of coffee and cigarettes.

'See,' he says, looking over at Rhys. 'I told you she didn't see me.'

I silently berate myself for walking into his obvious trap.

'That proves nothing, other than I have a lousy long-term memory,' I say, uncertain why I feel so compelled to defend myself. 'I repressed a lot of those painful memories, and I had all of sixty seconds to unpick them. I know what I saw.'

'I'll tell you why I know you're lying, Abbey. As I said, I *was* in the park that day. I was trying to lie low, because I needed to get to a pharmacy to buy medicine, and I didn't want anyone to see me doing it. I took a short cut through the park as I figured there was less chance of witnesses. I was wearing brown corduroys and a green and brown jumper, so I'd blend in easier with the trees. I was also wearing a hat and false beard.'

He pauses to study my reaction. Frustratingly, I actually believe he's telling the truth this time, and I shouldn't be surprised that he used a loaded deck when offering me pattern choices; just like Graves did yesterday when he showed me three cards.

'So, even if you had spotted me in the park, there is no way in hell you could have picked out my mugshot when the police showed you, as I was clean-shaven back then.'

He runs a hand over his scraggly goatee as he says this.

'I can see you still don't want to believe me, so I'm going to share something else with you, Abbey, to prove the truth of my words. I had already taken a child that week, and he was back at my house. But he was diabetic, you see, and I didn't know that at first. He became ill and that's why I needed to get to the pharmacy: to buy insulin. I didn't want anyone to be able to identify me to the police, which is why I disguised myself. The day the police came to arrest me, I had no idea who your sister was, until they showed me her picture and accused me.' He pauses, and reaches for the straw. 'Tell me, Abbey, am I telling the truth, or am I lying?'

I've heard enough and glance back at the door over my shoulder.

'I have a sickness, Abbey. I realise that now. The things I've done... are unforgiveable, and I am deeply ashamed. I've had a long time to reflect on my crimes, and I can hand-on-heart say the best thing that ever happened to me was being locked away in here. I'm not safe to be out there in the real world. What I have compelled me to act in the way that I did, but I've worked on myself whilst in here. I am more mindful and accepting of my sickness. And all I want to do is come to terms with what I've done before I face judgement from Him above. I have asked for His forgiveness every day since discovering His repentance. But I can't be forgiven for something I didn't do. My silence in here has allowed your sister's real killer to escape unpunished. It's time for me – for us – to set the record straight.'

I can't stand it any longer, and I race to the door, banging on the reinforced glass until the prison officer allows me to escape, and then the tears come.

14

I race into the ladies' as soon as I'm back in the visitors' centre, and lock myself inside a cubicle, allowing the tears of regret to flow freely. I'm angry at myself for allowing Anderson to see me so visibly upset, but mostly I can't stop thinking about how much I've let down Faye.

When the judges overturned Damian's conviction yesterday, I felt so elated that I could almost touch the sky. But right now, I've never felt so low. Between Graves's story, Sasha's financial revelation, learning about the documentary, and now finding myself sobbing in a cubicle, I can't believe how quickly I've fallen.

I cry until I have no tears left, and then I emerge from the cubicle and see the broken woman staring back at me from the mirror above the basins.

I learned a long time ago that no good comes from feeling sorry for yourself; the only person who can change my future is me, and it is with this mantra on repeat in my head that I wash my face and take a seat in the waiting room. Rhys joins me twenty minutes later, a look of concern stretched across his face.

'Are you okay?' he asks, but I'm not convinced the question comes from a place of empathy.

'Never better,' I lie, forcing a thin smile.

'Terry said he didn't mean to upset you. He's really keen to work with you to find the truth.'

All he wants is to ruin my future in the same way I did his, I think, but don't say.

'Can we go now? I need to get back,' I say instead.

He nods and leads the way back out to the car. I message Sasha to let her know that we're leaving, but that I'll probably head home as I'm exhausted.

I'm relieved when Rhys doesn't switch off the radio. I suspected he might lead an inquisition, but he seems comfortable with the journey being made without conversation.

As much as I regret coming here today, at least I've learned the angle Anderson is planning to use in his claim for wrongful conviction. I can't see how his defence team will be able to prove that he was wearing different clothes on the day Faye died, and that itself proves nothing. They are going to come after me. I imagine they'll call me as a witness and then unpick my original testimony.

All I need to do is stick to my story and pre-empt any challenging questions. And away from the courtroom, it's time for me to go on the attack. If the production company are serious about the series, then maybe there's a way we can negotiate some element of creative control. Anderson will want the episode to throw light on the strength of the evidence in his conviction, but maybe I can make sure it instead focuses on all his other crimes, and sway the audience. It's his word against mine, and who is really going to believe a convicted murderer and sex offender over that of the witness still grieving for her sister?

'I really do appreciate you coming here today,' Rhys says,

lowering the volume of the radio. 'I know it can't have been easy seeing him after all these years.'

I don't respond, hoping he'll take it as a sign that I really don't want to talk.

'If you take only one thing away from today, it's that he's only doing this because he wants to help you.'

I turn at this, frowning.

'I'm sure the money the production company are offering has nothing to do with it,' I reply sarcastically.

'He's only agreed to be interviewed to cover the cost of legal fees. He doesn't need money where he is; he has no dependants to leave any money to, and he has all the commissary he needs. This is not financially motivated.'

Whilst that might be partially true, I've no doubt that seeing his name in the headlines again will also be influencing Anderson's motivation, though he's probably kept that from his solicitor.

'With all due respect, Mr Morgan, you weren't there when my sister was killed. You're only learning about it second hand, and if I were you, I wouldn't put all your stake on winning this appeal.'

'Please call me Rhys. I'm not here to antagonise you. I was really hoping you'd be willing to work with me on this. My motivation for taking Terry on is the same as his: finally finding the person who really killed your sister. I can show you the mountain of correspondence between us where that's all he talks about.'

'Oh, please, I don't believe his act about finding God and changing.'

'Why not? He's dying, Abbey.'

'Are you sure about that? Have you actually seen the medical reports? I wouldn't put it past him to invent a story like that to make himself appear more sympathetic to the producers.'

'Stage IV prostate cancer, and it's spreading. I *have* seen the scans and medical diagnosis. He's telling the truth.'

My cheeks burn at this admission, and I grind my teeth.

'Well, that's as may be, but it doesn't mean he's telling the truth about what happened that day.'

'But ask yourself one question, Abbey: why would he lie? After all this time, he has nothing to gain.'

'Have you actually looked at his other convictions?' I snap. 'He manipulated teenagers and young adults to go home with him and then subjected them to all manner of abuse before killing them. Choosing his words carefully is second nature to him. He even admitted as much today: he knows how to read people and adopt a persona to win them over. Can't you see that that's exactly what he's doing with you now?'

I'm hoping my bluntness will break the spell, but he simply smiles through it.

'So, he's not convinced you yet, that's fine. He didn't think one meeting would be enough.'

'Nothing will be enough. I know he killed my sister and the jury convicted him for it. No amount of bluster and unprovable claims is going to shake that.'

He considers my response before replying.

'But ask yourself one thing, Abbey: what if he *is* telling the truth? Could you really live with yourself, knowing your sister's killer is still out there?'

I don't answer, refusing to be drawn into the conversation any further.

'Doesn't she deserve more? Doesn't Faye deserve justice?'

'She doesn't deserve to have her name once again dragged through the press because of what that monster did.'

I cross my arms and turn my head back to look out of the window. When he tries to speak again, I turn up the stereo's volume. I message Sasha again, this time asking her to meet me in Marylebone. I tell Rhys to drop me at the train station, and I see Sasha waiting patiently just inside, shivering.

'Are you sure you wouldn't rather I give you a lift home?'

'No, it's fine,' I say, grabbing my bag and coat, 'I'm meeting my friend for a drink.'

He reaches out and rests a hand on my arm.

'I promise you, Abbey, my intentions here are pure. I just want to find out the truth about what really happened. I understand we're approaching this from opposite ends of the spectrum, but I think we're both ultimately searching for the same thing. Take the weekend to think it over. And if on Monday, you decide to withdraw your support, then no hard feelings.'

If only it was that easy, I don't say.

I climb out and meet Sasha with a hug.

'How was it?' she asks, wincing in preparation for my response.

I wait until I see Rhys's car pull back into traffic.

'We can talk about it later. Right now, I need your help.'

'Anything.'

I take a deep breath.

'If we're going to do this, then we're doing it on my terms. We're going to march into the offices of *The Daily Bore*, and we're not leaving until we have the feature in a better state. Graves will try and push back, and he might even inject his editor into the conversation, and that's why I need full-on Sasha fighting my corner. You're better at arguing your points than I am, and I don't want you to hold back.'

She nods with quiet affirmation.

'We need to make it clear that Terry Anderson is nothing more than a shit-stirrer, using his terminal diagnosis to seek five minutes' more fame before he bites the bullet. I want to leave readers in no doubt that he's the bastard who murdered my sister, and that any claims to the contrary should be ignored.'

'Mate, I'm here to do whatever you need me to do. And can I make another suggestion? They asked me to send a profile shot of you over for the piece, and I sent the standard head and shoulders shot I hate. We don't want readers to see a timid version of you because that will call into question your reliability. Let me make you up and get a picture that shows them exactly who you are and why they should put their faith in what you're saying.'

'Deal,' I say, smiling, and so grateful to have her with me.

We link arms and march across the road. Graves, and Anderson, aren't going to know what's hit them.

15

SATURDAY

I'm relieved when the clock hits six and I no longer have to pretend I'm asleep. My brain has been motoring most of the night, in between snatches of nightmares where Anderson is chasing me through the dark and barren woods, rather than my sister. But as I push the duvet back, I'm not going to allow thoughts of him to ruin my day.

I make two cups of tea and a round of toast and then I sit on the bed and open my laptop. The same anxiety that kept me up most of the night is here now, but I persevere, and load up *The Daily Bore*'s website. There is an immediate pop-up message telling me I need to subscribe to continue, but I'm not prepared to waste my money on this rag. It's probably too early to find a paper copy of the feature in a local shop, so I select the free one-day trial, and search for my name.

The full-screen image of me that flashes up beside the headline almost looks like someone else. Gone are the puffy eyes, crow's feet and pale skin tone I'm so used to seeing staring back at me in the mirror; kudos to Sasha for making me look human. But the expression on my face is one of sincerity and determination. It says I'm ready to fight.

FIGHTING INJUSTICE IN MEMORY OF THE SISTER SHE LOST

The change to the headline was my idea, and by the time Sasha and I finished with Graves, I think he would have written anything just to get us out of his office. I didn't like how the original headline victimised me. I don't want people to think I'm *haunted* by Faye's death, and I dislike referring to myself as a *crusader for justice*. I support those who need my help because I can, and it's the right thing to do.

Graves's original article was factually correct, but made me sound so cold, so it is now interspersed with references to our happy childhood; how we were inseparable from a young age; and includes copies of a couple of scanned photographs I managed to find on my phone.

The first picture is of two-year-old me beaming next to the hospital cot where Faye is sleeping beside the unicorn with a rainbow-coloured horn, given to her by Dad, after her dramatic entrance into this world. She was delivered by caesarean after Mum spent nearly thirty-six hours in labour. The next is of Faye and me a few years later, splashing in the paddling pool in the garden on a hot summer's day, with the unicorn looking on. Even when she hit puberty, that stupid stuffed toy was never far from her grasp, like a comfort blanket she never grew out of. And finally, the last photograph taken of me and Faye together, both dressed in our school uniforms on the first day of term. Neither of us is smiling, but thankfully neither Graves nor Sasha asked why.

I send a message to Sasha to ask if she's read the article yet, but it remains unread, a sign that she's probably still fast asleep.

I feel satisfied with how the feature portrays my history, and it should be a big obstacle to Anderson's pathetic attempt to win people over to his proclamation of innocence. Given how badly yesterday started, I feel like I've wrenched some control back.

I finish my tea and toast, open the door to the built-in wardrobe in my bedroom, and extract the dusty box that has been hidden away inside since Mum passed. Right now, I need to feel her with me. When Dad died she told me it was us against the world, and it broke my heart that I could do nothing to stop her taking the overdose.

I carry the box back to my bed, and lift off the lid to a cloud of dust. Inside, I immediately see her old faux-leather jewellery box, weathered by age and neglect. I open it and see the few pieces that she didn't pawn when times were toughest. The gaudy brooch was her mother's and survived the Blitz by all accounts. The two bracelets only have a sentimental value as does the watch, which hasn't ticked for as long as I can remember. I put these treasures to one side, and lift out the thick photo album. Even with the advent of digital photography, she still preferred images she could hold close to her heart.

Hints of her favourite perfume fill the air as I open the heavy brown cover and see the images inside, each protected within the plastic sleeves inside. The first sheet has six black and white images, pictures of my parents when they were children, standing proudly with their parents. Both sets of grandparents passed before I was born, and having never met them, it doesn't feel right to refer to them as grandmas and grandpas. Below these pictures is one of my parents the night they met at a friend's birthday party. They look so young and innocent, and clueless about what their futures will hold. I really wish I could have met them at this age, to understand whether they experienced the same fears and uncertainty that still haunt me to this day. And the final photograph on this page is of the two of them standing outside the church where they married. Mum looks resplendent in a figure-hugging white gown and Dad looks like a true gent in his dark suit and tie. But it's their smiles that stand out most: it looks like the happiest day of their lives.

The plastic sheet crackles as I turn it over and see an image of Mum in a hospital gown, holding a tiny bundle I know to be me. She looks too exhausted to smile, but I can see the pride and love in her eyes as she rests her forehead against mine. And it's almost as if I can feel her warmth on my head now.

'I miss you, Mum,' I whisper as I feel tears sting the backs of my eyes.

Everything changed after Faye's death. I can see it in the pictures before me now. Mum and Dad are all smiles in each photograph, and there are dozens showing the two of us slowly growing; images of us on beaches, in snow, in school portraits, and at parties. We look like any normal family. And I know these pictures don't paint a true picture of what it was like in our family. They don't show the arguments, the tears, the lies; they are just the parts of the past we want to remember.

I press my fingers to the plastic covering the photo of John-Paul and me dressed for the Year 10 prom. I remember how awkward he was the day he asked me to go with him, sweat beading at his hairline, and the glasses slipping down his nose. He stuttered the words, and almost talked himself out of it, not realising how excited I was to be asked to prom by a boy in the year above. Mum looked so proud when she took the photo, and although at first I didn't think a relationship would develop between us, he kind of grew on me. Nothing was ever too much trouble, and he always insisted on paying for everything.

He was the first boy I ever loved, but like everything else, things changed after Faye's murder. It didn't feel right for me to enjoy myself knowing Faye never would again, and so I pushed him away, stopped answering his texts, and he eventually moved on to college, and I never saw him again. He did add me as a friend on Facebook years ago, and the last I checked he's a cosmetic surgeon with a beautiful wife, so at least things worked out for him.

My heart breaks as I turn to the next page, and immediately notice the difference: Mum's smile is gone and Dad looks as though he has aged a decade overnight. I can't believe there's actually a photograph of Faye's tombstone. It looks so shiny and new, the gold bevelled writing on the granite untainted by weather and age, unlike the last time I went back to visit. It must be years since I went to the cemetery to leave flowers. It was definitely before the Covid pandemic, but probably several years before.

My hand shoots up to my mouth as I realise it could be a decade since I last went to pay my respects, and the guilt overwhelms me.

I continue turning pages in the photo album, until I reach the final picture of me at my university graduation ceremony. I am standing with Mum and Dad and it is a bright and sunny day. At first glance, they look like any two parents watching on proudly as their daughter graduates top of her class, but all I see is two broken people forcing themselves to smile, all the while thinking about what they've lost. I've no doubt they were proud to see me graduate, but compare those thin smiles with the earlier pictures in this album and you'd see how hard they were having to work to appear normal that day.

They're not the only ones pretending.

I start as my phone vibrates on the bed beside me. It's probably Sasha responding to my message. I lift the phone and stare at the screen, but the text message is from an unknown number.

> I know you lied about what really happened to your sister in those woods.

I don't move for what feels like an eternity. I stare at the words as they fade in and out of focus. I can't breathe. It's as if someone has reached into my soul and pulled on my biggest fear. I start as a second message appears.

> Admit what you did, or I'll reveal everything that happened that day.

It's just a crank, I tell myself.

The feature was bound to bring some weirdos out of the woodwork, and that's all this is. I repeat the lie over and over, but I can't ignore the tiny voice scratching at the back of my mind: what if someone knows?

> You have three days. I'll be watching.

I am trembling as I return the photo album to the box and hide it away in the wardrobe again. I quickly dress and reach for my raincoat, carefully picking up my phone and putting it in my pocket. I've felt certain someone has been watching me over the last few days, and now I can't escape the possibility that they're coming for me. I send a message to Sasha and then I head out, double-checking my flat door is locked.

16

I open the front door of the building, but hesitate before stepping out, scouring the street for anyone surveilling the place. The road and pavement are soaking from the continuing downpour, and I consider returning to fetch an umbrella, but that will only make me easier to follow, and more difficult for me to be aware of my surroundings. Raising the collar of my jacket, I cross my arms over my chest to keep the jacket in place and then I slam the door behind me.

I hurry down the three steps and into the throng of people heading to the Saturday street market. With my headphones buried deep in my ears, I can barely hear the world around me as traders lift the shutters on their shopfronts, and consumers nip in and out of one retailer or another, dodging the rain shower. Whilst I can't hear them, I'm watching each one, assessing their potential danger to me.

I know you lied about what really happened to your sister in those woods.

Is he out here now? Watching me as I pace the pavement,

making an effort to avoid treading in puddles? If he has found my phone number, who's to say he hasn't also found my address?

I stop when I see a woman staring at me from outside of the estate agents on the corner up ahead. I don't recognise her, but I'm certain she's staring at me, rather than someone nearby. I force myself to look away, taking occasional glances back in her direction to check if she's still looking. Beneath the large red and white striped golfing umbrella, she must be in her mid-to-late fifties, her fair hair sprinkled with blossoming grey, and her face heavily made up to hide the signs of time. She's dressed in a paisley sweater and dark trousers, and is still watching me.

I stop at one of the market stalls ahead, and pretend to peruse the items on the table. It's only when the vendor starts speaking to me that I even realise I'm holding a padlock for a bicycle. He's trying to upsell the lock for a more expensive one, but I'm not listening to the sales patter, using the time to try and devise a plan to deal with this woman in case she approaches or begins following me. Ordinarily a stranger staring at me wouldn't be a concern, but my nerves are frazzled after the crank text, and suddenly it feels like the entire world is out to get me.

She is still there; still watching.

What does she want? Why is she watching me?

'You want buy?' the vendor is practically shouting at me, and I'm about to drop the padlock and walk away, when a fresh idea strikes.

I pull out my phone and tap it against the card machine in his hands, quickly pocketing the padlock. Its chain-like quality would make an effective weapon should I require one on my journey. I move behind the stall, trying to put distance and obstacles between me and the woman, but when I glance back over to the estate agents, she's vanished. I can't tell if she's gone inside, or moved on. I scan the road in both directions, but can't trace the red and white umbrella.

I take a deep breath and slowly exhale, the tension in my shoulders finally easing as I realise it was just paranoia getting the better of me. I continue along the pavement, reminding myself that most crank callers use the telephone because they don't have the courage to confront their victims face to face.

It takes another ten minutes of scanning faces as I walk, taking an elongated route to the office to try and determine if anyone is following me, but I finally see the sign for the wine bar, and feel my nerves begin to settle. If it was open I'd consider taking shelter inside, a quick glass of Pinot to settle my anxiety, but it's not even nine o'clock yet.

I unlock the door to the office, and lock it behind me, hurrying up the stairs, through the reception and into my office, peeking out from behind the blind, staring down at the road.

The street is deserted, but I can't stop thinking that he's watching me.

This is where I remain until I see Sasha hurrying along the pavement, carrying two paper cups and a brown bag. In the last twenty-five minutes, I've seen four men, five women, and two students. A mixture of couriers, and shoppers, at a guess. Nobody has stopped and looked up at any point.

I still turn and double-check when I hear footsteps on the stairs, relieved only when I see Sasha's face at the top.

'Hey, what's so urgent?' she pants.

'I think someone's stalking me,' I blurt out before I can stop myself.

Sasha looks me up and down before replying.

'Hardly surprising, you're a hottie.'

'Sasha, please, I'm serious.'

Her smile is quickly replaced by a concerned frown. She

crosses the room and hands me one of the paper cups and asks me to explain. I unlock my phone and show her the text messages from the unknown number.

'I don't follow,' she says, passing the phone back to me.

I take another glance out of the window before dropping in to my chair.

'My number isn't public,' I say. 'Whoever sent me this knows my number.'

'I hate to break it to you, Abbey, but nobody's number is private now. If you've ever bought something online, they demand a contact number and then these details get sold or stolen. I have a friend who dabbles with the dark web and he could get anybody's number you want; even celebrities. Why do you think so many criminals use burner phones that they use once and dispose of?'

I hadn't thought about it like that, though I wouldn't know where to begin trying to find somebody else's information, short of searching for them on social media.

'It's probably just some weirdo who saw you in the newspaper and is looking for attention,' Sasha concludes. 'Just block all unknown numbers in your phone's settings and you won't hear from them again.'

I wish I could be so blasé about it, but something won't let me dismiss it so easily.

'You don't look convinced,' she adds.

'It's just...'

I don't know where to begin, nor how much I should share. If she's right then I'm spending far too much time worrying about something so trivial. But I can't ignore the possibility that she's wrong.

I let out a heavy sigh.

'I feel like someone is watching me,' I say. 'Not just this morning, but for the last few days. I keep checking behind me, but haven't spotted who it is, but you know when you just get that sixth sense that makes you uncomfortable?'

She pouts.

'Not really, but then you're the one who is able to notice things the rest of us miss.'

'Do you think I should report this to the police?'

'Honestly? I'm not sure there's a lot they can do. There's no physical threat to your safety.'

'But this person might be trying to blackmail me. That's a crime.'

'But there's nothing in it, right? They say you lied about your sister, but what does that mean? What do you think they're alluding to?'

I stand and move back to the window, this time raising the blind fully and looking in both directions, trying to avoid the question. I can't see anyone I recognise on the street and turn to face Sasha when she stands and joins me.

'What's going on, mate?' she asks.

'Don't you think it's all just a bit coincidental, all this? First we're approached by *The Daily Bore*, then Rhys Morgan hires us to look through Anderson's case ahead of an appeal, and now I receive this text message.'

'Well, don't shoot the messenger, but you are a huge piece of what happened to Anderson; it was your testimony that was the final nail in his coffin. His appeal could all just be smoke and mirrors, one last dance with celebrity before he pops his clogs. Of course he'd try to drag you into it to discredit you. Maybe he gets his solicitor to generate the interest with the television production company, and that triggers Peter Graves to do some digging. Of course it's all linked.'

'And the text message?'

'Just some lone nutter with nothing better to do with their time. Or maybe it's some lackey Anderson has hired to knock you off balance.'

I move away from the window, suddenly feeling hot and needing space, my anxiety spiking.

'If it's bothering you that much, why don't you take a couple of days and get away from London?'

'And go where?'

'*Anywhere*. When was the last time you had a proper break?'

I must admit it's been a while since I switched off from work and actually rested. But guilt always overwhelms me when I try to relax, knowing there are more victims of misjustice rotting away in prison cells.

'You could have a weekend break at a spa, or jump on the Eurostar to Paris or Bruges. You didn't want to look at Anderson's appeal anyway, so it's not like there's anything keeping you here, is there?'

Admit what you did, or I'll reveal everything that happened that day.

This is the part that's worrying me most, but I can't share that with Sasha. But then I reconsider the words. It's so vague, suggesting that I've kept the truth hidden, but it doesn't detail anything about *what* that truth might be.

Maybe Sasha is right, and I'm just making a mountain out of a molehill. And maybe she's right about me booking somewhere away for a few days, to put all of this out of mind, and then figure out a plan to minimise the damage Anderson's documentary can do to me; to *us*. Time away would also stop the feeling that I'm being watched, especially if it's somewhere nobody would guess.

'Oh, that's interesting,' Sasha says, cutting through my thoughts.

I turn and see she is staring out of the window in my office.

'You know you said you thought someone was watching you? Well, guess who's just pulled up across the street?'

I stare blankly back at her.

'Who?'

'Anderson's solicitor. And just to warn you, he's holding a copy of *The Daily Bore*, and he doesn't look happy.'

I hurry to the window and look down just as he reaches our front door, and a moment later the buzzer sounds.

'What do you want me to do?' Sasha asks. 'Do we just ignore it, so he goes away?'

I'm about to respond, when Rhys steps back and stares straight up at the two of us.

'Too late,' I say. 'You'd better let him in.'

17

I take a long sip of the coffee Sasha bought for me, trying to compose my thoughts, ahead of what I'm sensing isn't going to be a pleasant meeting.

'What the bloody hell is this?' Rhys shouts as he enters the room and slams a copy of *The Daily Bore* down on the desk. Somehow, his anger makes him sound even more Welsh.

'Good morning, Rhys,' I say, trying to sound more in control than I'm feeling. 'What seems to be the problem?'

He glares back at me with disbelieving eyes, his face red and steam almost coming out of his ears like a cartoon character. He looks so different in jeans and a pullover, rather than the grubby suit and tie I saw him in yesterday.

'What seems to be the problem? You must think you're some kind of flipping comedian! The problem – as well you know, I'm sure – is that I hired you to help my client's appeal, and here you are – on the record – doing the exact opposite.'

I take a deep breath, choosing my words carefully, conscious that Sasha is hovering just outside the door, listening to everything.

'May I remind you, Rhys, that you approached us under false pretences? When you propositioned my business partner, you didn't make it clear that your client was Terry Anderson, otherwise we would have dismissed your request as an obvious conflict of interest.'

'Don't try and backtrack now. If that's what you really thought, you could have said as much when we met yesterday. But you didn't, nor did you say anything when you phoned and asked me to arrange for you to see Terry. You took our money, and then you stabbed us in the back.'

I keep my tone even.

'Please, Rhys, take a seat and we can discuss this like the professional people we are.'

He huffs, before pulling over a chair and dropping into it. I open the newspaper and flip to the feature, reading the headline that introduces it.

FIGHTING INJUSTICE IN MEMORY OF THE SISTER SHE LOST

She is the woman rarely noticed at the back of the courtroom. Whilst barristers claim the limelight, arguing and pontificating for their clients, the key to the appeal blends into the background. And even when the appellant is acquitted of their wrongful conviction, she still chooses not to claim her place front and centre. Yet without her insight and keen eye, the client would have remained just another casualty of war in the British justice system. But what drives this criminologist to step forward and put her neck on the line for a person she's only just met?

'It certainly isn't the money,' she says, when we meet for the second time to conclude our interview. But she isn't joking, as the majority of appeals she has supported have been undertaken on a pro bono basis.

Abbey Veritas (née Abigail Turnbull), 45, remains an enigma. Her face will be familiar to many who have seen her hailed as the Queen of Appeals after multiple interventions that secured the freedom of inmates wrongfully convicted of crimes. Most recently, it was Abbey's eagle-eyed expertise that led to the acquittal of Damian Johnson, a man who has spent the last seven years incarcerated for a crime he could not have committed. The police were so certain of Johnson's guilt that they stopped looking for other potential suspects, meaning the real killer of Rodrigo Johnson, Damian's husband, is still at large. We won't talk about the prejudices that might have played a key part in the police investigation, as the Metropolitan Police are set to launch an investigation into that themselves.

When I asked Abbey about her role in Damian's acquittal, she was self-deprecating, as I sense she often is, and hailed the hard work of the whole legal team who successfully argued for Damian's conviction to be overturned.

'I'm nothing special,' she told me when we first met earlier this week. But when you dig deeper, Abbey has a unique skill for reading people, predicting what they're thinking by reading their actions. I experienced this firsthand whilst we were talking when she accurately predicted my intentions in a card game. And I was keen to understand what drives someone to use that skill to the benefit of others.

'I suppose I've always had an interest in trying to understand how others think, and why they choose certain courses of action over others.'

But an upcoming true-crime documentary is about to question Abbey's integrity for the first time. Thirty years ago,

Abbey was a key witness for the prosecution when known sex offender, Terry Anderson, was convicted of multiple murders, including that of her sister Faye. Anderson maintains his innocence of that particular crime, a claim which is being explored as part of the new televised series that Abbey will be consulting on.

'I don't believe a word he's saying,' she says firmly. 'I know what I saw, and he is where he deserves to be.'

As you will see from the interviews that follow, the body of Abbey's 13-year-old sister, Faye, was discovered at the foot of a disused quarry less than a mile from where the Turnbull family lived. Anderson, now 70 and terminally ill, was the man police identified as Faye's killer, and when Abbey picked him out as the man she saw chasing after her sister, the police were able to include the crime as part of the multi-case trial that the Criminal Prosecution Service (CPS) was bringing against him. Abbey's testimony, played at the trial from a private room for her safety, was the final nail in the coffin for Anderson who was sentenced to multiple life sentences, with no chance of parole.

I met with Anderson and his solicitor earlier this month to ask why he's decided to appeal three decades after sentencing.

'Because I didn't do it,' he says in a tone so nonchalant that it sounds genuine. 'The doctor told me I don't have long left and should start to make final arrangements. I want that girl's family to know the truth: her real killer is still out there. They deserve justice.'

I ask him what justice means to him and he tells me it's accepting the truth and living by it. He is adamant that he did not kill Faye Turnbull and hopes the documentary will encourage the police to reopen the case.

'I've done a lot of bad things in my time,' he says, solemnly, 'and I've admitted to the other crimes, but my silence in here has allowed someone to escape justice. I'm not going to the grave until the truth is out there.'

'Truth and justice are two sides of the same coin,' Abbey quips when I share Anderson's responses with her. 'He speaks of truth, but all he wants is his own version of the truth. My sister deserves to rest in peace, and he is trampling on her memory. He killed her and he should stop trying to cash in.'

Anderson's solicitor has told me that his client intends to donate his fee to good causes. So, if money isn't his motivating factor, what else would drive him to such lengths?

'Everyone wants their fifteen minutes,' Abbey responds flatly. 'Real benevolence is about more than throwing money at an issue. He's had thirty years behind bars to make a real difference, and this just stinks of someone trying to make amends before they face judgement. It's too little and too late.'

You can read my full interviews with Abbey Veritas and Terry Anderson overleaf and when the documentary airs early next year, you'll be able to reach your own decision on which side of the debate you sit on. Having met and spoken to them both, I'm still on the fence.

I look up at Rhys.

'I don't see what the problem is,' I say flatly.

'You don't...' He puffs out his cheeks. 'You've called Terry a liar.'

'And that's what I firmly believe.'

'But have you even looked at the case files I sent over yesterday?'

'Not yet, but I am more than familiar with his case.'

'Are you though? You gave evidence relating to the charges for your sister's murder, but you weren't in court to hear the other charges against him. You only have your own *tainted* view of what happened.'

I resist the urge to rise to the bait.

'There is nothing in those files that will convince me that he didn't kill my sister.'

'You're wrong! If you look at the other victims – crimes he has now admitted committing, mind you – you will see he had a very distinctive modus operandi, and your sister's death doesn't fit the MO.'

I have no rebuttal to that, but I'm all too familiar with the kind of tricks solicitors and barristers use to obstruct the impact of truth.

'I've a good mind to advise Terry to sue you for libel,' Rhys adds.

'The writer makes it clear he is presenting two sides of the same story, and Anderson is accusing me just as much as I him. The point is for readers to choose which of us they believe, so don't make idle threats.'

'So, that's it, is it? You don't intend to look at the files? In that case, you can refund my fee.'

Sasha hurries into the room, before I have a chance to reply.

'Abbey didn't say she wouldn't look through them, but as you can imagine, all of this has been very triggering for her. Leave the files with us, and I assure you I will make sure they receive due care and attention.'

Sasha glares at me to concur.

'I will look over the files,' I say, trying not to grit my teeth.

Rhys looks from Sasha to me and then stands.

'You'd better do so. I'll expect an update early next week.'

With that he leaves, slamming the door behind him. I watch out of the window until I see his car pull away.

'I'll look at the files and make some notes,' Sasha says. 'You go home and pack and then go find somewhere to lie low for a few days. I'll keep Rhys at bay.'

I'm still not convinced, but agree. I hate leaving Sasha in the lurch, but Rhys was right about one thing, my view of Anderson is tainted. What he needs is someone independent to review the files.

I head back outside, once again raising the collar around my neck as the thick clouds overhead threaten to spill their load. I increase my pace, hoping I can make it back before the spitting becomes the inevitable downpour.

I hurry through the market stalls, no longer looking for undue attention, and feeling more determined than ever to stand up to Anderson's claims. I've just made it to the canopy over the entrance to the block of flats when the rumble of thunder is quickly followed by torrential rain, and I breathe a sigh of relief. Those still on the street scatter in search of shelter, and I unlock the door, almost tripping on the large cardboard box on the step. I'm surprised to see my name and address on the label, as I don't recall ordering anything online, but I pick it up and tuck it beneath my arm before ascending the stairs to the first floor. It's only when I'm inside my flat and have stripped out of my raincoat that my attention returns to the parcel. It's maybe a foot wide and half as tall. I reach for a cheese knife and cut through the brown parcel tape, lifting the flaps and pulling out handfuls of poly-styrene packing peanuts. I eventually find a much smaller wrapped box inside. The paper is shiny and striped, and I'm now assuming that it's a surprise gift from Sasha. I use the knife to cut the tape on the wrapping paper but frown when I pull out a matchbox. Curiosity gets the better of me and I shake it, but there's only a single rattle. Sliding it open, I drop the box when I see what's inside.

My hands shoot up to my mouth as I immediately recognise one of the hairclips that Faye was wearing when she ran off. The police found three in her hair, and assumed that the fourth must have fallen out while she was running from her killer.

Why would someone send this to me?

I dive back into the larger box, tipping the polystyrene peanuts to the floor, searching for any sign of who sent it, but find nothing inside. My gaze returns to the matchbox, and something on the inside of the wrapping paper catches my eye. I lift it so the shiny side is pointing away from me, and gasp as I read the message:

I CAN PROVE YOU LIED.

18

The message floats out of my hands and back into the box as I stare at it in disbelief. I'd almost convinced myself that the earlier text messages were from a crank, as Sasha suggested, but this parcel has to have come from the same person. I don't believe there can be two oddballs out there who've both targeted me in the same way following *The Daily Bore* feature. But who is doing this to me?

They have my phone number and my home address. I know Sasha said that kind of information can be harnessed through the dark web, but I don't think I know anyone with the skills to access the dark web.

I go through names in my head of all the people who already know my address and phone number, but I quickly lose track, and try writing them down.

Sasha knows everything about me, but there's no way she has anything to do with this. She's the closest thing I have to a best friend, and I didn't sense she was lying yesterday when I told her about my connection to Terry Anderson, nor when I showed her the anonymous text earlier.

Both Eddie Douglas and Robert Timmons-Drake have my phone number, but I don't think either know where I live, as I've always commuted to meet them in their offices. Damian Johnson also has my number, but like Eddie and Robert, there's no reason that he would have anything to do with this.

I turn my attention back to the hairclip in the matchbox and suddenly I see Faye's sweet face as we walked to the park that day. She was bouncing with excitement and kept asking me when John-Paul would meet us. To an observer you would have thought it was her boyfriend we were meeting.

I lift the matchbox up, studying the hairclip, wanting to lift it out, but conscious there may be fingerprints on it from whoever sent the parcel.

Would whoever sent it be smart enough to have worn gloves?

I stand and tip the matchbox up, the hairclip bouncing once on the tabletop before settling. I flick on the torch on my phone and shine it down, carefully inspecting the lower side, before using a packing peanut to try and flip it over.

I can't see anything obvious resembling a fingerprint and as I study it closer, I can't even be sure it is one of Faye's. I remember her asking me to help fix her hair in a high ponytail like mine, and I used four clips to keep the hairs around the tie from slipping out. She was always losing hairclips, much to Mum's annoyance, and this was one of the only sets where she still had four. The leopard print certainly resembles what I can see in my mind's eye, but my mind could just be playing tricks on me.

I don't recall the police making a big thing about the missing hairclip, because everyone assumed it had just fallen out like all the others, so I don't think it was ever reported in any of the newspapers. I can't see how anyone else would know about the missing hairclip, nor what it looked like, unless they were there and took it.

I hear Anderson's voice in my head: *My silence in here has allowed your sister's real killer to escape unpunished. It's time for me – for us – to set the record straight.*

If I were to take Anderson at face value, then the only conclusion I can draw is that Faye's real killer is the one who sent me the hairclip, but having evaded capture for thirty years, I can't understand why they would want me to know Anderson isn't responsible. And even if they did, it would be far easier for them to come and knock on my door and admit the truth, rather than play these games. It just doesn't make sense in my head.

If I stick to my guns and ignore Anderson's claims of innocence, wouldn't it make sense for him to be the one behind this? I've heard stories about prisoners being able to access hidden mobile phones in prison, so maybe he sent the three messages. But he wouldn't have been able to send me the hairclip from there, and I've no idea how he would have obtained my number and address.

I take a moment to compose myself, searching for an alternative explanation.

Just because Anderson couldn't send the parcel himself doesn't mean that he didn't get someone to help him. Maybe he told his solicitor of the little memento he'd taken all those years ago, and how sending it to me anonymously would mess with my head. My eyes widen. His appeal is based on his claim that I lied about seeing him that day, and if he can make me admit as much my reputation will be in tatters and he'll win his little battle.

It is the only explanation that makes any sense in my head, but I'm not totally convinced. There are too many big ifs, and I can't rule out the possibility that someone else could be trying to damage my reputation. It's not like I haven't made a few enemies along the way. Eddie Douglas and Robert Timmons-Drake would certainly be on that list, especially after the threat I made in their office yesterday morning. The fact that they still haven't emailed across the terms of payment speaks volumes.

I look back at the hairclip, and this time pick it up, holding it just beneath my nose and inhale as I close my eyes. I picture Faye's face as I smell the scent of Mum's shampoo. I feel a tear break free and blot on my cheek. I now have no doubt that this is the missing hairclip.

I see the text message flash behind my eyes: *You have three days. I'll be watching.*

Maybe this is the time I should contact the police. Although sending me the hairclip isn't directly threatening, it's what it implies which is causing me anguish. There might be a way they can track who sent the box, and that would reveal who is doing this to me. I close the flaps and study the label, only now realising it was sent from Hampshire where I grew up.

Is it possible that someone from back then is behind this? I don't know who or why anyone would hold a grudge that long. Is it someone I went to school with? Someone who was also in those woods that day, and saw what I did?

I collapse onto my bed, closing my eyes and trying to empty my mind of all these unanswerable questions.

This is like a nightmare I can't wake from, and as much as I'd like to follow Sasha's advice and run away from it, the thought of someone exposing the truth has me hyperventilating. I need to find out who is behind this, because there's one thing I'm feeling more certain of: this is not some loner craving attention; this is someone who knows me and wants to see me broken.

19

I spend the next hour trawling my memory for the names of anyone I shared a class with at secondary school. I even manage to locate an old yearbook from amongst Mum's old things in the wardrobe, but it doesn't help me narrow my search for suspects. I recognise faces of girls and boys I was friends with, some I couldn't stand, and some I don't even remember. But nobody leaps out as having anything to do with Faye or Terry Anderson.

So much water has passed under the bridge that I feel as though I'm wasting valuable time. And then I turn the page and see a photo of John-Paul in the yearbook. He looks even more geeky than I remember, his hair out of control, and his old-fashioned glasses. Behind the image I knew him to be a funny and compassionate boy, something his bullies never saw.

I feel bad about the way I pushed him away after Faye died. I couldn't cope with the intense scrutiny on our lives. At one point, my parents were both dragged into the police station to prove they weren't responsible for her death. But it's me who should have been under the microscope. I should have made sure she was safe, and not allowed her to run off.

I wipe the tears from my eyes; self-pity is not going to help me uncover the identity of this threat.

What I need is to speak to someone who was there at that time, and might remember things differently. My eyes fall back on John-Paul's picture, and I open a search page on my phone and type in his name. The address of a practice in Harley Street appears on the screen, along with a telephone number. I'm tempted to call, but given the sensitivity of what I want to ask him, it may be better to go in person. There's every chance he doesn't even remember who I am, but I need all the insight I can get.

I catch an Uber to the practice, with no energy to be watching for tails while walking or on the Tube. During the twenty-minute journey, I prepare what I want to ask him, trying to find the right words that won't make me sound like a nutcase, and hoping he is still as merciful as the boy I knew.

I exit the car, and walk up to the four-storey terraced building that looks exactly like all the others in the row, with black wrought-iron fences separating them from the pavement. It must cost an absolute fortune to be based here, but knowing John-Paul he's probably able to charge a fortune for his craft. He always excelled in maths and science, and always knew he wanted to be a doctor in some capacity.

I ascend the four steps to the large black door and buzz for reception.

'Can I take your name?'

'Abbey Ver—' I begin, before catching myself. 'Abbey Turnbull.'

'Do you have an appointment?' the shrill voice on the intercom responds.

'Um, no, not exactly. I'm an old friend of John-Paul Stafford. I need to speak to him urgently.'

'I'm afraid Mr Stafford has a full schedule of appointments today—'

'Please,' I interrupt, 'it's a real emergency. I need to speak to him now.'

'I'm afraid that's just not possible. The best thing I can suggest is you send an email to the practice account, explaining your emergency, and I'll make sure Mr Stafford receives it.'

I step back in frustration. I hadn't anticipated it would be this difficult to get into the building, nor that John-Paul would be so busy on a Saturday. I don't want to waste more time, but I imagine if I phone reception, she still won't connect me with him.

I'm about to search for a new Uber, when a man in a sling hurries along the road, and ascends the stairs.

'Would you mind buzzing for me?' he asks, his accent Scouse.

I press the buzzer, and step away, allowing him to talk to the receptionist. He provides his name and apologises for being late for his appointment. As soon as I hear the door unlock, I step forward and hold it open for him. He thanks me, without questioning why I'm following him through.

Signs on the wall indicate that reception is on the first floor, and we both follow the stairs up, but I allow him to enter first, hanging back, and assessing the layout of the area. The woman behind the reception desk reminds me of an old history teacher I had who I couldn't stand. Her voice when she speaks to the man in the sling is clipped and forthright. There's no way she's going to allow me to see John-Paul without an appointment, but then I see one of the closed doors at the far side of the space open, and a tall woman with a model's figure exit. And then I see him. Thirty years older, but still with that goofy charm I remember. He's put on weight since then, and his hairline is receding, and his glasses are now far more fashionable, but it's definitely him.

I hurry across the room, calling out his name, ignoring the

shouts of the receptionist. I push him back into the room, and close the door behind me.

'John-Paul,' I say, keen to say my piece before the staff have me forcibly removed from the building. 'I don't know if you remember me, but I'm—'

'Abbey Turnbull,' he says, a broad smile slowly spreading across his face. 'As I live and breathe. How are you? I didn't realise you were my next appointment. Please come in, come in. Sit down, and let me know how I can help.'

The door to the room bursts open, and the receptionist stands there, eyebrows raised in my direction.

'Madam, I already told you, Mr Stafford is very busy,' she begins, before he cuts her off.

'It's okay, Edith. This is an old school friend of mine. My next appointment isn't for another ten minutes. Just ask them to be patient.'

She leaves without another word, and I allow John-Paul to lead me over to one of the chairs across from his desk.

'How long has it been?' he says, his face still marvelling at seeing me again.

'Thirty years, give or take,' I say, wishing I was here under better circumstances.

'Thirty years? Bloody hell! Time sure does fly when you're having fun, right? Wow, are you a sight for sore eyes.'

His desk is neatly organised, his laptop perpendicular to the edge of the polished wood. Behind him is a row of immaculately clean filing cabinets, and in the corner of the room a healthy green houseplant. How I wish my own office was this well-maintained.

'I don't normally see potential patients without appointments – Edith is very strict with my schedule – but I'm happy to make an exception for an old friend. Now, what is it you're looking to have done?'

'Um, sorry, that's not why I'm here,' I say, though I can't help but feel as though he's already determined exactly what treatments would benefit my ageing face and body. 'I want to ask you what you remember of the day my sister went missing.'

His smile quickly fades, and I'm annoyed at myself for going off the script I'd prepared in the back of the taxi.

'You know what, I haven't thought about that in,' he sucks breath between his teeth, 'I don't know how long. I'm sorry, I'd totally forgotten that even happened. I know it wasn't easy for you back then. Sorry.'

Same John-Paul, still tripping over his words, and offering apologies when they're not required. I notice the framed photograph on his desk, showing him in a suit beside his beautiful bride. It makes me feel even guiltier for invading his space.

'It's fine, and I'm sorry for just showing up unannounced when you're clearly very busy. The thing is,' I take a deep breath, 'you were with us in the woods that day when she ran away, and I want to ask whether you remember seeing anyone else there who witnessed what happened.'

His cheeks flush.

'I don't mean that,' I quickly clarify. 'I mean, when she ran off, or before she did, did you see anyone you recognised from school watching us?'

His brow furrows.

'Watching us? No, not that I recall.'

I was afraid this would be his response.

'Anything out of the ordinary,' I persevere. 'Maybe something that you thought was insignificant, but might be really important?'

He continues to frown.

'No, I'm sorry. To be honest, I tried to push a lot of what happened from my memory, given what followed.' He sighs. 'What's this all about?'

'The man who was convicted of killing her, Terry Anderson, is now appealing his conviction, claiming he didn't kill Faye.'

The blood drains from his face.

'I think I'm being targeted as some sort of smear campaign,' I continue. 'Someone is claiming they know we lied about what happened that day, and I need to figure out who and why.'

'Wait, but you said—'

'I remember what I said,' I interrupt, 'but that's not relevant to what is happening now. If this person – whoever they are – saw what really happened and shares it, we both could face trouble.'

He pushes his chair back and stands, crossing to the net curtains over the only window in the room.

'I appreciate this will come as a shock, but the only way to prevent everything coming out is to find the person responsible. Sooner rather than later.'

He turns back to face me, his face still ashen.

'What do you need me to do?'

I compose myself.

'I need you to try and remember everything you can about that day. About where you went from when you woke to when the search party turned up. Every minute detail. Who you saw, when, where, and what you remember specifically about the moment Faye ran off.'

'I mean, I'll try,' he says sincerely, 'but it was thirty years ago, Abbey. I'm really not sure what help I will be to you. Have you spoken to the police about these threats you've received?'

'I don't think it's in either of our best interests for me to involve the police, do you?'

He returns to his seat without answering.

'Listen, my next appointment is in a few minutes, but I'm only working until midday. Let me deal with these patients and then maybe we can regroup for something to eat and put our heads together. How does that sound?'

I'm just relieved he hasn't chased me out or questioned my sanity.

I stand, trying to hold back the tears stinging at the edge of my eyes.

'Thank you, John-Paul. I'll be waiting outside at twelve.'

I show myself out of the room, and avoid the glare Edith is burning into the back of my head. As I exit back out onto the street, I finally allow myself a moment to breathe. The last thing I want to do is drag John-Paul into the mess of my making, but he's the only person I know who might be able to help me uncover who is threatening me. And I wasn't lying when I told him his reputation and freedom could be in just as much trouble as my own. We have three days to figure out if this threat is real or not, and who's behind it.

20

When John-Paul emerges, I'm half-expecting him to send me packing, but instead he tells me he managed to get through his remaining appointments early and is ready to help me in any way he can.

Just like old times.

He leads me to a local Italian restaurant where we are seated in the basement. He tells me he knows the manager and we won't be disturbed. He orders lunch and drinks for the both of us in perfect Italian, and even though I have no appetite, I tuck in to the bowl of carbonara like I haven't eaten in days.

He tells me to start from the beginning, and so I tell him about the approach from Graves for the feature in *The Daily Bore*, and am relieved when he tells me he doesn't read it. I tell him about Terry Anderson's appeal and the documentary, and how his solicitor tricked Sasha into roping us in to support his imminent appeal. John-Paul listens without interrupting, until I'm finished, and he then wipes his mouth with a serviette.

'I'm not going to lie and say I haven't seen the reputation you've created for yourself. So, I'm not surprised you're being approached by newspapers and television shows trying to ride on your coattails. And actually, I think you'd be a great series host if their offer is firmed up.'

'That's kind of you to say, but—'

'No,' he says, raising his hand, 'please don't do that, Abbey. I never said anything when we were younger because I didn't want you to think I was criticising but I used to hate how you always put yourself down. Self-deprecation and humility are one thing, but doing it all the time makes it seem like you're searching for reassurance.'

He's more right than he knows.

'Now, from what I remember, and what I've seen on the evening news, you're more than capable of achieving anything you want. You were always intelligent, but there is an authority to the way you speak that has others eating out of the palm of your hand. So, please don't put yourself down in my presence.'

I can feel the heat blazing in my cheeks, but the room is low-lit, so I hope he hasn't noticed.

'Now, tell me what had you hurtling across town to see me this morning,' he says, taking a sip of water.

'So, the feature in the newspaper was published this morning, presenting both sides of the case – mine and Anderson's – allowing the reader to make their own mind up. And after I woke I received three text messages from an unknown number claiming that I'm lying about my account of what happened that day, that they can prove it, and that I have three days to come clean or they'll expose me.'

He considers this in silence.

'And there's no way you can trace this number?' he eventually asks.

'None.'

'Why three days?'

The question throws me.

'Excuse me?'

'Why three days? What happens in three days? Why not today? Why not tomorrow? Why give you three days to admit the truth? Why wait?'

It's a valid question and not what I've considered until this point.

'I honestly don't know,' I reply, trying to think of an answer and coming up blank. 'Why do you think?'

He raises his eyebrows.

'Oh, I have no clue either, but it just seems an odd timeframe. In my mind, it either means it is a total bluff from someone hoping you'll admit something you later regret, or...'

'Or what?'

'Or this person wants you to try and find them.'

I know he's trying to help, but if anything, this only widens the net for potential suspects.

'You think it's some kind of trap?'

He wipes his mouth again, before dropping the serviette to his plate.

'Oh, no, that's not what I'm saying, or maybe it is, I don't know. Tell me, is there anybody who would want you distracted for the next three days for any reason?'

I immediately picture Eddie Douglas's face, but I can't say why.

'It was just a thought,' he says, dismissively.

'I was actually going through our old yearbook earlier, trying to work out whether it's someone who went to school with us. Can you think of anyone who would go to these kinds of lengths to get back at me or us for some reason?'

'A thirty-year grudge? No.'

'No, me neither,' I say, sighing. 'But I am sure it is connected to my sister in some way.' I extract the matchbox from my pocket and show him the hairclip. 'This was sent to my flat this morning. The postmark is Hampshire.'

He looks at the hairclip but there's no look of recognition.

'I think this was the hairclip my sister lost on the day. She had four in her hair when she showed up at the park, but when police discovered her body in the quarry, one of the hairclips was missing. That was never formally announced in the news coverage or the trial, so the only person who could have sent it to me must have been around at that time.'

His eyes widen in shock.

'You're not saying you think that *I* have anything to do with this?'

The thought had crossed my mind, but John-Paul is giving me no reason to suspect him, and I'm certain his reaction to the hairclip is genuine.

'No, but what if somebody else was there that day – someone we weren't aware of – who saw what happened, and then, I don't know, took the hairclip, hoping one day to use it to blackmail us or something.'

'Have they demanded money?'

'No, not yet, but even if they did I haven't got any I can give them.'

He drops a handful of notes on the table, and then stands confidently.

'Come on, let's go,' he says, heading for the stairs up, with me hurrying after him.

'Where are we going?' I ask, catching up to him on the street.

He stops, and fixes me with a firm stare.

'Ask yourself this: if you were a detective and someone gave you the story you've just told me, what would your next step be?'

'Refer them for a mental health assessment,' I say, shrugging.

'No, but what if you as detective believe the story? What lead would you pursue?'

I'm still not following his thought processes and am grateful when he reveals what he's getting at.

'You said the postmark on the box was Hampshire, right? So, let's go to Hampshire now, and see if we can figure out who sent it.'

I'm about to argue when he sets off again, eventually stopping at a top-of-the-range Land Rover parked outside the practice.

'This is insane, John-Paul. What are you planning to do? Go to every post office in the county and ask if the staff remember someone sending the box?'

'No,' he scoffs. 'But I reckon, if you post something on social media about travelling home, your stalker will see it, and follow you wherever you go. I'm suggesting we return to where this all began, and flush out whoever is behind this.'

I'm not convinced by the plan, and the thought of encouraging this person to follow me fills me with dread. But I can see how invested John-Paul is in helping me, and it's been a while since I felt someone was truly on my side.

He indicates before pulling out into traffic, and I send Sasha a message letting her know where I'm going and why.

21

It takes nearly two hours for us to reach Southampton through stop-start traffic, roadworks, and temporary speed limits. John-Paul seems keen on catching up on old times and peppers me with questions about how I got into my current line of work. I don't feel particularly chatty, and provide limited answers, whereas he chatters away, telling me about his wife Vanessa.

'She supports various humanitarian projects across the globe,' he tells me as we leave the motorway via the slip road. 'This week she's in Brussels, petitioning NATO to provide additional support to Ukraine.'

She sounds almost too impressive, but I am pleased that John-Paul managed to find someone more deserving of his love.

'So, she's not expecting me to be home tonight,' he adds.

I glance over to him, uncertain if I should be reading more into that statement.

'Listen, I appreciate you driving me here, John-Paul, but to be clear, I'm only here to try and find whoever is threatening us. This isn't some—'

'Oh, God, is that what you thought I was thinking? I'm sorry, no, I just meant, if we don't manage to find out anything today, we should find a hotel. Two rooms. I'm sorry if you thought I meant something else.'

My cheeks blaze with embarrassment. Of course he wasn't propositioning me. He's married and clearly head-over-heels in love. I wish the seat would just swallow me up.

'I'm sorry, John-Paul, I just didn't want the waters to be muddy. Forget I said anything.'

An uncomfortable silence descends as we head west of Southampton and to the outskirts of the New Forest.

It is so strange seeing sights that are so familiar and yet not quite as I remember them. We're practically on the doorstep of Ashford when we suddenly pull into the car park of a pub restaurant advertising bed and breakfast availability.

'I'll go in and check if they can accommodate us,' he says, opening his door and climbing out, before ducking his head back in. 'If they don't have two rooms, we'll try somewhere else.'

I watch as he walks towards the pub, but I still don't really know what his plan is. He said he knows someone who might be able to help us track the origins of the parcel, but hasn't said any more. He jogs back a few minutes later, and opens my door.

'Good news, I've managed to get two rooms for the night, so my suggestion is we freshen up, and then I'll see if my contact is free to meet.'

When I headed to Harley Street this morning, I hadn't anticipated that I might need fresh clothes and toiletries.

'And then in the morning,' he adds, 'I thought it might help freshen our memories if we went back to the woods in Ashford.'

I haven't been back since graduating university. Too many painful memories I couldn't confront, but if I really want to get to the bottom of this, then maybe it's time to stop running from the past.

I follow John-Paul into the pub, and he introduces me to the owner, Gwen, a woman with short white hair who looks as though she's worked in the trade most of her life. She shows us up into the roof, which has been converted into two adjacent rooms. She pushes the door open with some force, and leads me into a small room, with two windows fogged with condensation, where the limited heat is in contrast to the ice-cold temperature outside.

The room is barely long enough for the single bed, and being in the eaves of the roof means the only place where I can stand without crouching is the centre of the room. There is a small basin and toilet in what looks as though it was once a fitted wardrobe, but there's no obvious central heating up here.

'Excuse me,' I ask as she's heading back out, 'is there a super-market or grocery store nearby where I can pick up a few toiletries? We left in a hurry, you see.'

'We have a toiletry set that's available to purchase, which includes shampoo, a razor, toothbrush, toothpaste, needle and thread, and some moisturising cream. If you need anything more, there's a Morrisons about a twenty-minute drive away.'

'No, the set would be perfect, thank you,' I quickly say, though the room doesn't appear to have an obvious bathroom.

'Can you add it to our bill,' John-Paul says, 'and I'll come down and settle in a bit.'

'Very well. Breakfast is served from seven until nine,' she adds as she leads John-Paul into his almost identical room.

The single bed creaks as I perch on the end of it. I don't think I ever visited this pub when I was younger, and now that I've sat down, I feel as though I could easily fall asleep. I force myself up and huddle to the basin, running the tap until it's warm and then splash handfuls of water over my face. I dry myself with a towel, and then John-Paul knocks and enters.

'Sorry, I hadn't realised just how small the rooms would be. I can cancel and try somewhere else, if you'd prefer?'

'No, it's fine,' I say, forcing a smile. 'It'll be fine for the night.'

He smiles back, with an air of relief.

'Great. I've spoken to my friend, and he's currently on duty, but will come and meet us downstairs in an hour or so. Is that okay?'

'On duty? Who is he?'

He closes the door before coming over and sitting beside me on the bed.

'His name is Harry Maguire, an old friend from college, but he's a detective sergeant in Southampton, and owes me a favour, so I'm hoping he might be able to help us kick over a few stones.'

'I said we can't include the police. What if he starts asking questions about—'

'Relax, Abbey. We don't have to go into all of that. All we want is for him to have a look at some of the history of the case. Who the police interviewed, what wasn't included in the CPS case against whatever his name was.'

'Terry Anderson,' I say solemnly.

'Exactly. You don't have to give him your name; I'll just say you're a friend doing some background on the case. It'll be fine.'

I want to believe him, and he sounds convinced, but he's taking a huge chance involving others. For all we know, my stalker is already aware we're here and watching to see our next move. As much as I want to find him – or her – before the three-day deadline passes, I also don't want to piss them off and force them to accelerate the deadline.

'Rest up,' he says, standing and smiling again. 'I'll return when he gets here.'

I watch as John-Paul leaves my room, closing the door behind him. I pull out my phone, but the signal is weak. Sasha has responded to tell me to ask for anything I need, and to be careful. I wish she was here with me now, but it wouldn't be right to drag her into my mess.

I reply, asking her to chase up Eddie Douglas and Robert Timmons-Drake for the terms of our agreement, and then I search for Anderson's name online. There are several sites that have picked up his interview in *The Daily Bore* and have re-reported some of his claims in anticipation of the televised interviews in the new year. I'm looking to try and get a sense of public reaction to his claims, but all the reporting is just regurgitation of the Peter Graves feature. I was hoping for the warmth of outrage, but all I find is tepid indifference.

Have people really forgotten the other crimes he committed? He executed six innocent people to cover his own deviant behaviour. The world of social media has given a voice to people like Anderson who don't deserve anyone's time or acknowledgement.

These are thoughts that swirl through my head, as I lie back on the bed, unable to keep my eyes from closing.

22

_____

SUNDAY

I start awake. The room is so much darker, and I can see nothing of the garden from the window where the curtains remain closed. It takes a moment for me to gather my bearings, and then I remember John-Paul checking us in to this B&B within a pub.

How long have I been asleep?

The last thing I remember is messaging Sasha, but that was just before four. I'm sure John-Paul said his detective friend would be calling round in an hour, but my eyes widen when I check the time on my phone. It's almost 7 a.m., but I can't really have been asleep that long, can I?

I push the thick duvet off me, with no recollection of getting beneath it. The wooden floor is ice cold when I lower my feet to it, and I have to hop across to locate my socks, shoes and hoodie before putting them on. There is a small pink washbag now balanced on the basin and when I unzip it see a toothbrush, toothpaste, shampoo and a razor, as Gwen the host had promised. Someone must have brought it in, because it definitely wasn't here before I fell asleep.

I stifle a yawn as I stretch my arms above my head. I don't

understand why John-Paul didn't wake me, and it takes all my effort to prise open the wooden fire door separating my room from the tiny hallway. I think the wooden panels must be warped. I'm about to knock on John-Paul's closed door, when I hear the gentle rumble of snoring coming from beyond the door. I'm about to return to my room, when I catch the divine scent of fried bacon wafting up the stairs.

It's probably warmer downstairs than in my room, so I grab my phone and head down, following my nose into the dining section of the pub. I can hear someone – probably Gwen – singing away to the radio beyond the closed kitchen door, and it puts me off disturbing her. I pull out a chair at one of the smaller tables instead, and unlock my phone. I only have 40 per cent battery life, having not charged it overnight, but hopefully, John-Paul will have one in his car I can borrow later.

I start when I notice a young boy at one of the tables nearest the kitchen. He can't be much older than seven, and he smiles when he notices me, as he eats from his bowl of cereal, and I smile back.

'I'm Abbey,' I whisper. 'What's your name?'

He's about to respond when the door to the kitchen swings open, and Gwen appears, wrapped in an apron.

'How are you getting on with your breakfast, Jes—' she says, catching herself when she notices me in the darkness.

'Oh, goodness me, you gave me a fright,' she says, pressing a hand to her chest. 'It's Miss Veritas, isn't it?'

'Abbey,' I say, offering her a placatory smile.

'Is it seven o'clock already?' she asks rhetorically, checking the watch on her wrist.

'Oh, sorry,' I quickly say, 'I'm early. I woke up and couldn't get back to sleep.'

'Oh, that's no worry, dear. What's a few minutes between

friends?' She presses switches on the wall beside her and the dining area magically appears out of the darkness. 'Please help yourself to any of the items on the table,' she says, pointing at a long table against the wall. 'We have orange juice, apple juice and grapefruit juice, and there is sliced bread and a toaster over there, which you're free to use. There is bacon, eggs, and baked beans on the stove if you'd like something cooked?'

I feel bad that I've turned up early, but without dinner last night, my stomach is grumbling, so I order a plateful of bacon, eggs, beans and a slice of fried bread. Gwen heads off and I cross to the table to pour myself some orange juice from one of the ice-filled jugs beside a coffee machine. I am just carrying it back to my table when the boy appears beside me. He has finished his cereal and is holding out his empty glass.

'Do you want some juice?' I ask him, and he nods.

'Orange.'

I fill his glass from the same jug as before, selecting a black coffee from the machine. Gwen returns to the room and says my food will be out shortly.

'Jesse, where did you get that orange juice from?' she says, frowning at the child. 'I said one glass only. What will your mother say?'

'Oh, I'm sorry,' I quickly say. 'I filled it up for him. I didn't realise he wasn't allowed it.'

She waves away my concern.

'Oh, that's okay then. This is my grandson, Jesse,' she says proudly, resting hands on his shoulders. 'He knows exactly how to get what he wants when he's staying here with me.' She looks down at him affectionately. 'An extra glass of orange juice means extra teeth brushing for you, young man, doesn't it?'

He nods, still beaming at me.

'That's what grandmothers are for,' she continues. 'I'll be back with your breakfast in two shakes of a lamb's tail.'

I watch her leave, and Jesse follows behind. I never met either of my grandparents, but I believe they would have been as warm and welcoming as Jesse's.

'Here you go,' Gwen chimes when she returns a few minutes later, sliding the large plate of bacon, eggs and beans in front of me, and I salivate instantly.

'This smells so good,' I say, reaching for the bottle of ketchup, and am surprised when she sits down in the seat across from me.

'Are you staying long in Ashford or just passing through on the way to somewhere more glamorous?'

'I used to live here,' I tell her, swallowing a mouthful of fried bread.

'Oh, did you? So, you're here visiting family then?'

For some reason I picture Faye's gravestone but shake my head.

'Not exactly. Just a trip down memory lane really.'

'Does your family still reside nearby?'

'No, Mum and Dad... they passed a few years ago.'

'Oh, I'm sorry, I didn't mean to pry.'

'No, that's fine.'

'Whereabouts did you live? Maybe I knew them.'

'On Delabar Street, but it was over twenty years ago.'

'You're kidding! I used to live on Delabar Street, ooh, it must be thirty or so years ago.'

The coincidence is more than a little unnerving.

'We lived at number 26,' I say.

She exhales.

'I thought you looked familiar,' she says, gushing and slapping her hand on the table. 'You're Siobhan Turnbull's daughter, aren't you?'

The mouthful of bacon gets stuck in my throat as I try to swallow it down. I don't remember my parents being friends with anyone called Gwen, and there's nothing about her face that is ringing any bells in my head.

'Well, one of them, yes.'

Both hands shoot up to her mouth as her mind makes the connection.

'Oh my gosh, I'm so sorry, I wasn't thinking. So, it was your sister who...?'

I quickly nod so she doesn't have to complete the sentence.

'Oh, my dear, I am so sorry. Here you are, probably on some kind of pilgrimage, and I'm being a nosy busybody.'

I take a drink of the juice.

'That's okay, you weren't to know. Were you and my mum close?'

'We were colleagues, more than friends,' she says with a gentle shrug. 'We both worked at the old Cineplex theatre, before it closed down, and then we both got jobs on Old Man Turner's farm. Your mum used to tend to the cattle, while I cooked and cleaned inside the manor. I still remember the day the news broke. It didn't feel real. I think it impacted the whole area. It was like the security blanket that had been wrapped around us all was suddenly pulled away and we saw how evil the world beyond the rolling hills truly was. Of course, not the same impact as it had on you and yours, but it certainly changed the way a lot of folk behaved. Self-inflicted curfews were set up all over the place. I remember not letting my son and daughter go out unless there was a parent chaperoning nearby. Even to this day, I wouldn't let little Jesse go beyond the garden fence without being with him.'

My mum was similarly more security conscious in the weeks that followed discovery of Faye's body, and now that Gwen mentions it, I can remember not being able to see many of my friends unless we were in school. For a time, I believed it was because their parents saw me as some kind of hex; don't let your children hang out with that Abigail Turnbull, unless you want them to die next.

Years later, my therapist concluded that I was in such emotional turmoil that I was projecting my own guilt and insecurities on everyone I came into contact with. There's probably some truth in that, but I can remember some of the terrified looks I would get from those in my class.

Gwen stands and tends to another couple who enter the room and sit at a table across the room from me. I continue eating my food, mopping the bean sauce with the last of the fried bread. I feel guilty that I didn't wake John-Paul to join me, but given he didn't wake me for last night's meeting or dinner, I know I shouldn't feel guilty. Placing the knife and fork on my plate, I check my phone again, now plotting a route to Delabar Street to see how far away it is from here.

When I see it is only a twenty-minute hike, I decide that I need to go back there on my own. I'm not expecting to see a blanket of snow surrounding every inch of the car park. I had no idea it had been due to snow, but there's something almost angelic about the landscape. It looks like a fresh canvas has been laid out, hiding all the mistakes that went before. Downloading the directions, I follow the footpath until it reaches the pedestrian bridge over the A road, and then down the other side, along the canal bank, until I reach the edge of Ashford woods.

It's here I stop, too many memories clawing at the back of my mind, and it's only now I realise how isolated I am. I should have left a message for John-Paul to let him know I'd gone on ahead. Even as an adult, if I was to be set upon by a forty-year-old Terry Anderson, I'm not sure I would be able to escape him. For all his apologies now, he didn't do anything to curb his desires when he was out here. It shouldn't have taken multiple charges and prison sentences for him to be stopped.

I don't enter the woods, choosing to skirt through the overgrown grass that borders the smaller of the trees around the circumference. I stop when I reach the old stone well. Once upon a time, Faye and I would throw pennies into the well and make wishes, but it is long since filled in and covered by graffiti.

Back then we used to have to trample through mud and grass to get back to the public footpath that eventually leads back to Delabar Street, but there is a gravel pathway here now, and the stones crackle beneath my feet as I ascend the hill. I can practically hear Faye's voice on the wind, warning me to not go any further, but I need to open that Pandora's box, and remember what I've spent so long running from. I pass through the two yellow barriers, and onto the public footpath, which is as strewn now with empty crisp packets and squashed aluminium cans as it ever was. There is a dark shadow on the path where it looks like a rubbish bin may once have stood before being set on fire.

And when I reach the end of the public footpath, I stare out at Delabar Street, and am surprised by how different it looks beneath the thin blanket of snow. It never snowed like this when we were growing up; at least I've no memory of it being this crisp and clean looking. There are half a dozen children at one end of the street building miniature snowmen and trying to throw miniscule snowballs, but there really isn't sufficient coverage for either activity. I walk past the children, envious of their laughter and enthusiasm. I would give anything to have their level of innocence. And before I realise where I am, I see the old picket fence that still runs the length of the front garden, and the memories come flooding back.

23

It's almost as if the scenes are playing out before my eyes. I can see the large doll's house that I donated to Faye when I no longer wanted it. She would open the front of it and I can remember how certain she was that she'd own and live in a house like that one day. She would bring a handful of her dolls, and the stuffed unicorn with the rainbow-coloured horn down to the garden and host soirees whilst the sun shone overhead. She'd always ask if I would play with her but there were too many other teens from school who either lived in the street or close enough that they would walk past our house on the way to the woods. I should have played with her more. I could easily have suggested we take the toys inside to play with, but at that age she was just my annoying little sister.

And then I recall the times when Dad would be mowing the lawn and would stumble across one of the figures or a piece of furniture that had fallen from the doll's house and he'd go ballistic, telling her she wouldn't be allowed nice things if she didn't look after them. He used to hate this lawn. I can remember him pleading with Mum to let him dig it up and replace it with a patio or some gravel, but Mum said she wouldn't even consider it whilst Faye and I were still around.

I don't remember him asking again after Faye passed.

'Oh, you're still here, thank God,' I hear someone say and the breath catches in my throat.

Turning, I see a woman in a navy business suit, holding a tablet and with a face heavily made up. Her dark brown hair is frizzy and flopping about in the wind. I don't recognise her.

'Sorry I'm late,' she continues. 'Bloody snow has caused havoc on the main road into town. I don't see a car. Are you local then?'

'Sorry, I think maybe you have me confused with—'

'You're Mrs Johnstone, right? Here for a ten o'clock viewing of the house?'

So, she's an estate agent; I hadn't even noticed the small For Sale sign at the edge of the house. I'm about to correct her, when a fresh thought strikes.

'Um, yes, sorry, I am Mrs Johnstone. Sorry, my mind is all over the place today.'

'No need to apologise,' she beams. 'I had a late one last night too. How about we head inside and I'll fix us both a cup of tea and then we can view the inside of the property?'

I don't know what I'm going to say if the real Mrs Johnstone shows up, but it's already quarter past, so if she was coming there's every chance she's been and gone. I follow the agent into the property, carefully wiping my feet on the welcome mat and stepping inside. I'm instantly struck by how different it smells inside. Gone is the stale smell of Dad's cigarettes and Mum's over-the-top perfume. The aesthetic looks different too. The walls have been painted white, rather than the honey colour I remember, and it has brightened the hallway so much.

'It's this way to the kitchen,' the agent says, leading the way. 'I'll see if I can get some central heating on too. I usually get here ten minutes before a viewing to sort things like that out, but anyway, enough about me, what are *your* initial thoughts?'

The old linoleum floor is gone, replaced by wooden struts, and there are triple-glazed windows where the single-pane glass used to be. I'd swear the sink and gas hob are the same though. There used to be a small square table in the corner of the room where Faye and I would eat dinner on school nights, while Mum prepared separate meals for her and Dad, but that's long gone.

'There's plenty of space for cooking feasts in here,' the agent continues, without missing a beat and filling the kettle at the sink. 'I know the property looks quite small from the outside, but it goes back a fair way, so I think it hides its real potential.'

It feels so odd being back in here. I feel like I'm trespassing and although the property layout is the same, the changes to the walls and floors make it feel less like home. I almost feel as though I've woken in an alternate reality and am seeing how another family would have lived here if we hadn't. I bet they would have done things differently.

'Why don't you take a look around upstairs while I make the tea?'

I nod gratefully, and head back out of the kitchen and gaze up at the carpeted staircase. Faye always used to sit in the corner where it bends round, snuggling with that damned unicorn. Whenever she was in a strop about something that's where she'd take herself, glowering at anyone who dared to ask what was wrong. She was nearly always there when John-Paul would come around and I'd tell her to leave us alone.

Why are all my memories of me being cruel to Faye? Was I really that bad a sister? Why can't I remember any of the happier times when I would go out of my way to cheer her up, or we'd form a little gang when Mum and Dad were arguing about money?

'Go on up, it's fine,' the agent calls from the kitchen, seeing me hesitating. 'The owner is away and won't be back until after Christmas, so you won't be disturbing anything.'

I place a tentative foot on the first step, already anticipating the creaks I'll hear on steps three, six, and eight. I deliberately tread on them, needing the validation that this is actually the house I grew up in. The stairs don't let me down, and I hurry up the rest, bending around onto the landing. Faye's room was the smallest, immediately to my left, then there was Mum and Dad's room, also at the front of the house, then my old bedroom, and then the bathroom and toilet. All the doors are closed, but I can't resist heading to my room first. But as I open the door and walk through, I'm disappointed at how different it looks. The doors of the two built-in wardrobes directly across from me no longer have mirrors hanging from them, and my trundle bed has been replaced by a double, pushed up against the wall where my desk used to stand. I didn't expect it to look exactly the same thirty years later, but it looks so different that it's unnerving, and I'd definitely argue the white walls and lack of posters make it feel less homely than when I was here.

Disappointed, I leave the room, and glance into the bathroom, which doesn't look a lot different to what I remember. The bath has been replaced by a walk-in shower, but the airing cupboard door looks the same, as does the basin beneath the window. I don't bother looking into Mum and Dad's old room, but my hands are physically trembling as I stand outside Faye's old room.

She used to have a small poster stuck to the door saying only fairies and happy people were allowed to enter. It's just as well that's gone as I'm feeling neither magical nor happy. The door creaks as I open it, and initially it's as if I've stepped back in time. I see the old bunkbed we shared once upon a time until Dad turned his office into Faye's bedroom when I hit puberty. I see her Care Bears duvet and pillow set, all her teddies lined up on one side of the bed against the wall. I see her small dressing table and mirror where she'd sit and pretend to put on makeup every morning, and I see the small plastic keyboard she begged Santa for, but never actually learned to play.

But then I blink and the façade quickly fades away. There is no longer a bed in here, just a large oak desk, and a desktop computer and monitor. Gone is the yellow wallpaper, now painted the same white as the rest of the property. I'd hoped I'd be able to still smell her inside, but there isn't a trace that she ever existed here.

I close my eyes and search for the memory of how it used to look, and what I see is Faye sitting in a heap, crying because she'd fallen over and grazed her knee. She must have been about nine and she whispered that one of the boys in her class had pushed her over in the playground. Mum must have been out because I remember cleaning it with cotton wool and water, before fastening a large plaster over the top. I hear my younger self telling her to point out the boy to me the next day and I'd have a word with him to make sure he knew that I would come for him if he ever laid hands on her again. I swore I would protect her for the rest of her life, and at the time I meant it.

My hand rushes to my eye and catches the tear as it breaks free.

I failed to live up to that promise and if – and it's a big if – Anderson isn't lying, then I've spent the last thirty years failing to do what I promised.

'Ah, you've found the office.'

I start, having not heard the agent approaching, and quickly shield my face so she can't see my tears.

'You and Mr Johnstone just have the one child, am I right?

This room would make a great nursery if another should arrive, or could easily be turned into a playroom if not. I don't recall where your husband said you lived when he booked this appointment.'

'London,' I say without really thinking.

'London? But I thought you said you walked here today?'

I don't have the mental capacity to maintain this lie much longer.

'I stayed over with a friend last night.'

I see the frown on her face, and can feel her now questioning exactly who I am. It must be dumb luck that she hasn't recognised me from the news of Graves's article in *The Daily Bore*.

'I love the house,' I say quickly, squeezing past her towards the staircase, 'but I'll need to talk it over with my husband before we can make an offer.'

I'm already at the foot of the stairs when I hear her hurrying after me.

'Let me give you my card. It has my mobile number on it and you can reach me at any time, day or night, when you're ready to make your offer.'

I accept the card, promising I'll call one way or another as soon as I've spoken to my pretend husband. I'm desperate to get out of the house before she realises that I'm not a prospective client and calls the police.

I open the front door and step out onto the porch, but immediately stop when something catches my eye just beyond the welcome mat. I crouch down to check it's what I think it is, and then my heart breaks a little more when I read the message scratched into the tile: *A & F 4eva.*

24

Tears blur my vision as I stomp away from the place I once called home, now so alien to me. I don't know where I'm going, I just need to get away. Too many memories are flooding my mind, and the guilt is painfully overwhelming. I knew I wasn't ready to open this Pandora's box, but it's too late to close it.

The tears break free and feel as though they're freezing on my cheeks as I head into the bitter wind.

You're the reason I'm appealing, Abbey. You deserve to find the person who really pushed your sister into that quarry.

I scream out loud as Anderson's voice taunts me.

The police manipulated you... you were just a pawn in their game.

'You son of a bitch!' I roar, only stopping when I see a dog-walking teenager staring back at me with fear in his eyes.

I try to mouth an apology, but he hurries away before I can get the words out. Is this really what I've become: a liar who terrifies children?

Are you sure this is the man you saw in the woods? Did you see him abduct Faye?

I freeze when I realise where my subconscious has brought

me. The wooden sign is badly weathered, to the point it's hard to make out the name of the cemetery. The gothic gates are open, and there is no sign of snow on the tarmacked path leading inside, almost as if it's melted away under the hellish heat coming from below. It's been years since I've been here, and as much as I want to turn and run in the opposite direction, I can't help but feel like I've been drawn here for a reason; as if there is somebody else out there controlling my destiny.

I wipe the tears from my face with the sleeve of my thick coat, and take a deep breath, before moving forwards. If I'd realised this is where I would end up today, I would have brought flowers, but Faye deserves so much more.

I remember first laying eyes on the coffin at the front of the church. It was so much smaller than I'd expected. I'd only ever seen coffins in movies and on the television; naively I didn't even realise they came in child sizes too. I sobbed so loud that Mum had to take me to one side and ask me to control myself. It felt like the whole congregation were staring at me, reading the guilt emanating in waves from my soul.

Even after I'd made my statement to the police, and forced John-Paul to corroborate it, I wasn't convinced it would be enough. I had nightmares every night in the weeks that followed; in some, I saw myself in the dock at court; in others, I saw the police tearing my statement to shreds and demanding the truth.

Innocent people don't go to prison is the mantra I rehearsed every day. That is the foundation that the British justice system is built on. We are all innocent until *proven* guilty. So, the fact that the case made it as far as court only encouraged my belief that I had done the right thing. This evil monster wouldn't be able to hurt anyone else any longer.

I stop when I make it to the plot. Mum and Dad are buried

together, with Faye beside them. There is space on her headstone for my name and date of death, as their intention was always that we would be reunited in death. This is what my future is supposed to bring, but I can't imagine anyone stopping by to bring me flowers or offer words of condolence when they realise what I did.

I crouch down, and look at both gravestones.

'I am so sorry,' I whisper, hoping my words are carried by the wind to wherever they all are. 'It was all my fault. I should have protected you, Faye, like I promised I would. And I don't know how to begin telling you how sorry I am that I didn't.'

Fresh tears escape, but I make no effort to wipe them away.

'You'll have seen that Terry Anderson is claiming he didn't do it, and I no longer know what to believe... what if he's right? What if I...?'

I stop myself from finishing the sentence as I always have. Someone else attacked Faye and caused her to fall into the quarry. The alternative doesn't bear thinking about.

'I thought I'd find you here.'

I jolt, only now realising I'm not alone. I crane my neck round, and am relieved that it's John-Paul and not the police.

'I'm sorry if I'm intruding,' he quickly adds, offering his palms out apologetically. 'Sorry, I should have waited by the gates. I'll leave you to it.'

'No, don't go. You have just as much right to be here as I do. Maybe more so.'

I hold out my hand and he quickly clasps it, helping me back to my feet, and leading me over to a nearby bench, brushing the snow off and there we both sit. I hadn't realised how cold I was until I felt the warmth of his touch.

'When I woke up, Gwen said you'd gone out for a walk, and I was worried about you. I saw a single pair of footprints on the bridge over the road, and took a chance I might find you here. Sorry, I probably should have brought some flowers.'

There's no reason for him to apologise, as I didn't think about flowers either.

'I really miss her,' I say, the words disappearing as condensation in the cold air.

'Yeah, she was a really sweet kid. Had a high opinion of herself, but her heart was in the right place.'

This makes me smile; never a truer word spoken. Mum always said she saw me as a role model, but if that was true, I don't know why she was always such a pain when I tried to meet up with John-Paul.

'Oh, hey, what happened last night?' I ask when my mind returns to the present. 'You were going to collect me when your detective friend arrived.'

'I tried, but you were fast asleep. I was knocking on the door when Gwen brought up the washbag and she let me into your room. You were in a deep sleep, so I tucked you in and figured I'd talk to you at breakfast.'

At least that explains why the duvet was over me when I woke.

'So, what did your friend say?'

'Harry? Well, not a lot as it goes. I asked what he could remember from that time, and whether he'd be able to do some subtle digging into whether there were any other witnesses, or contradictory evidence suppressed from the trial. He wanted to know why, and so I told him that Anderson is appealing the conviction and the victim's sister wants to make sure there are no grounds. I didn't name you as such, but said you were an old girlfriend.'

'What about the post office the box was sent from?'

John-Paul sighs.

'Unfortunately, he said he'd need solid justification to go around requesting access to security camera footage, and that would mean you coming forward and explaining everything else. I'm sorry.'

I can't say I'm surprised. Disappointed, but not surprised. And even if I did report what had been sent, along with the three text messages, I doubt it would be tangible enough to warrant checking the footage.

I pull out my phone to check the time, and see a message notification. I swallow hard when I open the message. I instantly recognise the house in the background of the attached image, and the estate agent leading me into the property. There is a four-word message above the image:

TRIP DOWN MEMORY LANE?

He was here, and followed me to my parental home. I try to think back to this morning and whether I saw anybody hanging around, but I only recall seeing the children playing in the snow.

Does that mean he knows where I am now?

The thought sends a shiver the length of my body, but then I feel the length of John-Paul's leg against mine, and a fresh thought smacks my head: the only other person who knows what happened is sitting beside me now.

'I want to see your phone,' I quickly say to John-Paul, and he looks nervously back at me.

'Why, what's happened?'

'Your phone, now,' I say, thinking back to what he said about following my footprints over the bridge. It wouldn't have led him to the cemetery without passing my old home. And I couldn't work out why he was being so helpful, offering to drive me down here.

I hold my hand out, until he reluctantly hands it over. I hold it up to his face to unlock the screen, and then I search through his message folder.

'What are you looking for?' he asks defensively.

I show him the message I've just received from the unknown number.

'Wait, you think I sent that? I don't even know your number.'

The messages folder has no history of a message being sent today, and when I double-check his photo gallery, there are none taken in the last week. I search in his recycle bin as well, but it's empty.

I reluctantly hand the phone back to him, and stand to try and get the feeling back into my feet and legs.

'How could you think I could be behind these threats?' he says, and in truth it was just a moment of paranoia. It doesn't serve him for the truth to be revealed either.

'I'm sorry,' I offer, 'but whoever is behind this, they were following me today.'

I catch myself, and suddenly look to the horizon, arcing around, checking to see if there is anyone observing me now.

'That is why you posted our destination on social media, remember?' John-Paul stands beside me, and tries to put a comforting arm around me, but I shirk it away.

'I just want to go home,' I say, and set off for the cemetery gates, with John-Paul hurrying after me.

I came back here looking for answers, but all I've managed to stir up is my own guilt at not doing more to protect my sister.

There has to be more I can do to stop whoever this is from exposing the truth. Most of the reading British public will now know about his appeal after Graves's feature. I've spent so long trying to avoid the spotlight, but it's found me regardless.

'Abbey, please wait,' I hear John-Paul panting. 'Let's go back to the pub, collect our stuff and then I'll drive you back if that's what you want, but we're no closer to finding out who's behind this. I think we need to go to the police and come clean.'

I stop and glare at him, unable to speak.

'What you did – I mean what *we* did – if it is revealed by someone else, there will be no coming back from it for either of us. I have spent decades building a reputation and my practice, and I'm not prepared to let someone snatch it away from me. But if we get out ahead of it, we might be better able to manage the fallout.'

On that day, Faye was upset, so her mind might not have been thinking clearly. The quarry was in the opposite direction to our home, and I've never understood why she ended up in that part of the forest. But maybe she couldn't see clearly through her tears and ended up lost; it would certainly explain why John-Paul and I were unable to find her when we searched.

I try to put myself in her shoes at that age. If she was lost, would she have approached an adult to ask for help? Or would she have called out my name when she realised she couldn't find her way home? Could that have brought her to Anderson's attention?

John-Paul is still waiting for me to respond, but then I hear Sasha's voice in my head: *maybe it's some lackey Anderson has hired to knock you off balance.*

There is a ring of truth to that possibility, but I feel certain there's more I'm missing. What was it Anderson said when I visited him?

I didn't see you or your sister that day, and that's why I know you lied about seeing me there too.

If that's the truth he wants me to come clean with, it would certainly help his appeal, but it would also destroy my reputation and the business. But if the actual truth comes out, it could mean greater punishment than that.

25

We walk back to the pub in silence, with me leading the way, playing various scenarios through my mind, but failing to make sense of it all. I feel awful for accusing John-Paul of being behind it, especially after all the kindness he's shown despite the way I pushed him away thirty years ago. That's twice I've incorrectly accused him of wrongdoing; it's a wonder he doesn't tell me to make my own way back to London. I can't imagine he and Vanessa will be adding me to their Christmas card list anytime soon. I used to think I was good at sensing when people were being honest, but my radar must be misfiring.

The pub appears in the distance, and I decide to try and make things right, otherwise the journey back is going to be even more uncomfortable than it was on the way.

'I'm sorry, John-Paul,' I say without breaking stride. 'I shouldn't have doubted your motives for helping me, and I am sorry for any offence I may have caused you.'

I look over to him when he doesn't respond, but he just silently nods.

Oh, that's not good. I remember he also went into a kind of

non-verbal state when he felt rejected when we were younger. My therapist once told me he probably had extremely low self-esteem and that was just his way of hiding his emotions.

'I've reached a decision,' I continue, as we cross the bridge. 'None of what happened was your fault, so I'm going to bear the brunt of it. I still can't be certain that whoever's following me isn't...'

I freeze, hearing Sasha's words playing in my head again: *maybe it's some lackey Anderson has hired to knock you off balance.*

I pull out my phone. My battery is now below 20 per cent, but I search for Rhys Morgan's number and dial it. It goes unanswered until the voice messaging service cuts in, but I don't leave a message.

I can't believe I didn't think of it sooner. I didn't believe it when he told me his only motivation for helping Anderson was to clear an innocent man's name. It would have been easy for him to get a burner phone to message me with. And when I was walking to the office yesterday morning, certain I was being watched, he magically appeared outside our office not long after. If Anderson has convinced him I'm lying about seeing him in the woods, then it would be far easier to prove if I fall on my own sword.

Who's to say he didn't hand deliver the box to my address after he left the office yesterday? Or maybe he drove to Southampton to post it. I know he drives, so he could have followed John-Paul and me here. I didn't see him outside the house on Delabar Street, but he could have taken the picture from behind the wheel of a parked car. The fact that he isn't answering his phone now speaks volumes too.

'What is it?' John-Paul asks.

'I think I know who's been stalking me.'

'Who?'

'Anderson's solicitor. Could you message your detective friend and see if he can run an ANPR check for Rhys's car?'

'I can ask. What's the registration number?'

I've seen his car a couple of times, but I have no memory of what make or model it is, nor the registration number.

'Can't he look it up if we give his name? I think the car was a light grey – maybe silver – colour. Sorry, I know it's not a lot to go on, but the police have contact with the DVLA, so I'm sure he can figure it out and then check to see whether the car has been in Hampshire today.'

John-Paul looks slightly lost, but he nods, and puts the phone to his ear as he walks on ahead and moves towards his snow-covered 4x4.

I head back into the pub, up the stairs and grab the washbag, checking around the tiny room to make sure I haven't left anything else, before I hurry back down the stairs, waiting at the bar while Gwen pours a pint for one of her customers.

I can hear her grandson, Jesse, playing with his toys at the table behind me, and it makes me remember when Faye used to set up tea parties for her stuffed animals and would put on voices for them so they could interact. I turn and see that Jesse is using his to battle one another, but each to their own.

Gwen comes over, and I hand her my room key.

'We're checking out now,' I tell her. 'I'll ask my friend to bring his key in when he finishes his call.'

'Oh, that's all right, dear, he already has.' She moves past me towards her grandson. 'Oh, Jesse, I do wish you wouldn't be so violent with your toys,' she says. 'Oh, and where did you get this from? It looks so old and tattered. This isn't one of your usual toys, is it?'

'A man gave it to me,' the boy replies, and my ears prick up.

'What man?' Gwen says. 'Where did you get this from?'

'He said it used to be his daughter's, but she was too big to play with it now, and he said I could have it, because I don't have a horse.'

The hairs on the back of my neck stand.

'This is a unicorn, Jesse, not a horse.'

I spin around, and when I see Gwen holding the threadbare, grubby white unicorn with the rainbow horn, my legs go from beneath me. I have no doubt it's the same one that Faye had the day she disappeared.

'Are you okay?' Gwen asks, hurrying to my aid.

With the unicorn now much closer, I am certain it is the same one she used to play with all the time. She wouldn't go anywhere without it. I snatch it from Gwen's hands and study the hooves. And sure enough there is the 'F.T.' marking on the right hind hoof that Mum drew the first day Faye went to preschool and insisted on taking the toy with her. She used to suck on the horn when she was anxious, which is why it looks so shabby now.

I crawl towards Jesse's chair.

'You have to tell me who gave this to you,' I say in a loud whisper.

The blood drains from his face, and he shuffles as far from me as his chair will allow.

'Please, Jesse, who gave this to you?'

Gwen moves behind him, and glares at me in admonishment.

'Stop it, you're scaring him,' she says.

'I'm sorry, I'm sorry,' I say, trying to smile to show I mean him no harm. 'I just need to know who this man was. Did you catch his name?'

Jesse shakes his head.

'Can you tell me what he looked like then? Was he tall, was he short? Did he have light hair, or dark? Was he thin or overweight? Please, Jesse, just think.'

'I don't know,' he says as his lower lip trembles. 'I don't know who he was. He was just walking past the garden fence and saw me playing.'

'What have I told you about accepting things from strangers?' Gwen chastises.

'I know, but he said he knew you and you wouldn't mind.'

'He said he knew your grandma?' I say, desperate for any additional detail he can give me, and I then look to Gwen to see if she can shed any light on who the man is, but she stares back at me blankly.

The door to the pub opens, and John-Paul enters, staring at me on all fours, a quizzical look on his face.

'What's going on?'

I show him the unicorn.

'Do you remember this toy? It was Faye's. She had it the day she ran away from us. Do you remember it?'

He frowns at the toy in my hand, my knuckles whitening from the pressure of my grip.

'Sure, I think so,' John-Paul says. 'But that doesn't mean it's hers though.'

I twist the toy around so he can see the initials Mum drew.

'He was here, John-Paul. The man who's messing with me. He was here and he gave this boy the toy while we were out.'

'Can you describe him to us, Jesse?' Gwen tries again.

'He was wearing a dark coat and a dark bobble hat,' Jesse says. 'He was bending down, so I didn't see how tall he was.'

I look back to John-Paul.

'It has to be the solicitor. Anderson must have kept the toy and hairclip as mementoes, and he's told Rhys to send them to me to put me under pressure. We need to find him. What did your friend say?'

'He didn't answer, so I left a message asking him to phone me back urgently. What do you want to do?'

I look from John-Paul to Jesse, and then up to Gwen.

'Is there any kind of security cameras on the outside of the building that would have recorded this man?'

She shakes her head with a melancholy pout.

'I'm sorry, dear, but there's no call for it to be honest. They're generally a good bunch who come in here.'

John-Paul helps me to my feet, but then I feel my phone vibrate in my pocket, and I already sense who it's going to be from. My hand shakes as I pull the phone out and press my thumb to the sensor. Sure enough, the message is from the same unknown number. It's another photo message, only this time it's of me and John-Paul siting on the bench in the cemetery. The message reads:

> TWO GUILTY BIRDS, ONE SHOT.

'Oh my God, he *was* there!' I gasp, showing the picture to John-Paul, whose face pales instantly.

I looked to see if we were being watched but saw nobody. But he must have got the picture before we checked and then come back this way to deposit the unicorn. I feel sick.

'What does he mean by two guilty birds?' John-Paul whispers.

'I think it means he knows you lied too, John-Paul.'

'But you said...'

I fix my eyes on the phone, and type a reply.

> I know this is you, Rhys. Do what you want.

> We both know your client is the only guilty one.

'What the hell are you doing?' John-Paul gasps when I've pressed send. 'What if he...?'

'He has nothing. I should have done as Sasha suggested originally and blocked his ability to message me. If I'm right and this is Rhys, then we've got nothing to worry about. Stick to our story, and we'll be fine.'

His lips chatter, but I don't wait to hear his response.

'Let's head back to London.'

'What about Harry running the ANPR check?'

'When he phones you back, you should still request it, because that's evidence that he's been tampering with witnesses, and we can report him for that.'

I move towards the door.

'Wait, you've got Jesse's toy,' Gwen calls after me.

I fix her with a hard stare.

'This was my sister's favourite toy, and I'm not letting it go. I'm sorry.'

I head out and march towards John-Paul's car, finally feeling as though I'm wrestling back some control.

26

MONDAY

I wake early, relieved to see I've had no response from Rhys's burner phone. I quickly open a search engine and type in my name, but there are no new stories beyond the syndication of *The Daily Bore*'s feature. I message Sasha to tell her I'll meet her in the office later, but I have somewhere more critical to be first.

My preliminary stop is at the offices of Woodley and Douglas solicitors in Ruislip, the black signage and darkened windows looking less welcoming than ever. Eddie's sister Kayla is on the phone when I enter, but I can see her shooting daggers in my direction, as I march on past in the direction of Eddie's office. When I push the door open, he is not inside. His business partner, Jake Woodley, is also not in his office. I return to the waiting room and as soon as her call is finished, Kayla tells me Eddie will be gone all day. I can't immediately tell if she's lying, though it wouldn't surprise me if Eddie had warned her I'd be on the warpath.

'My brother is in court all day,' she says defiantly. 'I can make you an appointment for some time later in the week, if that would help?'

I sense the question is rhetorical because we both know that won't help.

'Which court is he at?'

'That's none of your business.'

The nearest courts to here are the County Court and Magistrates' Court in Uxbridge. Whilst it is feasible he could be elsewhere, I'd say the latter is most likely.

'He's at Uxbridge Magistrates' Court, isn't he?'

She makes a poor effort of showing her shock.

'How did you...?'

'Because you just told me,' I say smugly, and march outside and back to Ruislip Manor Tube station.

It takes the Piccadilly line Tube sixteen minutes to get to Uxbridge, and then it's another five or so minutes until I am standing across the road from the court. It's an old brown building from the nineties, and if it wasn't for the people coming and going every few minutes, I'd have thought the place was abandoned. There are even wooden boards over two of the lower windows.

There is a flow of suited and well-dressed people entering and leaving, presumably a mixture of those who've committed speeding offences and public disorders. It throws up memories of when I had to go to court to present my evidence against Anderson. I was told I wouldn't need to appear in court due to my age, but that they would hear my evidence via a television in the court, with me in a room just down the hall. My mum insisted I dress up for the occasion, and so I wore the same outfit she'd bought me for Faye's memorial. It certainly helped put me in an emotional state as I gave my testimony.

I'd very briefly met both barristers the morning of the trial so I would know who was who when it came to the questions. Anderson's barrister was far more sinister when he was in action.

Accusing me of lying and claiming I was a troublemaker as I'd been caught bunking school on a couple of occasions the previous year. It didn't feel right that he could attack me in this way, but the judge did nothing to stop him; it genuinely felt like I was the one on trial.

Mercifully, it's not raining at the moment, though the sky is covered by light grey clouds, and the wind is bitter. I'm just crossing to enter the court in search of shelter, when I see Eddie Douglas emerge, immediately pressing a cigarette between his lips. His grey suit looks shabby, and his stocky build makes him look more like one of the accused than a defender of justice.

'Oh, what do you want now? Come to gloat?' he says, his brow creased and a look of disgust on his face.

'Nice to see you too, Eddie. Bad day in court?'

'I have nothing to say to you,' he says, looking back over his shoulder, as if wondering whether to go back inside and hide.

'Well, that's good because I have plenty to say to you. I thought I made myself clear on Friday: you were to send me terms of our settlement agreement via email, or I would speak to Damian. I even gave you the weekend, but we've received nothing, Eddie, and now you're avoiding my partner's calls and emails.'

'You've got some nerve showing up like this and accusing me of wrongdoing,' he huffs.

'I've got a nerve? You and Robert Timmons-Drake have been conspiring against me from the very beginning. I remembered something after our last chat. When you and Robert approached me in my office, you specifically said if we could find a way of getting Damian acquitted, the civil case could be worth millions.'

'And?'

'*And* you implied we would all receive our fair share.'

'Implication is not a promise, and has no legal standing in court; you know that.'

'You said if I helped you win the acquittal at no cost, then you'd see me all right in a civil case.'

'Did I? Have you got any proof of that?'

He knows I don't, and I am angry that I didn't make them sign terms there and then. Had Sasha not been out at the time, I'm sure she would have pointed out my error.

'And it's as Robert said to you the other day: all you did was identify an inconsistency in the barman's statement. That's it. It was me who then had to dig out the truth, and locate the CCTV footage of when he left, and for Robert to prove it in court. I don't know where you get such a high opinion of yourself.'

He's trying to bully me into submission, but I'm not willing to back down. Not today.

'I will carry out my threat. Is that what you want? You want me to find Damian alternative representation? We both know he listens to me.'

He pulls the unlit cigarette from his lips and spits on the grubby pavement.

'Like that's not what you've already done.'

'No, I think I've been incredibly patient until now, but I will go and speak to him today if you don't give me something in writing. I'm not bluffing, Eddie.'

He puts the cigarette back between his dry and cracked lips, and lights it, exhaling a cloud of smoke in my direction.

'No smoking outside the court,' a security guard calls out, and Eddie moves away from the building, crossing the road, with me swiftly following.

'You can drop the act,' he says, almost breathless at the short walk. 'Damian already told me he's going elsewhere.'

My brow furrows.

'He what?'

'Stop playing games, Abbey. He told us on Saturday morning. *That's* why we never bothered sending across the terms you demanded.'

'He told you he's found alternative representation?'

He shakes his head in disbelief.

'We know you went and spoke to him. Whether that was the moment you left my office or when we didn't meet your Friday evening deadline. At least he had the decency to tell me to my face.'

This is certainly news to me, but sounds so out of character for Damian. It's exactly the sort of dirty trick I'd expect from Eddie though: telling me one thing until he's forced Damian to sign terms for the civil suit.

'You said you wanted a third of mine and Robert's shares, and then left the office and decided you wanted more, so you told Damian to fuck us over. What share are you getting now?'

'Cut the crap, Eddie!'

'Who did you lead him to? Coffey and Co? Gordon and Slater? Tell me you didn't go to Hemlock and Kellerman? They make grandiose guarantees that aren't worth the paper they're not printed on. They rarely deliver and even when they do they take an even bigger cut of the package than we were proposing.'

'I haven't spoken to Damian yet,' I say firmly. 'I haven't told him to go elsewhere, but I will if you keep up this bullshit.'

He throws his cigarette to the floor and squashes it in the remnants of a puddle before lighting another.

'Oh, really! Then why did he come into my office on Saturday and tell me he no longer wants to seek compensation?'

I want to believe this is more of his bluster, but my instinct is telling me this isn't a lie.

'If you're lying to me, I swear to—'

'I'm not the one lying. Ask my sister if you don't believe me, or call Robert. They'll both confirm what I'm saying.'

When I spoke to Damian on Friday he said he would swap any settlement to have Rodrigo back, but he didn't give any impression that he'd changed his mind about suing for wrongful conviction. He spent seven years in prison, his reputation was dragged through the gutter, he lost his job, his flat, and his husband. I can't understand why he would tell Eddie he no longer wishes to proceed.

'Did he give any reason for the change of heart?'

'No, just that he was considering all his options. It sounded exactly like *someone* had fed him that line so she could take him to a different firm.'

'I swear I have nothing to do with that.'

'Yeah, well, whatever. I've got to head back into court.' He squashes the second cigarette in the same puddle. 'If I find out that you are behind this and you're just here to stick the knife in, then... it'll be the last business I ever throw your way.'

He doesn't wait for me to remind him that so far I've worked for him for free, and don't need to give away any more of my valuable time. I try to call Damian, but his phone is switched off. The only conclusion I can draw is that he must have seen in the article in *The Daily Bore*, and that somehow influenced his decision. I don't want to have to tell Sasha that our future recompense has gone up in smoke, but if I can find Damian, and try to understand what's going on, then maybe I can persuade him to reconsider.

27

I feel exhausted by the time I make it to Ealing Broadway. I've tried calling Damian several times, but his phone remains switched off. I've sent him a message asking him to call me as soon as he sees it, but it remains undelivered. I think back to the last time I spoke to Damian on Friday at the small café in Ruislip. He told me his freedom felt like a dream from which he would wake at any moment, but he never gave any indication that he wouldn't pursue the civil case Eddie had pinned his hopes on. So, this U-turn now feels so out of character for the man I've come to consider as a friend over these last few months.

I'm guessing that he's switched his phone off because he doesn't want me to contact him, but I'm now worried about his mental health. I could see he was still grieving for Rodrigo, and the fact that his in-laws still considered him guilty of Rodrigo's murder. But what if it was more than that? I sensed he was sombre, but maybe I underestimated just how bad a state he was in. I can't think of any other reason he would walk away from the potential compensation set to come his way.

I would swap it all to have Rodrigo back, even for a few seconds.

Eddie told me Damian had moved back in to the home he shared with Rodrigo, so that is where I'm heading now, in the hope that I'm not too late. I turn left out of the station, and march along the sodden pavement in the direction of the town centre, but turn left onto The Mall, past several bars and restaurants, until I make it to Hamilton Road and then stop when I reach Hazel Court. The orange brick building is about eight large houses wide, and one of several such buildings scattered along this road, amongst the impossibly unaffordable homes along this street. Damian and Rodrigo's two-bed flat is worth close to three-quarters of a million pounds according to the last estimate that was made, and used as collateral to secure the services of Eddie and Robert Timmons-Drake for the appeal. And from the outside, it really isn't anything special-looking for that price.

I head through the gate and along the path to the main entrance, buzzing for Flat 12 on the fourth floor. There's no answer on the intercom, and I take several steps backwards, craning my neck up to try and see if there's any movement beyond the net curtains, but I'm too low down to see anything. I buzz again, before calling out his name, but if he is home, he's got no intention of speaking to me.

I could go and visit his mum to see if she knows where he is, but I don't want to worry her unnecessarily. He could just be out, and it would be a long walk or a bus journey to Hanwell to visit her flat. I pocket the idea, as a moment of inspiration strikes. When I returned home on Sunday, I went to Faye's graveside to pay my respects. It's possible that Damian could be visiting Rodrigo. South Ealing Cemetery is a good thirty-minute walk from here, but half that time by bus, so I hurry back to the main road just as a number 65 double-decker is approaching. I hop on, and try Damian's number again, but disconnect when his voice-mail cuts in.

The bus reaches Chilton Avenue at 12.30 and I disembark, seeing the large fenced estate ahead. It was established in the mid-nineteenth century from what I read online on the bus, and covers over twenty acres. Finding Damian may be like searching for a needle in a haystack. Damian told me how angry he was at not being able to attend the funeral as he was on remand and not granted permission, at the wishes of Rodrigo's family.

I enter through the wrought-iron gates and beneath the gothic-looking stone chapel ruins. The path beyond is surrounded by leafless trees, their branches like bony fingers stretching as far as the eye can see. From what I read on my phone, the most recent graves are in a specific section in the southwest corner of the grounds, so I head there, trying Damian's number again without success. It is starting to spit again, but there is a lack of shelter, and so I pull the collar of my raincoat around my neck to keep the chill off.

There doesn't appear to be a single other person here. I've almost made it to the end of the cemetery and into Brentford, when I see a figure crouching beside a grave. My shoes squelch in the muddy grass as I get closer, trying to get a better look at the figure. He must hear me approaching because he suddenly straightens and stares at me.

'Abbey? What are you doing here?'

'Looking for you. Please take your time, I didn't mean to interrupt.'

I bow my head, now conscious that I'm intruding.

He kisses his hand and rests it on the tombstone, before turning and moving closer to me.

'It's all right, I'm done,' he says.

I link my arm through his, and we squelch back to the concrete path.

'I was worried about you,' I say quietly, as we slowly make our way back towards the South Ealing entrance.

'It's been a long time since I had anybody to worry about me,' he says, patting my hand.

'I spoke to Eddie,' I continue. 'He told me you'd withdrawn your permission to seek civil recompense for your ordeal.'

He doesn't respond at first, and we continue to walk solemnly.

'Is it just Eddie you don't want to use? Or have you changed your mind altogether?'

He sighs loudly.

'I... I don't feel right about profiting from Rodrigo's death.'

That makes sense, and feels like the kind of thing I'd expect to hear Damian say.

'But it isn't profiting,' I counter. 'Your whole life was wrongly destroyed: your reputation left in tatters and you were denied the right to earn a living for nearly eight years. And all because the police tried the wrong man.'

'I know you're only looking out for me, but that's not how Rodrigo's family will see it. I need to build bridges with them.'

I understand exactly how he's feeling. When Faye died, and I knew I was responsible, I felt like I was constantly trying to make it back up to my parents, but no matter how hard I tried, the distance between us continued to grow. And I can't help feeling like Damian is fighting a losing battle. I don't want him wasting the opportunity to get his life back on track.

'What would Rodrigo want?' I ask instead.

He sighs again.

'I don't even know how to answer that question any more. I can't feel him beside me like I once could. And I miss him so much.'

I feel a lump forming in my throat.

'Can I share something with you?' I ask next. 'My sister died thirty years ago when I was fifteen. And I've spent every day since blaming myself for not preventing what happened. But that's time wasted. That's why I try to pay my penance by helping innocent people like you avoid injustice. It's great to feel like I'm making a difference but it doesn't take away any of that guilt. The pain and regret is still there, and it always will be.'

'What are you saying?'

'I'm saying don't give up on your future because of your past. Once the police find the person who did kill Rodrigo, I'm sure his family will come running back, begging for your forgiveness. Wouldn't it be better for them to see that you've managed to secure your future in spite of all their doubt and ill will?'

'I'm tired, Abbey. Tired of fighting. In some ways, I wish we hadn't appealed. It was hell in prison, but being out here without him is no better.'

I hear Terry Anderson's voice mocking me inside my head: *Is that what you're here to do, Miss Veritas? Do you come in search of the truth?*

'I don't think Rodrigo would agree with you. I think—'

'You don't know what my husband would be thinking,' he shouts, breaking the link of our arms. 'You didn't know him! What gives you the right to come here and try to give me advice?'

I take an unsteady step backwards.

'Calm down, Damian, I didn't mean to—'

'Just get out of here, Abbey. You want me to sue the authorities so you can get a nice chunk of money for your time. At least admit that's why you're here!'

I take another uncertain step backwards.

'Damian, I'm sorry. That's really not why I came here. I'm worried about you.'

'I never asked you to worry about me. Did I?'

'Well, no, but we're friends, and—'

'Oh, you think we're friends, do you?' he scoffs. 'You really think you know me, Abbey? You've no... you've really no fucking idea who I am, or what I'm capable of.'

He is foaming at the mouth as he rants, his eyes blazing in a way I've never seen before.

And just like that, I hear the detective's voice in my head: *You're so quick to forget that your pal Damian Johnson twice put the victim in hospital in the months prior to his passing. Leopards don't change their spots, Miss Veritas.*

Damian admitted to the violent arguments, but always insisted it was Rodrigo who started them, but is it possible that wasn't the truth? I wasn't involved in his first trial, and although I've read the court transcripts, I never got to see him deny the allegations. My head is spinning.

'I read in the newspaper that you're supposed to be some kind of fucking human lie detector,' he shouts next. 'What a fucking joke!'

He was seen snorting coke off one of the toilet cisterns in the club. Rodrigo was also heard arguing with someone in their flat less than an hour before he died.

The bartender at the nightclub originally claimed he saw Damian leaving the club just before eleven, but the CCTV footage had him leaving through the main entrance after midnight, which meant he couldn't have been the person arguing at the flat. And yet there's something no longer sitting comfortably with me as I see this new side of Damian.

'You should just get away from me, Abbey. I'm not the man you think I am.'

The club he was in had a rear garden that backs onto a railway line, but there are no security cameras out there, and the ones owned by the rail authorities was broken. Is it possible that Damian could have made an escape from the back of the club, killed Rodrigo and then snuck back in, making sure he was seen leaving after midnight?

No, this is insane. Damian's mum convinced me he was innocent, and at no point have I had reason to question that. I've met Damian several times, and never sensed any dishonesty from him.

But I've never outright asked him whether he killed Rodrigo, and it's like I said to Peter Graves, the best lies are partially based on fact.

'I can see from your face that you want to ask me,' he says next, almost as if the hard stare is buried deep in my mind and he can read what I'm thinking. 'Go ahead. Ask me, and I promise I'll tell you the truth.'

I hear the detective's scoffing in my head: *You know as well as I do that ninety-nine times out of a hundred, the victim's spouse or partner is the most likely perpetrator of a murder.*

I swallow hard, fighting against the sting at the back of my eyes.

'Did you kill Rodrigo?'

A single tear drops from his left eye.

'Yes.'

28

The whispered answer is like a kick to the gut.

No, this can't be happening.

'I blocked out what happened that night,' Damian continues quietly, his legs giving way, and his knees crashing hard against the wet concrete. 'I couldn't face what I'd done, so I convinced myself it never happened. It was easier than the truth.'

How could I have got it so wrong? I've prided myself on being able to see through others' bullshit, but I never saw this. What else have I missed?

'But your mum... the appeal...?'

He hangs his head, planting his hands on the floor to keep himself from fully collapsing.

'Sh-she doesn't know. How could I tell her?'

He's panting, as if confessing is sapping all of his strength. The rain is heavier now, but it's as if my feet have sprouted roots and are holding me here even though I desperately want to run and hide.

Damian's head and shoulders are bobbing as he cries and wails, his clothes already soaked through, his umbrella discarded.

I should phone the police, or maybe I should be recording his confession on my phone, but I don't reach for it. As terrified as I am, I know I can't escape the truth.

'Tell me what happened that night at the club,' I say, but I can't tell if it is loud enough for him to hear.

He slowly raises his face and I can see the shame deeply rooted in his eyes.

'He... he told me he wanted a divorce. H-he said he loved me, but couldn't live with me any more. When things were good, they were great, but when things were bad, they were awful.'

Rodrigo twice ended up in hospital as a result of injuries inflicted by Damian, and regardless of who started the violence, it is clear who came out on top each time. How many other fights ended with injuries that didn't require hospital intervention?

'He left the club, saying he was going home, and begged me not to follow. He promised we would talk in the morning, so I stayed on at the club, but I couldn't stop picturing a life without him. I was desperate to change his mind. I wanted him to know I would do whatever it took to change.'

We are both soaked through, but I can't even feel the rain falling any more. It's as if we are the last two people left in the world, and everything else has faded into a void.

'I stole a car, trying to get back to the flat to reason with him, but when I got there, he'd already packed two cases with his belongings. I pleaded with him for a second chance, but it was like he was a different person. So cold. I told him I wasn't going to let him go, and he handed me a letter, telling me to read it. He couldn't even tell me to my face. He tried to push past me, and we fought, and before I knew it, he was lying dead on the floor. I don't remember exactly what happened.'

The crime scene photos showed fragments of a broken vase in amongst the pool of blood that seeped from the crack in the back

of Rodrigo's head. According to what I read in the court transcripts, the medical examiner said that had Rodrigo received
urgent medical care, there is a chance he would have survived. I
don't remind Damian of this now.

'It... it didn't feel real. I was high and drunk but seeing him
there had a sobering effect. I drove back to the club and dumped
the car and snuck back in over the fence. I made a scene inside, so
people would remember me there, and then I eventually
returned home, but the police were already there. One of our
neighbours had heard us arguing, and had seen a dark figure
leaving, and so I was arrested. I was pretty wasted and when I
woke in the cell the following morning, it genuinely just felt like a
bad dream. I couldn't initially remember leaving the club, and I
leaned into the narrative my imagination created. And for years
I've allowed that story to protect me, but now it's too real. Everything I touch and see reminds me of what I have done. I don't
suppose you know what that feels like.'

I know only too well, I don't say.

'I don't deserve to be free. That is why I can't seek damages.
They were right all along.'

'So why did you appeal, Damian? Why did you maintain your
innocence for so long?'

He meets my hard stare with one of deep shame, and utters a
solitary word.

'Mum.'

I picture her the day she approached me earlier this year,
begging me to look into her son's case. She drew me in with her
passionate assertion that he couldn't have killed Rodrigo.

'I was too scared to tell her what I'd done. It would break her
heart. She doesn't have long left, and I wanted her to go to her
grave still believing I'm the innocent child she brought into the
world.'

I feel my own heart break a little.

'What now?' I ask him.

But he isn't able to respond as fresh tears splash into the mass of puddles surrounding his hands and knees.

* * *

I escort Damian back to his flat and put him to bed with a mild sedative, telling him I'll return to check on him tonight and then I'll help him figure out a plan for his next steps.

The Tube journey back to the office is quiet, as I'm lost in my own thoughts. I can't believe I got it so wrong with Damian. How could I have missed the signs? When I looked over to him the moment he was acquitted, he mouthed his thanks, and buried his head in his hands. I thought that was because he was finally free, but now I can see it was the feelings of guilt consuming him.

Under UK law, an acquitted person can only be retried for the same offence in exceptional circumstances, otherwise the principle of 'double jeopardy' applies. A retrial is only permitted if the new evidence is considered 'compelling', meaning it's highly persuasive and significantly changes the assessment of guilt. I could make a statement to the police confirming Damian's confession to me, but it would be a case of my word against his. He could deny the conversation occurred and I have no evidence to substantiate my claim. I suppose if he were to confess to the police, then maybe it would be enough, but with his mum still alive, I don't think he will. I don't know how he will be able to balance his overwhelming guilt with his newfound freedom.

'Are you okay?' Sasha asks when I get inside, and to be honest my red face probably isn't creating the best impression.

'I'm fine,' I lie.

'Well, I'm not. Rhys Morgan phoned this morning and said we're in breach of contract, and he wants his fee refunded.'

I don't think he'll be making such demands when John-Paul's friend sends over the ANPR confirmation.

'We don't have it, Abbey,' Sasha continues, pressing a hand to her eyes to restrain the tears. 'It's over.'

'I wouldn't be so sure,' I say with more confidence than I'm actually feeling. 'I'm certain there's something just around the corner that will save us.'

'I know you're trying to be optimistic, Abbey, but I think we seriously need to consider packing things up before the bailiffs are sent round.'

It's like a dagger to the heart. I promised myself I wouldn't allow things to come to that, but maybe I should have considered that before forcing Graves to rewrite the feature.

'Is it really that bad?' I ask, and she nods, her eyes watering slightly.

I don't have the heart to tell her that any hopes of a payout from Damian's acquittal have also gone up in smoke.

'Have we had any calls for new business following the interview?'

Her face brightens slightly.

'A couple of emails came through over the weekend, but ultimately they're talking about the new year, and only one hasn't asked for voluntary support.'

'So, our only option is the television show, right? The real-life *Murder, She Wrote* series you mentioned.'

'It probably won't pay until too late.'

'Then I'll demand payment upfront, or at least a retainer. I'm not going to let this business go under, Sasha. Even if it means I have to go and stack shelves overnight in a supermarket, I'll get something.'

She smiles empathetically, but we both know it won't be that easy.

'How was your weekend?' she asks, dropping in to the chair across from me, and snatching up the remaining Jaffa Cake in the packet.

'I'm not sure you'd believe me if I told you...'

'That good, huh?'

I shake my head and proceed to tell her about the messages that came through last night, as well as finding my sister's unicorn toy.

'Holy shit!' she gasps when I'm through. 'Who do you think is behind the threats?'

'Oh, I know who's behind it. I figured out it was Rhys yesterday. I'm pretty sure that's why he's trying to claim a breach of contract.'

'What makes you so sure it's him?'

'Because he works for Terry Anderson, who is the only person who could have kept mementoes of pushing Faye into that quarry. Think about it. Anderson wants to appeal his conviction for whatever reason – probably just to spite me – so he hires an unknown solicitor, with the offer of big money should he file the appeal. Anderson tells him to contact a television production company offering to reveal the gruesome details, and Anderson promises any payment to the solicitor. But they don't have any fresh evidence for the appeal unless they can call my original testimony into question.'

Sasha sits there speechless.

'I know it sounds far-fetched, and I sound like some kind of conspiracy theorist, but I can't make any other sense of it.'

Sasha blinks several times before speaking.

'Bloody hell, mate. Do you really think Rhys would do something like that?'

'I'd like to think not because it's not only immoral, but also illegal, but I can't see who else has anything to gain from it, aside from Anderson.' I pause, choosing my next words carefully. 'Do you still know that tech guy who can access the dark web?'

'Max? Sure. Why?'

'Can you ask him if he has any means of...' I pause again, summoning the courage to utter the words. 'Is he able to access Rhys's emails and text messages?'

She raises her eyebrows at me, and I smile feebly.

'I need proof that he's the one behind these threats.'

The intercom buzzes, but I tell Sasha I'll answer the door so she can call Max straight away. I head down the stairs as I hear knocking on the door.

'I'm coming,' I call out, increasing my pace. 'What's so important?' I add as I open the door, but my mouth drops when I see two police officers in high-visibility vests blinking against the downpour.

'Abbey Veritas?' one of them asks.

'Yes,' I say, already worried about who they may inform me has died.

'Abbey Veritas, I am arresting you on suspicion of perverting the course of justice. You do not have to say anything, but it may harm your defence if you do not mention when questioned something that you later rely on in court. Anything you do say may be given in evidence.'

29

My fight-or-flight response fails me, as I am spun around and my hands are cuffed behind my back. I want to call out to Sasha for help, but my throat is paralysed with fear. The two officers escort me through the rain and into the waiting transit van, where I'm secured in a small cage.

This can't be happening.

I clamp my eyes shut, willing my brain to wake me from this nightmare, but when I open them again, all I can see is the reinforced door only inches from my face.

What was it they charged me with? Perverting the course of justice? Me? I've spent my entire adult life correcting the course of justice. I don't know why but I picture Detective Roach and what he said to me immediately after Damian's acquittal: *I really don't know how you can sleep at night, knowing you've colluded to set a convicted killer free.*

I left Damian sleeping in his flat, but if his conscience has been gnawing away at him, then I shouldn't be surprised that he's turned himself in. And as much as Detective Roach would take immense pleasure in trying to pin something on me, I know I didn't do anything wrong. I didn't collude with Damian to lie in court. That was all of his own doing.

These are the thoughts that remain with me as we reach our destination, and I am released from the cage and led in through the back door of a building and into the custody suite. I am taken to the desk where the custody sergeant takes my details and checks I'm not inebriated by drugs or alcohol. They confiscate my phone, but rather than taking me to a holding cell, I am led into a small, dark room, and seated in one of four chairs around a table. My cuffs are removed and I'm asked if I would like them to contact a solicitor on my behalf.

Who would I call, I want to ask, but don't. I wouldn't trust Eddie Douglas as far as I can throw him, and besides, it would be a conflict of interest for him to represent me when it's Damian who has landed me here.

'I've done nothing wrong,' I say firmly, 'so why would I need a solicitor?'

'Can I get you a drink of anything? Water? Tea? Coffee?'

I'm about to refuse when I realise how dehydrated I'm feeling and request water. I watch as the officer heads out, closing the door behind him. He's back within minutes, placing a plastic cup of chilled water before me, and then a woman in an all-in-one trouser suit enters, followed by a portly man with a shaved head and grey handlebar moustache whom I instantly recognise.

I shouldn't have left Damian alone in the state he was. I thought the mild sedative I gave him would keep him sleeping until morning, but I should have stayed with him and made sure he was okay.

The two detectives sit across from me, and Roach starts the tape recorder, introducing himself and his colleague and then reminding me I remain under caution.

'For the DIR, Miss Veritas has refused legal advice from a

solicitor, but before we begin, Miss Veritas, are you certain you wouldn't like us to find you a solicitor?'

'I have nothing to hide,' I say with more confidence than I'm feeling. 'Let's get on with this, shall we?'

The two of them exchange a glance, before Roach nods.

'Can you describe your job, Miss Veritas?' he asks.

I clear my throat.

'I am a professional criminologist who specialises in reviewing miscarriages of justice, as well you know, Detective Roach.'

'Can you tell us what that means?'

I hate the formality of this, especially as I know it's not going to lead anywhere. Roach is just enjoying the opportunity to waste my time and make me feel guilty.

'I am hired by solicitors who believe their clients were wrongfully convicted and are usually serving a prison sentence.'

'And what exactly is it that you do when you're hired?'

This is so pointless!

'I am provided with copies of all the evidence that was presented during the appellant's trial and I search for inconsistencies.'

'So, you look for loopholes to set these convicted prisoners free?'

I clamp my jaw tight, aware that he's baiting me.

'No, that isn't what I said, Detective Roach, though it is disheartening to witness you, yet again, misinterpreting what you've been told.'

His eyes narrow, and I feel like I've scored a point there.

'Do you ever ask whether your clients are guilty of their crimes?'

'No, but I'm a pretty good judge of character, and I'm good at spotting when I'm being lied to.'

My skin crawls as I say this, given what's been happening these last few days.

Roach whispers something to his colleague and she scribbles something on the paper before her.

'Can we just cut through the bullshit?' I say. 'Tell me what it is I'm supposed to have done, and then I'll clarify why it isn't perverting the course of justice.'

They exchange glances again, only this time I see something far more sinister In Roach's eyes when he turns back to face me.

'What is your relationship with Terry Anderson?'

The question throws me.

'That has nothing to do with Damian Johnson.'

'Please just answer the question for the digital recording, Miss Veritas.'

'Terry Anderson is a convicted serial killer; I have no relationship with him.'

'So, he isn't one of your current clients?'

I close my eyes as I realise what is going on here. This is Rhys at work behind the scenes.

'As I guess you probably already know, Anderson's solicitor hired our firm under false pretences, and now that I've made it clear to him that it would be a conflict of interest to be anywhere near Anderson's attempted appeal, he is trying to make things awkward. I bet he's told you we're in breach of contract. I can assure you we will be more than happy to refund his retainer. Was it really necessary to go to all of this drama over what's at best a civil dispute? In fact, if anything you should be pulling him for wasting police time.'

I take a sip of water, trying to compose myself.

Roach just sits there, staring at me.

'Is that it?' I say, giving way to my frustration. 'Are we done now? Am I free to go?'

'No,' Roach replies evenly. 'Tell us when you first became acquainted with Terry Anderson.'

I take another sip of water, uncertain where he's going with this.

'I've never been *acquainted* with Terry Anderson.'

'But you did testify at his trial when you were a teenager, no? Back then your name was Abigail Turnbull, but it was you who testified in court, wasn't it?'

I think back to the text message I sent to Rhys yesterday: *I know this is you, Rhys. Do what you want. We both know your client is the only guilty one.*

So, not satisfied with his attempts to make me 'come clean', he's now set the police on to me to try and freak me out.

'Yes, I testified against Terry Anderson when I was fifteen.'

'And what was it you said in court?'

'It was thirty years ago, Detective Roach, so I can't remember my words exactly.'

'Summarise for us. It doesn't have to be word for word.'

I deliberately sigh to show them how frustrating I'm finding this whole experience.

'I told the court that I saw Anderson chasing after my sister shortly after she'd run away, and before she...' I pause and take a breath. 'Before her body was found in a disused quarry.'

'You saw him, did you?'

I swallow hard.

'Yes.'

'And how could you be sure it was him?'

'Because when you see a monster in real life, it's hard to forget about them.'

He looks at something on the page before him, before meeting my gaze again.

'We have it on good authority that you didn't actually see Terry Anderson in the woods that day, and that you lied in court.'

I hear Anderson's words playing out in my head: *I didn't see you or your sister that day, and that's why I know you lied about seeing me there too.*

'Good authority?' I scoff. 'The word of a convicted murderer is not what I'd call *good authority*. And I'm surprised you'd put so much faith in the words of a monster like Terry Anderson.'

Roach smirks momentarily but it vanishes as quickly as it appeared.

'Terry Anderson isn't our source. Someone else has come forward to reveal you lied about seeing Anderson in the woods.'

The breath catches in my throat.

'Rhys Morgan is Anderson's solicitor and he wasn't there, so, again I'd argue your source isn't reliable.'

He slowly shakes his head.

'I can't say I know a Rhys Morgan. No, the person we've spoken to witnessed exactly what happened the day your sister disappeared.'

I think back to the message to the unknown number; I convinced myself that Rhys was on the other end, but what if he wasn't?

'Would you like to tell us what *really* happened in the woods that day?'

I don't answer, as my mind races with thoughts, searching for angles out.

'You have my account on record already, and I have nothing further to say,' I eventually respond.

'Very well. What usually happens at this point is called discovery, where we would share some of our evidence with your solicitor, but as you've declined legal support, I'm going to share it with you instead, Miss Veritas. We'll then pause the recording and give you some time to think very carefully about your next steps.'

I take a long drink of the water, unable to stop my hand from shaking, terrified by what's to come. There's no way they can know what actually happened.

'We have been told that you and your sister had an argument that day; that the two of you got into a fight, and that you pushed her. She fell, and bashed her head on a rock of some kind, before running off into the woods. You didn't give chase until some time later when she hadn't returned. You disposed of the bloodied rock, before informing your parents that she was missing. And when her body was recovered from the quarry, you lied about seeing Terry Anderson in those woods and sent an innocent man to prison.'

My heart sinks.

I know you lied about what really happened to your sister in those woods. Admit what you did, or I'll reveal everything that happened that day. You have three days. I'll be watching.

I dared them to expose my lies, and now that I'm confronted with them, I have no way out.

30

I'm still in the room where the interview occurred, and I'd give anything to be able to open the door and just run. But there's an officer guarding the door from the outside, and I'd never manage to get through the various security installations between me and the outside world.

I can't stop thinking about that day. Faye was being more obnoxious than ever. She knew I wanted to spend some time alone with John-Paul, but every time I tried to kiss him, she'd make a fuss or say something vindictive. It wasn't even my idea that she come to the park with me, but Mum insisted. She kept going on about how much Faye was struggling at school and how she and Dad had to talk about her future. She practically begged me to take Faye with me. I wish I'd just been honest and told her I was going to meet John-Paul, but I know she wouldn't have approved.

I wipe the free-flowing tears from my eyes, but they won't stop. I didn't realise how badly she was hurt. She didn't pass out at any point, and it didn't seem like there was a lot of blood on the rock. And the way she ran off... someone with a fatal wound wouldn't be able to run off like that. But what if she was worse than I thought and became confused and lost in the woods? And then she stumbled through the gap in the fence and tumbled headfirst into the quarry.

I've always told myself that such an explanation is too far-fetched, and that she must have come across someone like Anderson who meant her harm. I guess it's easier to convince yourself when you so desperately want something to be true.

There must have been someone else in the woods that we didn't spot. Roach said he knows we didn't immediately chase after her, so whoever was watching us must have seen us fooling about in the long grass. I wanted to show John-Paul how much he meant to me, but he wouldn't go past first base because I was only fifteen. I was sure that if Faye saw we were ignoring her she'd come running back. In fairness, I didn't even notice the blood on the rock until we gathered after our original search. I took it into the woods and threw it into the river, assuming the water would wash it away, but what if the witness saw that and collected the rock? They'd have proof I'm the reason Faye died.

I'm letting my imagination get the better of me. Why didn't this witness come forward sooner? Why would they allow thirty years to pass before turning me in? Unless I was right all along and it was Anderson who witnessed what happened. But it still doesn't make sense as to why he would wait to expose my lie. If he'd testified about what he saw, the judge might have ruled my testimony inadmissible, and that might have been enough for him not to be found guilty; the verdict wasn't unanimous, after all.

I start at a knock on the door and a moment later, Roach and his colleague return, asking whether I've reconsidered seeking legal advice. The truth is, I have, but I don't want to waste any more time in here. I need to get out, regroup, and find a solicitor who can try and help me steer through this.

They start the digital interview recorder again, and fire various questions at me about the day Faye went missing. I meet each question with a stone-faced, 'No comment,' as I've seen so many arrestees do when they don't want to give anything away. Roach tries to convince me that a 'No comment' interview can reflect badly when a case goes to court, but I don't budge, just willing the time to tick by.

When he eventually stops the recorder, he leaves, but his colleague remains in the room with me this time. I can't meet her gaze, and am grateful when she doesn't attempt to stimulate conversation. After what feels like an age, Roach returns and advises me I am no longer under arrest, but they will be in touch in the next day or so. The last thing he says is that it would be in my best interests to find a good solicitor.

I exit the station but don't truly breathe until I'm several hundred yards away, at which point I duck behind a wall, and release the tension in my shoulders. I pull out my phone and call John-Paul to warn him that the police might be on their way to him next, but he doesn't answer, which could mean they've already got to him too. I leave him a message, asking him to call me back as soon as he can.

My next call is to Sasha, to tell her what happened, and she says she saw the convoy of vehicles driving away and figured I must be involved when I didn't return having answered the door. She urges me to come back to the office, but adds that Peter Graves has been trying to get hold of me. I ask why, but she says she doesn't know and suggests I call him on my return to the office. It's nearly three o'clock, and I don't have a jacket, but I actually feel grateful to feel the cold air and rain on my face. For all I know, my freedom to walk where and when I want might be snatched away from me.

I buy a sandwich and an energy drink from a newsagent's that I pass, and then find a canopy over a shuttered retail shop to shiver under while I place the call to *The Daily Bore* front desk. I'm connected through to Graves seconds later.

'I hope this is just a call to tell me we set a record for sales with Saturday's edition,' I say, trying to lighten my own mood.

'I'm sorry, Abbey, but my call is more official. I need to ask you something on the record.'

I've not heard him sound so serious before, and I'm instantly dreading something that is going to make my day even worse.

'I have a source who tells me that you were arrested earlier today and police are asking questions about your involvement in your sister's murder.'

I shouldn't be surprised that Roach's first call upon my release was to a tabloid hack. It would be typical for his response to the CPS saying he doesn't have enough to charge me to muddy my name in the press instead.

'No comment,' I say, sticking to my tried and tested method.

He sighs.

'I have a secondary source who has gone on record to say you lied about seeing Terry Anderson in the woods that day to cover your own complicity.'

Is this the same person who turned me in to the police?

'No comment,' I croak as the words catch in my throat.

'Okay. My source also tells me they have evidence that you conspired to cover up your own involvement in your sister's death. They say you lied to police about why you and your sister became separated. How do you respond to that?'

Shit, shit, shit. This cannot be happening. Not now.

'Tell me who's doing this, Peter. I deserve to know who is slandering me.'

'I'm sorry, Abbey, my source wishes to remain anonymous.'

'Even if they're lying?'

'Are they lying, Abbey? Because if they're not that really calls into question everything you told me on Friday night. And if you've lied about Terry Anderson's involvement, now that it's published, you could be sued for libel. This is your chance to set the record straight. But if you continue to deny the allegation and then I print my source's evidence, things will be far worse. I don't want to put you through that, Abbey.'

Everything is falling apart. Maybe John-Paul was right and we should have got ahead of the truth breaking. He's leaving me little other choice.

'Okay, Peter, listen, I'm willing to go on the record with you, and tell you *everything*, but first, I need to meet your source.'

'I'm not sure my source will agree to that.'

'Please, Peter. Ask them to meet me and show me their evidence and then we'll speak. I just need to know who's doing this to me.'

'Okay, I'll try, but I can't guarantee anything. I'll call you back once I've spoken to them.'

I hang up the phone and bury my head in my hands. It's no less than I deserve, but if I'm going down, I'm going to do my utmost to ensure I don't drag Sasha and John-Paul down with me, and that starts with telling them the truth about what happened the day I last saw Faye.

31

I've been back at my desk for ten minutes and have reread the same sheet of paper before me three times, without taking any of it in. It's a transcript of the police interview with Anderson shortly after his arrest. I figured it would make sense to reacquaint myself with how the investigation and subsequent trial played out. I have no chance of coming out of this clean, but now it's all about damage limitation.

Reading the dialogue isn't the same as hearing it. There are no sidenotes to indicate the tone of Anderson's 'No comment' responses. Did he sound worried? Did he sound cocky? How can I know what was going through his mind without being able to hear his voice?

I just wish his interview had been video recorded, but at the time of his arrest the use of the technology wasn't widespread. I sigh and close the flap of the paper folder on my desk. What is the point of me looking at the case file if I can't properly assess and evaluate the detail? And given how bad a job I clearly did with Damian, it's naïve of me to assume I will find the splinter which will prove Anderson's guilt once and for all.

I stare at my phone, contemplating whether to call Damian and ask what his next steps are, but I can't bring myself to hear his voice again. I can still hear the cries of anguish from Rodrigo's brother and sister in the courtroom. My interference has denied them justice, and that makes me as guilty as Damian for their feelings of loss. I've helped turn what I thought was a miscarriage of justice into an *actual* miscarriage of justice. And when that fact becomes common knowledge, it is sure to be the final nail in my coffin.

'Sorry to disturb your thoughts,' Sasha says, popping her head through the doorway. 'I've spoken to Max about... well, what you asked. He says he managed to get into Rhys Morgan's emails, and has sent over all emails sent and received in the last month, but there's nothing jumping out at me in terms of him having any kind of vendetta against you.'

It was a longshot.

'Hey, do me one more favour,' I say, as she's turning to leave. 'I can't get hold of my friend John-Paul. Can you keep trying him, and ask Max if he can locate where his mobile signal is? I'm worried he's been arrested too, and I want to do what I can to keep him from facing the same charges as me. He only lied to the police because I asked him to.'

Sasha scribbles the note on her hand, and attempts to offer a reassuring smile.

'You know I've got your back no matter what happens. And if there is anything you want me to do, just say.'

I appreciate her support, and it almost brings fresh tears to my eyes, but I force them down. I don't want her to see how hopeless and helpless I feel.

It's now dark beyond the blinds over the windows. With less than a week until Christmas, I'm going to be lucky not to be eating Christmas dinner on remand somewhere. I'm just grateful my parents aren't alive to see how far their firstborn has fallen.

I grab my mobile the second it rings.

'Abbey? It's Peter Graves. Further to your request, I've spoken with my source, and they've agreed to meet you tonight, but it has to be at the offices here.'

It isn't the response I was expecting. I want to get evidence of who they are and how they've been threatening me this past week. It's the only leverage I have to try and keep Roach and his team at bay.

'Fine. Can you now tell me who they are?'

'Not over the phone, but you'll come face to face with them here. Come to the reception desk. I've added you to the visitors list, so they'll call me the moment you arrive.'

He makes it all sound so formal.

'Oh, and Abbey, I want you to confirm what we agreed in terms of you providing me with an exclusive.'

I can see Sasha pacing while on the phone in her office.

'You'll have it,' I say to Graves.

'Good. Can you be here in the next hour?'

I agree and hang up, quickly sending Sasha a message to tell her where I'm going. It's still raining when I make it to street level, and so I head out to the main road and hail a passing black cab, giving the driver the address of *The Daily Bore* building in Marylebone. Traffic is slow and it probably would have been quicker to walk.

Graves is waiting for me in reception, and as a flurry of casually dressed workers head for the exits, I enter, now wishing I'd never agreed to the original interview with him. On Thursday I was riding the crest of a wave, and now I've hit rock bottom.

We ride the lift up to the top floor once more, and he silently leads me back to the same large conference room with darkened windows. This must be what it feels like walking from death row towards execution: knowing the end is near and unable to do anything about it.

The large screen shows one other participant in the meeting, but their video is off, so I can't see their face, and their name shows only as 'Guest'.

'You said me and your source would meet face to face,' I challenge, once again feeling as though he has misled me.

'You will. Sort of. Sit down, Abbey, and all will be explained. Can I get you a drink before we start?'

I reach for one of the glass bottles of mineral water in the centre of the table, my hands shaking as I twist the cap off and pour the sparkling water into a glass. I sit down in one of the two chairs that have been pulled out, and Graves sits down beside me.

'Before we begin, we are currently on mute, so my source can't hear us. When I phoned you earlier and told you my source said you lied about seeing Terry Anderson with your sister the day she disappeared, you said it wasn't true. And when I revealed that my source also told me they have evidence that you conspired to cover up your own involvement in your sister's death, you also denied the allegation. We are on the record now. I will introduce you to my source, as requested, but I will repeat my questions at the end, and I will quote you in my story. I just want to make sure that is clearly understood.'

I swallow hard, but nod. I look up at the screen, trying to determine who is putting me through this shit. Someone I used to go to school with? Rhys Morgan, maybe? Or someone I haven't even considered?

Graves unmutes the call.

'Okay, we're both here,' he says, 'and Abbey is aware that what follows is on the record.'

There's a flickering of the screen and slowly the black fades to a backlit room, the dark figure coming into focus. The grey sweat-shirt continues to hang from his emaciated frame, and his scraggly white goatee somehow makes him look even older, but maybe it's the video software.

'Hello again, Abbey,' Anderson's voice echoes through the speaker on the desk before me.

'You?' I say, the breath catching in my throat, before I turn back to face Graves. 'This is your source? A convicted serial killer? Are you winding me up?'

But there's no trace of mirth on Graves's face.

'Terry has been able to provide additional information about what he saw in the woods that day; information that was excluded from his original trial, but makes the case for a retrial more compelling.'

'I told you the other day,' Anderson picks up, 'I *was* in those woods that day, but I didn't kill your sister.'

'Is that it? That's your evidence?' I scoff. 'No court in the land will just accept the word of a murderer.'

'They will when I tell them *exactly* what I saw, Abbey.'

I stand, frustrated, ready to storm out of the room, but some-thing holds me back.

'Did you see who killed my sister then?'

His wrinkled jaw widens into a smile.

'I certainly saw you arguing with her. I was passing through the trees when I heard a scream, and I moved closer to investi-gate. I saw two teenagers arguing and pushing at one another.'

'Last time we met you said you didn't see me, and that's why you claimed I didn't see you.'

He smirks at this.

'Oh, I saw you, Abbey, and you'd know that *had* you seen me too. I saw you push your sister, and I heard you tell her you wished she'd never been born.'

The heat rises to my cheeks, as I hear the words in my own voice in my head. They were the last words I ever said to my sister, and I hate myself for it.

'And then when she ran off, rather than chasing after her, I saw you and some lanky lad fumbling about in the grass. For some reason that salient fact never came up in your testimony. Is that because you didn't share it with the police as your boyfriend would have been charged with having sex with a minor?'

'We weren't having sex,' I say, determined to keep John-Paul's name out of my account.

'I thought about going after the other girl,' Anderson continues. 'She looked like she needed attention, but as I said on Friday, I already had a situation to take care of.'

'Is that all you've got? Why not mention it at your original trial?'

'Because then I would have had to admit that I was in those woods, and the reason why. My barrister had me believing the jury would side with us, because the other evidence was pretty circumstantial. After they found me guilty of all counts, there seemed little point in appealing the one I didn't do. It wouldn't have got me out any sooner.'

'So why share it now? Other than to screw with my life?'

He laughs at this; a long, raucous laugh that has him wheezing and reaching for a drink of water.

'I want to go to my death with a clear conscience. I continued on my way to the pharmacy to collect the insulin I needed for the lad I'd already snatched. But it was on my way back that I spotted you and your boyfriend, scrambling around in the same long grass, only this time you were upright and looked proper panicked. I saw him lift a rock and hand it to you, and heard him say something about blood. I couldn't believe what I was seeing. It was like one of those old *Crimewatch* reconstructions playing

out before my eyes. You see, I know what it's like when the immediate panic sets in when you've taken your first life. It can be so
terrifying, and yet exhilarating. For some of us, it's a feeling we
desperately chase after for the years that follow. But either way,
it's a time when most mistakes are made.'

I feel sick to my stomach hearing him comparing my accident
with his own urges.

'You and I are not the same,' I tell him through gritted teeth.

He grins widely at the screen.

'Yeah, you're probably right about that, but we do share one
trait: we know what it is to lose someone we love.'

I've heard enough and stand, pressing my hands against the
desk to support myself as I glare at the screen.

'It's your word against mine. All I have to do is deny your
version of events and stick to my guns. Your allegations will make
it difficult for me for a bit, but it won't end anything. When the
TV series launches I'll make sure not a single person on this
earth believes a word you're saying.' I turn and look at Graves
dismissively. 'I can't believe you've been so taken in by this made-
up bullshit.'

'So, you're now denying that you pushed your sister, that she
cracked her head on a rock, and you proceeded to dispose of the
evidence with your boyfriend.'

'You're damn right I am,' I shout back, even though it pains
me to lie.

'She can deny it all she likes, Petey, you and I know the truth: I
was at a pharmacy collecting your insulin when that girl died.'

I turn to look at Graves, and suddenly the dots connect.

32

'You're the diabetic kid he'd already abducted,' I say, unable to quite make sense of what is happening.

'No, I was the kid he rescued from abusive foster family after abusive foster family,' Graves replies icily.

I knew nothing about this other child he claimed to have taken, until he mentioned it when Rhys and I visited him in Belmarsh. I should have thought to validate the claim, but I didn't think about it after I ran from the meeting. I figured Anderson must have had someone on the outside helping him, but I never once thought it might have been Graves.

'Do you know what it's like growing up in a home where you're treated as nothing more than an inconvenience?' Graves continues. 'My conception was the result of my mother – and I use that term loosely – being assaulted by her local priest. And being from a good Roman Catholic family, she couldn't have me aborted. And so, I was born, and quickly given up for adoption. I was made a ward of the state, and bounced from one foster home to another. Some were better than others, but nobody was willing to keep me long term.'

After Faye's passing, I often felt like an inconvenience to my parents, to the point that at times it felt like they wished I was the daughter they lost.

'I was at my lowest point, living on the street, when I first met Terry. He offered me food and shelter. He is the only person to ever want me with him. And although our time together was brief, he has been a constant support to me. He helped me gain an education and offered me advice when I needed it. You call him a monster, but you don't know what he's really like.'

A classic case of Stockholm syndrome; when a kidnapped person falls in love with their captor.

'He killed at least six other people – children, even.'

'He wasn't well. He's admitted as much to you. And he has acknowledged his former behaviour was abhorrent and he is paying for those crimes. But that doesn't mean he should pay for something he didn't do.'

I take a breath, knowing that if it really is Stockholm syndrome, there is no point trying to reason with him.

'And he's right,' Graves adds. 'He left me at exactly 2 p.m. that day to go to the pharmacy and was back in less than an hour. Given where his house was, he didn't have time to stop and kill your sister.'

'If you're so certain he didn't kill my sister, why didn't you speak up at his trial?'

'He didn't want me dragged into it, and as he's already explained, he didn't believe the jury would find him guilty. Besides, they would have made out like I was going to be his next victim—'

'How can you be so naïve?' I interrupt. 'You probably would have been his next victim had the police not arrested him.'

He scoffs at this.

'If he wanted me dead, all he needed to do was deprive me of my insulin. But he didn't. He wanted to help me; he wanted to support me. What's more, he wouldn't have been arrested had he not risked everything to get my medication.'

I take a moment, playing all of this through my mind.

'But even if you're right, none of this changes anything. If his conviction for killing my sister is overturned, he'll still be where he is. I don't understand why you'd go to such lengths when—'

'Because he's innocent of that crime, and the real perpetrator – you – have made a life at his expense.'

He lifts something from the chair beside him, and I immediately recognise the paper copy of the Damian Johnson case file that was stolen on Thursday night. The penny finally drops.

'It was you,' I say. 'You followed me to my office and stole the file. Why?'

'I needed to understand how your mind worked, and I thought I might find other proof of your lies.'

I stare down at the file, and briefly hear Damian's voice in my head: *He tried to push past me, and we fought, and before I knew it, he was lying dead on the floor.*

I pause, as my mind makes further leaps. I stare at Graves. '*You're* the one who's been messaging me. You sent the hairclip and left the unicorn.'

Graves looks over to Anderson, as if searching for permission to speak, but I can already see the guilt etched across his face.

'I think I should show her what you gave—'

'Not yet,' Anderson interrupts him. 'She needs to hear the rest first. Abbey, I did not kill your sister, but I was the one who discovered her body.'

I double over, as if someone has just plunged a dagger into my gut.

'Reports of a missing child were all over the local news, and I couldn't be sure, but I thought it sounded like the girl you'd pushed. So, the following morning, I returned to the woods, but took a short cut through the gap in the fence towards the abandoned quarry, out of fear I'd be spotted by some eagle-eyed bobby. It was so slippery, with loose rocks, and I nearly fell a couple of times, and then I saw her. From that height she resembled a discarded toy. But I recognised the denim dress. I figured she must have slipped and fallen, but she was long dead by the time I got down to her. Her eyes were glassy and her skin frozen to the touch.'

'Stop it!' I scream out, tears burning in my sockets.

'I'm not lying, Abbey. She looked like a porcelain doll. I wanted to make sure she was found and returned to her family, so I followed the steps back up to the other side of the quarry, and managed to slip out onto the main road, before I made an anonymous 999 call.'

'Stop lying!' I scream out again, thumping my hands against the desk.

He remains silent for a moment, before sighing.

'Show her the box.'

Graves slides out the chair beside him, and lifts out a battered shoe box, opening the lid. He pulls on a single latex glove, before slowly reaching inside and withdrawing an A5 notebook with a pink cover.

'I recovered this book from your sister's body,' Anderson's low voice rumbles through the speaker. 'It's your sister's diary.'

After she died, Mum was adamant that Faye was keeping a diary, but there was no sign of it at home. She searched every nook and cranny for it; even accused me of stealing it. Dad told me she was under a lot of pressure, and probably just imagined the diary. Eventually we all stopped talking about it.

Graves opens the cover and my hand shoots up to my mouth

as I see my sister's handwritten warning that nobody is to read her private thoughts.

'It makes very interesting reading,' Anderson says. 'The police might even go so far as to say it is evidence of motive.'

I reach my hand out to take the book, but Graves withdraws it from my grasp and tuts.

'This is what is going to see you put on trial for your sister's murder, as well as perjury,' Graves says with such certainty that I can feel the room spinning. 'On the record, Abbey, did you know your sister was infatuated with your boyfriend?'

The question throws me.

'What?'

'She describes in great detail how much she hated you because she was in love with your boyfriend. She's written countless stories in the back of the diary where she is a damsel in distress, and he her proverbial knight in shining armour.'

'You're lying,' I snap, but this news shifts the focus of that day in my mind.

She was so upset when John-Paul and I were talking and kissing. I assumed it was because we were deliberately pushing her away, but the way she went for me... it was me she was jealous of, and not John-Paul.

'The closer I got to John-Paul, the angrier she got; calling me names, and then eventually charging at me. I was embarrassed that she was acting in that way in front of him, and my immature mind feared that he'd lose interest in me because of my annoying sister.'

I no longer care that I'm confessing everything to Graves.

'I wanted to show I was in control, which is why I pushed her and told her... I wished she'd never been born.' I sit forward, speaking louder now, trying to convince us all. 'I didn't mean it. Obviously, I didn't mean it. It was just one of those things you say in the moment, and it has haunted me every day since. I loved my sister, and I would give anything to have her back with me now.'

I should stop talking. My whole life is on the table, doused in accelerant, and here I am holding a match beside it. But the weight of it has become too much, and I just want to be free of it now.

Graves clears his throat again.

'So, Abbey, on the record, did you see Terry Anderson in the woods that day?'

I grind my teeth and take a deep breath.

'No, I did not.'

'And, again on the record, did you conspire with the police to cover up your role in the disappearance of your sister and to lay the blame at Terry Anderson's door?'

Are you sure this is the man you saw in the woods? Did you see him abduct Faye?

I don't like how he has worded the question. It wasn't a conscious decision to frame Anderson. The police seemed sure he was behind it, and I went with the flow. I needed someone to be responsible for what had happened, and it was an easy way out.

'You claimed you didn't see your sister after the argument in the clearing, but I don't think that's true,' Graves continues. 'I saw how you reacted when I mentioned your sister that day we met for hot chocolate. You told me the best lies are partially based on fact, but as soon as I brought her up, you ran off. You've been running away from the truth for the last thirty years, Abbey. You did see Faye once again, didn't you? And you pushed her into that quarry.'

I leap to my feet and slam my hands against the desk.

'No, I did not! I pushed her and she hit her head on the rock, but I swear to God that was the last time I saw my sister.'

'Then who the hell tried to choke her?' Anderson shouts.

I frown at the question.

'There was bruising around her neck, caused by some kind of cotton scarf or shirt sleeve, the coroner said. Cotton fibres were recovered from her skin, but they tested those fibres against every shirt in my closet and there were no matches.'

I have no idea what he's talking about. Because I was due to testify in court, I wasn't permitted to sit in the public gallery, and my parents refused to let me see any of the newspaper or television coverage of the case. In my head, I knew how Faye died, so I've never felt the need to dig into it.

'I didn't try to choke Faye,' I repeat.

'Well, someone did!'

'Are you sure that's right?'

'Every word,' Graves says dryly.

'Then that means...' I don't know whether I should say it aloud, but there are too many other thoughts jumbling in my head. 'The rock didn't kill her.'

'No, the push into the quarry is what killed her,' Anderson states. 'A fall from that distance, she never stood a chance.'

'I didn't kill my sister.'

'So you say.'

'I do say.'

'Well, I don't believe you, and Petey here is going to take your sister's diary to the police and tell them everything we've just discussed.'

I've heard enough, and march away from the table.

'You can't keep running from the truth, Abbey,' I hear Graves call over my shoulder.

He's right, I know he is, but if Anderson is telling the truth, then that means my sister's killer is still out there, and my only chance of clearing my name is to find them.

33

I phone Sasha the moment I'm out of the building.

'Oh, thank God,' she says, 'I was beginning to worry. Is everything okay?'

I don't even know how to begin answering that question. I'm about to ad-lib a response when a black Land Rover pulls up to the kerb and the darkened window opens. I see John-Paul leaning over, and offering me a lift, and I climb inside.

'You look dehydrated,' he whispers. 'There's a bottle of mineral water in the glovebox if you're thirsty.'

I mouth a thank you and tear into the bottle, taking a long drink.

'Abbey? Can you hear me? I asked if everything was okay.'

'Not exactly,' I swallow and answer, 'but I'll tell you all about it when we get back.'

'We?'

'I'm with John-Paul.'

'Oh, good, he got hold of you. He phoned not long after you left here and I told him where you'd be.'

I switch the call to speaker as I fasten my belt, and John-Paul pulls out into traffic. It's so dark outside already as we near the shortest day of the year. I'm so tired, but I can't afford to rest until I finish putting the puzzle together.

'Wait, is this the John-Paul you were away with at the weekend? The one you—'

'You're on loudspeaker, Sasha,' I quickly warn.

'Oh. Hey, John-Paul, you'd better take good care of my friend there. Do you hear me?'

'Yes, ma'am,' he says, smiling that goofy grin I remember so well from school.

'Did Graves reveal his source?' Sasha asks next.

'Yeah, and it's Terry Anderson.'

'Anderson's his source?'

'Evidently.' I sigh. 'It's a long story, but apparently Anderson has been a father-like figure to him, and Graves can give him an alibi for the time Faye died, so it looks like his appeal will go ahead.'

'Shit!'

'My thoughts exactly.'

'So, he was the one who shopped you to the cops?'

'Yeah, he must have been. He also admitted to being the one who was sending those messages.'

But Sasha's question has something stirring in the back of my mind. Anderson's final words to me don't make sense: *Petey here is going to take your sister's diary to the police and tell them everything we've just discussed.*

If Graves had already shopped me to the police, he could have given them the diary then. Why hold on to it until after I'd called round?

'So, it wasn't that solicitor threatening you then?' John-Paul asks.

'Rhys Morgan? Apparently not. I guess that's why your detective mate couldn't find him on the ANPR tracker.'

'Yeah, right. I guess so. What are we saying here then? That it was this journalist who's been pulling all the strings?'

'Yeah, sort of. Ultimately, it's all been Anderson, but he's been pulling Graves's strings.'

'You should go straight to the police and report him,' Sasha says. 'The weird messages, sending hidden evidence and threatening you. You can't let him get away with it.'

'Yeah, I know, you're right. But Anderson is adamant he didn't kill her.'

'Are you surprised? He's had decades to rehearse his claims.'

'I know, I get that, but I have to be honest: I think he's telling the truth.'

'What?'

'Can you do me a favour, Sasha? Go through the files Rhys left and see if you can find anything about my sister's cause of death. Graves and Anderson said something about short fibres being recovered from around her neck, as if someone had tried to throttle her.'

John-Paul slams his hand down on the car's horn as someone cuts in front of us without indicating. I rest my hand on the dashboard as we suddenly brake.

'Sorry,' he murmurs, accelerating again.

'Let me have a look,' Sasha says, and I hear her place the phone on a desk.

I take another long drink from the bottle, amazed at how parched I feel.

'So, what did you tell the police?' I ask John-Paul while we wait for Sasha to return.

The car judders as his hand slips on the steering wheel.

'What? What do you mean? I didn't tell the police anything.'

I frown at this.

'You weren't brought in for questioning about the day Faye ran off. Like I was?'

'What? Oh, yeah, *that*,' he says nervously. 'Sorry, I thought you meant... Never mind.'

'Wait, what were you going to say?'

'It doesn't matter. I told them what you said, I guess: the story we agreed all those years ago.'

I'm about to ask him to go into more detail, when Sasha returns to the line.

'Are you still there?'

'Yeah, we're here.'

'Great. I've managed to find a photocopy of the ME's report. It's pretty grainy and difficult to read. It says cause of death was blunt force trauma to the back of the head, consistent with a fall from a great distance.'

'There you go,' John-Paul quickly says. 'They're just making shit up to cover their tracks.'

'No, wait,' Sasha continues, 'the medical examiner also notes discolouration of the skin around the jugular, consistent with some kind of ligature. Recovered fibres were being sent for forensic examination.'

It's a partial relief to hear it confirmed that it wasn't my push that caused her to stumble into that quarry, although it still begs the question of who she came into contact with after she ran off.

'Oh, shoot, my battery is running low,' Sasha says. 'I'll try and see if I can find the forensics report amongst the papers while I find a charger. I'll call you back.'

The call disconnects, and as I look out of the window, I don't recognise my bearings. It's pitch black and overcast, but not the usual array of city-centre lights I'm used to seeing.

'I thought you were taking me back to my office,' I say.

'Yeah, I was, but I missed the turn and now we're on the A40, so I'll have to turn around at the next junction. You look beat. It's okay if you want to take a little nap. I'll wake you when we get there.'

I tell him I don't need a nap, but have to stifle a yawn as I say it.

He lowers the volume of the radio and I try to replay my conversation with Graves and Anderson in my head. Graves must have followed me from my office to Harley Street when I went to speak to John-Paul on Saturday, and then followed us to Hampshire, and watched and waited for us to visit Faye's grave and saw me going into my old house. He must also have been the one to give little Jesse my sister's unicorn.

It angers me that he could be so willing to cross the line for someone like Anderson. Not only were his actions illegal, they were immoral. And that whole time when he was plying me with hot chocolate, and flattering my ego, he was just trying to set me up for a greater fall. It's no wonder he was so willing to yield control of the feature to Sasha and me on Friday night. It's like he handed me a shovel and allowed me to dig my own grave.

I yawn again, the small bright lights of houses beyond my window starting to blur.

Poor Faye. She remains the greatest victim in all of this. If I'd known how she felt about John-Paul, I would have tried to speak to her about it. I would have explained that as a sixteen-year-old, he'd have no interest in a girl three years younger than him...

Something scratches at the back of my mind, but I can't quite place what it is. I can see a glimmer of something, but then it disappears as fatigue tightens its grip on my mind.

My head bumps against the window beside me, and jars me awake again. I picture John-Paul and I sitting on the bench by her graveside, and his words pop to the front of my mind: *Had a high opinion of herself, but her heart was in the right place.*

I don't know why that has come back to me now. But the more I replay his words, the stranger they seem. I don't know why I didn't pick up on it sooner. I can probably count John-Paul's inter-actions with Faye on one hand, and I was with them on *every* occasion. She acted out each time, but why would he draw that conclusion? I don't recall them exchanging a single word beyond a greeting.

'Are we nearly there?' I ask, feeling as though I'll actually fall asleep without some fresh air. 'Why's it so hot in here?' I try to say, but my words slur.

I can't tell if it's the stress of the last three days, the impending trouble on the horizon, or just that I'm overthinking, but some-thing doesn't add up in my head. I feel like I need to say it out loud, just for someone to shoot down the hypothesis that is slowly starting to knit itself together.

I hear Anderson shouting: *Who the hell tried to choke her?*

And then it's Detective Roach's voice I hear next: *Terry Anderson isn't our source. Someone else has come forward to reveal you lied about seeing Anderson in the woods.*

I hear Anderson again: *Petey here is going to take your sister's diary to the police and tell them everything we've just discussed.*

So, if Anderson isn't Roach's source, and Graves had yet to speak to him, that can only leave Rhys.

But then I hear Roach's voice again: *I can't say I know a Rhys Morgan. No, the person we've spoken to witnessed exactly what happened the day your sister disappeared.*

The only people that I know who witnessed me push my sister are Faye herself, John-Paul and me. But if neither Faye nor I spoke to the police, that can only mean...

I try to focus on John-Paul's face, but my vision is blurring in and out of focus.

What is wrong with me?

I try to take another sip from the water bottle, but miss my mouth and it trickles down my chin and onto my jacket.

It's almost as if I've been drugged...

The bottle slips from my fingers, and bounces on the mat between my feet.

'John...' I try to say, desperate for him to help me.

'Why do you always have to be so smart?' I hear him say, but his voice is distorted, almost as if he is talking through a megaphone. 'You had to go and piece it all together, didn't you? If only you'd let sleeping dogs lie, then it wouldn't have come to this.'

I don't hear what he says after this as the world around me fades to black.

34

When I come to, my head feels as though I've been on the world's biggest bender. It throbs in ways it never has before, and when I open my eyes I see I'm still strapped in to John-Paul's Land Rover, though there is no sign of him beside me.

I quickly straighten as my last thoughts come flooding back to me: *John-Paul killed Faye.*

It sounds ridiculous, but that's where my logic took me. Sasha said the medical examiner found cotton fibres near the bruising around Faye's neck, and when I picture John-Paul and me frolicking in the tall grass that day, I remember him saying he was too hot, and then he stripped out of his Ben Sherman long-sleeved shirt. He bundled it and placed it beneath my head like a pillow, and I remember thinking how tender that was.

I choke back vomit as I now picture him tying it around Faye's throat, but chase the image away.

I hear his voice echo somewhere in the back of my head: *You had to go and piece it all together, didn't you? If only you'd let sleeping dogs lie...*

I can't make sense of this. The biggest difficulty is understanding why he would want to kill her. He was never violent towards me, and I don't ever remember seeing him get angry. Was it all a mask all along?

I unfasten my seatbelt and open the car door as quietly as I can. The internal light comes on, and I duck down in case he's out there somewhere in the darkness watching me. But even if he is, it's impossible to see because it's like we're parked in a blackhole. I slide my legs out of the car, my feet crunching on twigs or branches, but when I try to stand, my legs feel as though they're made of jelly. I grip the frame of the car to steady myself.

Where the hell am I?

I check my coat pocket, but there's no sign of my phone. I turn and look back inside the car in case it slipped out, but John-Paul must have taken it with him. I do notice the now empty plastic bottle of water, and can only assume he must have spiked it with something before I got in the car, though I have no idea what or why.

The car's interior glow provides a small arc of light immediately around this side of the car, and I see the ground is dark, and is covered in muddy bark chippings. The ground is damp from recent rainfall, but as I breathe the air deeply in my lungs, I sense I'm not in London any more; it tastes less polluted than I've grown accustomed to.

I try looking around the immediate vicinity, willing my eyes to become accustomed to the darkness. I head towards the outline of what looks like a tree of some kind, and then beyond it there are more trees.

We're in some kind of forest.

I can't remember where John-Paul said he lived, but it was somewhere out in the sticks. Was it Chalfont? I can't quite remember, but why would he bring me back to his home? Sasha must be wondering why we haven't made it back to the office, but would she have the sense to realise I'm in danger and phone the police? I hope so. She knew I was in John-Paul's car, so maybe we can be tracked using ANPR, although I'm not convinced.

There is no obvious way through the trees beyond the front of the car. It would appear he stopped here because he couldn't drive any further, but that doesn't narrow down where we are.

I stumble back towards the rear of the car, opening the boot, and looking for anything that might help me find a way out, but there's no torch. I do spot the tyre iron, and quickly pick it up, the steel cold against my palms. I'm hoping I won't need to fight off any attackers, but there could be anything in these woods, and I'm not prepared to take the chance.

With a deep breath, I place one unsteady foot in front of the next, holding out both arms, like a blind person searching for obstacles. All I can hear above the sound of my own haggard breathing is the buzzing of indistinct wildlife all around me. I could call out to John-Paul to find out where he is, but if I'm right about him, and he's driven me to this isolated woodland, there's no telling what he might have planned.

The fingertips of my left hand brush against rough bark, and I feel around the stump, taking a few seconds to lean against it to support my wobbly knees. I step forward again, and almost trip as the bottom of my trainer catches on something hard and sharp on the floor. I just about stay upright, and then tap my trainer against it. I move slowly forward, still tapping against this long structure.

It's some kind of wooden border.

I lower myself to the floor, and scramble my hands about. I feel large, smooth, treated stones directly in front of me, and if I had to guess, I'd say I've stumbled upon a footpath of some kind through the trees. Straightening, I slide my left foot against the wooden border, as I continue forwards, my left arm out to the side, feeling for more bark as I make slow progress. Glancing back over my shoulder, I can still just about make out the glow of the car's interior light from where I left the door open.

It's so cold out here, despite my raincoat, and there's part of me tempted to return to the car and wait it out until dawn, but that probably won't be until at least eight o'clock. I've no idea what the time is now, but I imagine John-Paul will be back this way before then. I have no choice but to keep going. Maybe if I can find some kind of enclosure or bushes to hide in, I'll be safe until first light and then I can figure out how to get to safety.

I continue to shuffle along the path, the strength in my legs starting to improve, but when I glance back this time, I can no longer see the car. It would be easy to lose my bearings, though there is a glimmer of moonlight poking from the shadow of a cloud, and I can see the path a little better. There's something unnervingly familiar about it, but I don't want to think about that right now.

I freeze at the sound of a twig snapping somewhere up ahead. I hold my breath, straining to hear any further sound. If that's John-Paul and he's returning from wherever he's been, then I don't want him to see me. I step over the wooden border, and do my best to tiptoe between the trees, but every step crunches, and I eventually stop, once again straining to see or hear anything, but there is nothing beyond the silvery glow of the steam escaping from my mouth.

It could have just been an animal of some kind. A rabbit, or a deer maybe.

I remain there for a few seconds more, before deciding it's safe and step back onto the gravel path. The moon is now poking further out from the cloud, and I can see the layout of the foot-path several metres ahead of me. It twists and turns, meandering through the trees, but I can't be sure if this is the most direct route

I should be taking. Would it be quicker to cut directly through the trees? The difficulty is I don't know where the nearest road or help would be. With no phone, no compass, and no light, I have no choice but to continue onwards.

An owl coos somewhere up ahead, but that only serves to make this area creepier. I recall all the scary fairytales I would tell Faye when we were huddled in my bed late at night. Nearly all of them started in a creepy wood, with werewolves and witches stalking nearby.

Directly ahead of me, the pathway widens into more of a clearing, and beyond that I see four large logs set out in a square, surrounding what was once probably a firepit. It's a picnic area, akin to those my parents would take us to when we were younger. To the left and right there are more logs laid out in a similar fashion.

The sense of familiarity resurfaces, and deep down I know where he's brought me. And then a bright light is suddenly shone into my face, and I have to bow my head and close my eyes, my outstretched arms doing little to prevent the sting.

'Is that to kill me with?' I hear John-Paul's voice call out in the darkness.

He must be looking at the tyre iron, and I now wish I'd tucked it in my waistbelt or beneath my coat so he didn't know I was armed.

'You come near me, and you'll soon find out,' I spit back, taking several unsteady steps backwards, to try and get away from the torch light.

'I don't mean you any harm, Abbey.'

'Oh, no? You drugged and abducted me and brought me to wherever the hell this is.'

He raises his arms into the air, the torch beam creating a spotlight over him as he slowly twirls around.

'I don't have any kind of weapon. I just... I just want to talk.'

'What about? How you murdered my sister?'

'No,' he begins to shout, before catching himself. 'That isn't what happened. Please, if you just let me explain what happened, you'll see that it was an accident.'

'How is strangling a defenceless child an accident?'

'No,' he shouts again, 'it wasn't...' He breathes heavily for several moments. 'Please just let me explain, and then, if you still want to attack me with that tyre iron, I won't stop you.'

I take another step backwards, trying to calculate how far I could run in the darkness before he would catch up with me and drag me back here. Despite the extra weight he's carrying, my legs are still feeling the effects of whatever was in that water.

He slips one of his legs over the nearest of the large logs and sits, placing the torch in the ashes of the pit.

'If you want to run, go ahead,' he says, his voice calmer now. 'I won't stop you and I won't give chase. But if you want to know what really happened that day, then please sit and let me explain.'

I should demand my phone and the car keys so I can call the police, and have them interrogate him, but given I don't have any evidence to prove his guilt over my own, I move forward and sit on the log across from him, the tyre iron gripped tightly in my right hand, in case he leaps at me.

35

His face remains frozen initially, as if he doesn't know how to begin. Eventually his brow furrows, and he places his palms on his knees and meets my gaze.

'I've thought about this moment more times than I can remember,' he says, a hollowness to his tone, 'but now that it's here, I can't find the words.'

'Where's my phone?' I say, my teeth chattering against the cold night air.

He reaches into his trouser pocket and pulls it out.

'I switched it off before we left the M25, so it won't be traceable here. I'll give it back to you when you've heard my confession, and I've answered all of your questions. And then you'll be able to choose what happens next.'

My eyes don't leave the phone as he rests it on the log beside him.

'What do you remember of that day?' he asks, but I don't want to think about any of that, so I remain silent. 'Okay, how about I tell you what I remember? Your parents really weren't happy when they found us alone in your room. And even though we

..firmed nothing had happened, your dad phoned mine,
 rbade you from seeing me again. I protested my innocence
to my parents, but they said I should make more of an effort with
girls my own age. They couldn't see how in love with you I was.'
His lips form a regretful smile.

'When you told me you'd sneak to the park on the Saturday, I
could barely contain my excitement. I knew I would treasure
every second that you were with me, and I was ready to tell you
how I felt, and how I would wait as long as it took for you to feel
the same way.'

I'm struggling not to empathise with him, remembering that
shy and awkward teenager, but then I remind myself of why we're
here and bury those feelings.

'I saw you arriving as soon as you passed the old well, and I
was so happy, and then I saw you'd brought your sister with you.
It was like someone had burst my bubble. I'd been so sure of how
the day would play out, but I wouldn't be able to talk to you with
her hanging around. It made me question whether you didn't
trust me to be alone with you.'

'Don't throw this back on me,' I quickly snap. 'I explained why
Faye was there; my parents gave me no choice.'

'I know, I know,' he hastens to add, raising his hands in a
passive gesture. 'I didn't blame you then, and I don't blame you
now. I just want you to understand where my head was at when
all of this was happening. Okay? Can I continue?'

I reluctantly nod, wishing he'd given me my phone back so I
could record his confession.

'I could see she was riling you, and that's why I suggested we
should take her to the playground. I figured, if she found some
other children her age she'd go off with them so we'd be alone,
but I couldn't get a word in edgeways the way the two of you were
bickering.'

I open my mouth to interrupt, but he keeps speaking.

'You were. She was pushing your buttons. Every time you came near to me, she was making snide comments, and just being an awkward brat. I could see how frustrated you were, and I felt so sorry that she was ruining what should have been a really special moment for us. And then when she threatened to run home and tell your parents, something in your eyes changed. It was like a red mist descended or something and you charged at her. She was already falling backwards before I could react and then, do you remember the way she screeched when she caught her head on that rock? That shriek still returns to me in my darkest nightmares.'

I can hear it echoing in my own head, and I bite down to stop the tears breaking free.

'Your demeanour changed in an instant. You were straight by her side, checking if she was okay, and desperately sorry for what had happened. I remember you saying that you should take her home, but she sat up and pushed you backwards, and then took off, running into the tall grass. I remember saying we should go after her, but your reaction was so blasé. Do you remember what you said to me?'

I remember thinking how unfair it was that my parents had forced me to take her with me, and how they were dictating who I could be friends with.

'You said, "Fuck it. If I'm going to get in trouble anyway, I might as well get something out of it." It was then you took my hand and started kissing me, and I'll be honest, I quickly forgot about your sister as well.' He pauses, staring down at the ground between his feet. 'I wish she had gone straight home to tell your parents.'

I echo the thought, but I don't see how this would lead to him pushing her into the quarry.

'I started to worry when she hadn't returned with them after twenty minutes,' I say, the ghost of the memory forced into my mind's eye.

'It was when we split up to look for her, I found her hunched over crying. I tried to help her; tried to be like a big brother. She snuggled into my chest, and I managed to calm her, and told her I would walk her back to find you, but she refused to go, saying she didn't feel safe being around you. She asked me to protect her, and I said I would. I told her you'd be getting worried, and she said she didn't care. She said she was going to hide out until dark and then walk home so your parents would be angry and probably ground you for a few weeks. She was so spiteful, and I dreaded the idea of not being able to see you for that long.'

That definitely sounds like the kind of thing Faye would have said, but although she would have threatened it, she'd have been home the moment the sun started to set, because she was terrified of being out alone in the dark.

'Why didn't you tell me any of this at the time?' I croak.

'Because I was playing along with her plan. She made me promise not to tell you I'd seen her. I begged her to come back with me, but she refused, and so I walked back to the clearing to wait for you.'

I narrow my eyes but I can't see his whole face because of the angle he's sitting at. In my head, I was expecting him to confess to killing her, so I'm thrown by what he's said.

'You left her in the woods?'

'I knew where she was, and I figured that if I sent you back to your parents to look for her, I'd be able to convince her to come back with me, and then your parents would stop thinking of me as a threat, and instead as the guy who rescued your sister, or whatever. I know it sounds stupid now, but back then I really believed it. I was so desperate for your parents to like me that I would have done literally anything.'

I don't want to ask the next question, but I can't stop myself.

'So, why didn't you bring her back, if that was your big plan?'

'When I went back to her, I told her she'd had her fun and games, but she still refused to come with me. I told her she would get you in a lot of trouble and she said she didn't care. She said I was too good for you, and the sooner we split up, the better. I tried to reason with her. I told her how much I cared for you, and how one day I'd be her brother when you married me, but this only seemed to make her angrier. She started screaming, and it was all I could do to keep her quiet. I tried putting my hand over her mouth, but then she kicked my shin with her heel, and said she was going to tell your parents that I tried to have sex with her, and then they'd get the police involved and I'd never see you again. I couldn't believe such venom was coming out of her mouth.'

Right now, I have no choice but to accept that he's telling the truth, as I have no way of verifying whether this was an argument they had.

'I pleaded for her not to mess things up, but then she started laughing at me, and said she would only agree if I got down on my knees and begged her. I was getting desperate by this point and was worried that a random passerby would get the wrong idea if they heard her scream out again. So, I did as she asked, and I clambered down onto my hands and knees.'

I don't know if this is purely for effect, but I watch him drop onto his knees now, in front of the log.

'I begged her to stop messing around, and I promised I would buy her something if she agreed to keep quiet about you and me meeting and you pushing her over. She then reached up and touched the back of her head and showed me the blood on her fingertips. She told me she didn't want me to buy her anything, but she would keep quiet if I agreed to break up with you. It sounded so juvenile, but I thought if I could convince her that I would go through with it, then she would agree to drop all the trouble for you. I thought if I walked her back to your house and told you I didn't want to see you again, then everything would be sorted with you and your parents. And then I thought I could fix it when I saw you before school the following week.'

I don't like how much closer he now is since sliding off the log, and so I lift the tyre iron into his eyeline, and he reluctantly shuffles back into his place.

'She initially agreed, and I started standing, and we walked back out towards the clearing. I figured you were probably back at your house by this point, and your parents would be going crazy, so I wanted to get her back there as soon as I could, but she grabbed my hand and pulled me towards her, and before I knew it she was kissing me. I swear I didn't know she was going to do it, and I had to push her off me. I demanded what she thought she was doing, and she smiled coyly and said as I was breaking up with you, I was now free to date her instead. Can you believe the insanity of it?'

I hear Graves's voice crowing in my head: *On the record, Abbey, did you know your sister was infatuated with your boyfriend?*

I really didn't know she had feelings for him, but there's no way John-Paul could know unless it was true.

'I told her that I was too old for her, but she said it would all be different once she was sixteen, and that nobody would worry that she was dating a nineteen-year-old. She told me she would keep our relationship a secret until then, and I didn't know what to say or do. The fact that she'd changed the rules so quickly made me suspect that if I tried to lie now, as soon as I told her I was lying, she'd still drop us in it with your parents. She tried to kiss me again, and I firmly told her I didn't want a relationship with her. I said the age difference was bad enough, but that it was her sister I was in love with. She burst into tears, and before I could stop her, she ran back into the woods.'

I'm not sure I can listen to any more. I do now believe he killed her, and I should just hit him with the tyre iron and avenge her death, but that wouldn't be justice. John-Paul needs to be arrested, charged and prosecuted in full view of the public. He has lied and betrayed all of us by keeping this a secret for thirty years.

'Is that why you killed her then? You thought she would ruin everything for us, and so she was better off dead? Give me my phone now.'

He shakes his head.

'No, there's so much more you need to understand before I do that.'

36

I am so cold now that I can barely feel my fingers. It's tempting to suggest we reconvene this conversation back in the warmth of the Land Rover, but I don't want to let him get that close to me ever again.

'I caught up with her pretty quickly,' he says, his face a mess of remorse and fatigue. 'I grabbed her by the arm, and asked her not to ruin everything. She was sobbing at this point, and told me it didn't matter what I said any more. She was going to tell everyone that I tried to assault her and that even if the police didn't arrest me, everyone would find out what a sleaze I was. It was like a nightmare playing out before my eyes, but I decided to call her bluff, and turned my back, walking away instead. I remember thinking how much I wished you didn't have a sister to complicate everything. But she ran up behind me and hit my head with a fallen branch. I didn't mean for my hand to swing out, but I was trying to defend myself, and I caught her cheek. She started laughing and proceeded to hit me with the branch again until I smacked it out of her hand.

'Her cheek was glowing pink and when she noticed it was

stinging, she laughed harder, telling me how your dad would have me arrested for hitting his daughter, and so I rushed towards her, desperate for her to stop laughing, but then she stumbled over something and fell to the floor again. I started to walk away, but stopped when she didn't get up to follow me. She was just lying there, and I thought she was pretending to be hurt to annoy me, but she was silent. Frustrated, I walked back to her. Her eyes were closed and she looked like she was sleeping. I told her to stop messing about and get up, but she didn't move. I figured I'd just lift her up and carry her back to the clearing, but as I crouched I saw blood was flowing from the back of her head. I guess the fall had worsened the previous trauma.'

I clench my jaw, suppressing the urge to scream out and sob. I fight to keep the growing pool of tears at bay.

'I shook her, trying to get her to wake, but she wasn't moving. It was all her fault. If she'd listened to me, she wouldn't have hit her head. I wanted to run away and pretend nothing had happened, but I thought if you came past and saw her you'd assume I was responsible, so I panicked and decided I should hide her. That way, when she was found, I would be far away and nobody would connect the dots. It was an accident. You can see that, right?'

When I returned to the clearing after discovering she wasn't at home, John-Paul did look uncomfortable, but I never imagined what he was hiding. I just thought he was as worried as me about how my parents would react to her running off.

'Please, Abbey, you have to understand what I was going through at the time. I didn't mean to hurt her, but it just kind of happened, and I panicked.'

'How did she end up in the quarry?' I ask, my voice cracking under the strain.

'I knew there was a hole in the fence, because I knew some

lads who used to go through to smoke weed. I carried her over and put her just inside the hole, figuring they'd find her when they next stopped by. But she started moaning, and I realised she wasn't dead. I was so relieved, and I tried to help her. She was crying because her head hurt so much, but I told her everything would be okay and that I'd call for an ambulance to help her, but she started accusing me of hurting her on purpose. She told me she was going to tell you what I'd done and then you would finish with me. I tried to reason with her, but she said she was going to tell everyone I pushed her over on purpose.'

John-Paul drops to his knees again, and starts shuffling towards me.

'I don't remember exactly how it happened,' he says, his face screwed up in confusion. 'She was shouting and trying to hit me, and then it's kind of a blank. My eyes were closed, and when I opened them, she was just lying there, her eyes motionless.'

'Sasha said shirt fibres were recovered from around her neck; that doesn't just happen. You have to have removed your shirt and coiled the sleeve around her throat.'

He's still shuffling towards me, and it's enough to force me to my feet. Pins and needles quickly spike at my feet, but I'm able to hobble over my log and put distance between us.

'I – I don't know how it happened,' he says, wailing now. 'One minute she was hitting me and the next... I don't remember.'

I spy my phone over on the log he has vacated, and I don't hesitate, sprinting off towards it, before he has time to realise where I'm going, but he does see and as I bend to scoop it up, his full weight crashes into the side of me and sends me flying across the bark chippings and twigs.

'What are you doing?' I hear him groan from somewhere beyond the log. 'I haven't finished yet. The deal was you could have your phone when I'm finished.'

'Semantics!' I holler back. 'Do you really expect me to feel sorry for you? Is that what this is all about? You want me to forgive you and tell you everything is going to be okay? Well, it isn't okay, John-Paul. You fucking murdered my sister!'

His head suddenly appears above the log, startling me.

'But I did it for *you*, Abbey. I did it for *us*.'

I can't believe he's trying to lay the blame at my door again.

'I never asked you to kill my sister,' I grizzle.

'But I heard you tell her you wished she hadn't been born. People don't say shit like that unless they really mean it.'

'It was in the heat of the moment. I didn't *mean* it. I didn't want her dead.'

'No, but she was going to ruin everything for us. What should I have done?'

'You should have just told me where she was when you first located her. I would have convinced her to come back to the house.'

'No,' he says, standing now and waving his arm in my direction. 'You didn't hear what she was saying about you. She said she hated you and would do everything she could to make sure that you couldn't be with me.'

'That doesn't make it right to kill her. We were children, for Christ's sake, John-Paul. How can you not see how wrong this was?'

'You think I don't know it was wrong? She haunts my dreams most nights. But there's nothing I can do about it now. I can't bring her magically back to life.'

'No, but you could have admitted what had happened back then. Terry Anderson has spent the last thirty years in prison because you didn't.'

He's pointing at me again.

'No, no, no, that was your fault, not mine. You were the one who told the police you'd seen him in the woods. I told you we shouldn't blame someone else, but you *begged* me to go along with it. You made me tell the police that I'd seen him too. I did that for you, because I loved you, Abbey.'

I try to sit up, but I'm so cold that it's a struggle to even prop myself on my elbow. I don't like how close John-Paul is now, and I want to wave the tyre iron in his direction, but I can't move.

He leans down and snatches it from my hand, before hurling it away into the darkness. He then places his hands on my upper arms, and lifts me up into a standing position.

'We are responsible,' he says to me firmly, squeezing my arms. 'Let me hear you say it.'

'You k-killed my sister,' I stammer.

'No, Abbey, *we* killed her. Don't you see? Haven't I explained it well enough? You pushed her first, and then I finished the job.'

'She was st-still alive after I pushed her.'

'Technically, yes, but you don't know she wouldn't have died as a result of her cut head. She could have had concussion for all you know. And if the police had found out you pushed her, you'd have spent the best part of your life behind bars. But I saved you from that scenario.'

'How did she end up in the quarry?' I ask again. 'What did you do after you choked her?'

His brow ruffles at the question.

'I moved her to the edge of the quarry hole and rolled her in, of course. I figured the police would assume she'd snuck through the hole in the fence to hide and had then tripped or stumbled into it. In the days and weeks that followed, I was certain the police would come calling for me. But they believed our lie about seeing Anderson, and I started to believe that things would work out in the end.'

I hear Detective Roach's voice in the back of my head: *Someone else has come forward to reveal you lied about seeing Anderson in the woods.*

'W-why did you tell the police I lied about seeing Anderson?'

'Because I panicked. When you just showed up at the practice, and said someone was threatening to spill what had happened, it suddenly felt like I was going to be found out. I was terrified, so I took you for lunch so I could try and find out as much as I could about how much they knew, and how much they'd told you. That's why I drove us to Southampton that day. I was more desperate than you to know who had witnessed what had happened.'

'So, did you even speak to your detective friend whilst I was asleep?'

'Yes, I did. He was there, I swear. But I was glad you weren't, because it meant I was able to ask him things I wouldn't have with you around. We spoke off the record, and he was adamant that we should get ahead of it and speak to the police. But I couldn't convince you, so I had no other choice.'

'You told them I killed Faye and then colluded with the police to cover it up.'

'And I'm sorry, but if it's a choice between protecting you and protecting Vanessa, it's no contest.'

'What does your wife have to do with this?'

'I told you, she supports various humanitarian projects across the globe. She's almost as famous as Greta Thunberg. How will it look if her husband is arrested on suspicion of murder? It would ruin her, and the knock-on effect is that desperate people around the world will suffer more.'

'And what about my future and career? I've spent the last three decades believing it was my push that killed her. You son of a bitch!'

'I know, I know, and I'm sorry, but I wouldn't survive in prison.'

I try to shake off his grip, but he's stronger than he looks.

'Listen,' he says, squeezing tighter, 'I have a plan that will fix all of this. That's why I brought us here.'

I'm not following his train of thought, and the torch has been knocked out of position from when he leapt across the pit, so I can see even less of our surroundings.

'I don't understand. What is this place?'

'You mean you *don't* recognise it? We're home, Abbey. It was these woods where you and I used to sneak off and meet. It is these woods where... where Faye died.'

37

If it wasn't for John-Paul holding me up, my entire body would crumple to the floor. I knew there was something familiar, but when I was briefly here yesterday, the floor and branches were covered in a layer of snow, and it looks so different bare and in the dark.

'Why would you bring us back here?' I ask, but he's no longer in a conversational mood.

Instead, he places my feet on the floor and links his arm through mine.

'Don't worry, it isn't far.'

He collects the torch from the floor and shines it into the trees beyond the clearing. Not even idle curiosity would want me to see the exact spot where he tried to choke my sister with his shirt, but I have no fight left in me. I didn't see what he did with my phone, but am assuming it must be in one of his trouser pockets again. My only chance of escape is to get hold of my phone and make an emergency call to get help.

'Hey, listen,' I try. 'I don't need to see where it happened. You've told me what you did, and how sorry you are, and I believe you. Why don't we head back to your car, and then we can drive together to a police station and tell them everything.'

'No, because then Vanessa's name will be tarred.'

'Okay, okay, how about you drive *me* to the police station and I'll tell them I did it. You've described your actions in enough detail that I reckon I could make them my own. That way, Vanessa's reputation remains intact, and the two of you can live happily ever after.'

'You'd really do that for me?'

'Yes, John-Paul. Come on, let's go there now.'

He stops and fixes me with a firm stare.

'You must really think I was born yesterday. If I take you to the police station you'll blame it all on me, and tell them that I abducted you too. No, that doesn't work.'

'What is your master plan then?'

He doesn't answer, dragging me further into the darkness, and the deeper we go, the greater my fear rises. Sasha knows I was in his car, but she wouldn't necessarily think he would bring me back to Ashford with him. If he is planning to kill and bury me, I may never be found. With Graves sharing his notes with the police, everyone will just assume I couldn't live with the guilt and ran away.

He drags me through a nest of intertwined branches and suddenly I see the large metal fence, and the large sign tied to it warning trespassers will be prosecuted. I try to pull back, but he swings me into the clearing and I collapse to the floor, thorns and stones grazing my palms. He doesn't seem to care, proceeding to the fence, before extracting something from his jacket pocket. A moment later something snaps, and I see now he is clipping a fresh hole in the fence. With his back to me, I should try and run, but without the torch, I have no way of finding my way back to the car.

I scramble my fingers around in the dirt before me, but all I can feel is limp leaves and twigs until I touch something smooth and cold. I coil my fingers around the large shape, measuring its mass in my palm. It won't do as much damage as the tyre iron would have, but if I strike him right, it might buy me enough time to get away. I quickly scurry it behind me as the torch beam falls on me and I see he is watching.

'It won't be long until we're through and then you'll have that choice to make.'

His attention returns to snipping the wire fence. I roll onto my side and then force myself back onto my feet, the heavy stone gripped tightly in my right hand, but when I see his balding crown, I can't do it. Despite everything John-Paul has done, I don't have it in me to kill him. What if I hit him too hard and he dies? Or what if I don't hit him hard enough and he retaliates, choking me as he did my sister?

One thing I'm sure of is I don't want to crawl through that fence with him.

Just as I'm about to raise the stone over my head, he shines the torch into my eyes and I lose momentum as I'm forced to look away. He pulls the fence up at one side, the aluminium creaking under the strain, and then he grabs my sleeve and pulls me towards the fence.

'I don't want to!' I shout.

'You don't have a choice, Abbey. This is where it has to happen.'

He steps behind me, and pushes me through and I collapse the other side, dangerously close to the edge of the dark pit. He then steps through and squats down beside me.

Did Faye feel this vulnerable when she awoke and saw what he was planning?

'Here we are,' he says, tilting his head in an empathetic manner. 'This is where it happened.'

I picture my sister, dazed and confused, wondering whether she knew she was about to die.

'How does that make you feel, Abbey?'

'I feel sorry,' I say. 'Sorry that I wasn't a better sister to Faye; sorry that I ever brought you into our circle; sorry that I didn't go after her; sorry that I allowed you to get away with it for this long.'

'Good, good,' he says, his voice rising an octave. 'I bet you'd like nothing more than to kill me right now. Right?'

'What? No, I don't want to kill you, John-Paul.'

'Of course you do! I killed your sister and I left you blaming yourself. Avenge her death!'

I don't like how he's now leaning closer, and the manic look in his eyes.

'You know you want to; you know Faye would want you to get vengeance.'

'No,' I scream back at him. 'She deserves justice, and killing you isn't justice. You need to be tried by a jury of your peers, and then sentenced. That's the only thing my sister would want.'

He rolls his eyes and an elongated groan escapes.

'No, I am not going to prison. I already told you that won't help Vanessa and all the good causes she supports.'

'And killing you would?'

'It would do a damn sight more than humiliating her in the press.'

I'm not following his logic, though I sense he has been planning this for longer than the last few days.

'But you'd still be guilty of killing my sister and perverting the course of justice.'

'That's as may be, but Vanessa will be able to deny all knowledge of it. At first she'll be vilified, but once the public learn I was executed by the victim's sister, they'll start to feel sorry for her, and then they'll gather and raise her back up to the heights she's at. That's the only way this works.'

Heavy rain has started falling, and with the temperature this low, I don't imagine it will be long before it turns to hail or snow.

'I am not going to kill you, John-Paul. Despite everything, I still care for you, and I want to help ensure you receive a fair trial.'

He throws his arms up in the air and walks off in frustration.

'I confessed to you so you'd want to kill me. What more can I do?'

'You can drive us to a police station and tell them—'

'No!'

He yells so loud that I actually jump backwards.

'One of us must die here today, Abbey. I don't want it to be you, but if you refuse to kill me, then you leave me no other choice.'

'What will killing me help?'

'Think about it: the police already know you pushed your sister and cut her head. I will simply tell them you forced me to drive here, confessed to killing her, and then took your own life.'

I feel winded.

'You're fucking insane.'

'No, I'm not, I'm just pragmatic. I told you: I won't survive in prison. So, the choice is yours. Kill me, or I'm going to kill you.'

The fat raindrops are now bashing against the uneven ground, sounding like bullets fired through a sound-suppresser.

He charges towards me, and I quickly sidestep, but he shines the torch into my eyes again, and I lose my bearings. His shoulder collides into my midriff, and the stone falls from my hand. Before I can react, he crawls on top of me, pinning my legs with his body and my wrists with his hands.

I try to raise my knee to catch him in the groin, but he is much taller than me, and his bottom prevents me bending my legs. I blink as the raindrops splash against my face.

His body weight suddenly shifts, and he releases my wrists, only to press his large hands around my throat. The sudden pressure is overwhelming, and I picture younger Faye in this same position.

Did she feel this helpless too? Did she try to fight back?

I swing my arms at his, but the contact does nothing to ease their rigidity. I try stretching up and clawing at his face, but my fingertips barely make contact with his chin. I try wriggling my legs, but my efforts are in vain.

I begin to choke, my airway totally blocked, and I've never wanted a fresh breath more in my entire life. I continue to swing my limbs at him, but they feel like heavy logs as my vision blurs.

Is this it? Is this how my story is going to end?

I have one last play to try, and I close my eyes, and stop wriggling. If I can convince him I'm already dead, then maybe I'll buy myself a few more seconds to think of a fresh plan. My chest is burning as I will the milliseconds to quickly pass.

I must temporarily pass out, because the next thing I feel is something pulling on my wet hair. It's him dragging me across the mud towards the edge of the quarry. I grip my hands around the hair at my crown and yank back, ends splitting as I struggle for control. His grip slips and I stop moving, but it's all I can do to dig my feet into the ground and try to swivel my body around. I see him, with the torch raised above his head, ready to strike me. I manage to roll onto my side, but not quick enough and feel the full force of the torch's edge against my cheek.

38

I scream out in agony, but it's the adrenaline shot my body needs, and I manage to kick out my legs, catching John-Paul's shins. He falls to his knees, and I quickly sit up, throwing a fist at his face. I must catch his jaw as my knuckle immediately erupts in a hot shooting pain, and he falls sideways. I am so exhausted, but I manage to push him onto his back and search his pockets for my phone.

'Finish me,' I hear him slur in the darkness, but I ignore his request, and locate his keys.

I can no longer see the torch, which must mean it broke when he hit me with it. My wet and muddy fingers struggle to type the PIN into my phone, and then he grabs my wrist with a firm hand.

'No, you can't go,' he says, but the words are difficult to understand.

I can't break his grip on my wrist, so I use my left elbow, to slam against his chest, and the shock of the move causes him to release his grip. I push myself up and off him, and use the faint glow of my phone's security screen to guide me towards the opening in the fence. I hear him groaning after me, as I duck through the gap. My phone finally accepts the number, and the screen fills with my apps. I swipe my thumb down the screen and stab at the torch app. The ground immediately before me is showered in bright white light, but as I hurry towards the tree line, I can't see where we came through. There are no obvious gaps, so I can't be sure how to make it back to the curved pathway and where he abandoned the car.

I press the key remote, straining to hear the sound of it unlocking, but I can't hear anything over the hail. I hear a sound behind me, and as I spin around, the light falls on John-Paul, dragging himself through the fence. I don't hesitate, running straight at the trees, twisting my body one way and then the next, trying to squeeze through the narrowest of gaps. The phone's light helps me see the trees before I walk into them, but it's also going to show John-Paul exactly where I am, so I take the decision to switch it off, casting everything into total darkness once again. I keep trying to recall whether he pulled me through here in a straight line, or whether there were any turns, but my memory fails me.

I hear him yelping and branches snapping as he reaches the tree line. I can only estimate how far he is behind me, but I need to increase the distance. My mobile vibrates in my hand, notifying me of missed calls and messages from Sasha, but if I stop to call her, he'll be on me. Branches scratch at my cheeks like bony fingers and nails, but I don't stop, my breathing becoming heavier, as there seems to be no end to the trees.

What if I'm going in the wrong direction, and he gets back to the car first?

The paranoid thought isn't helpful, but I don't remember us moving through the dense trees for this long.

I almost fall out into the clearing as there's a sudden break in the branches. I can just about make out the row of logs surrounding firepits, but I don't know which of the areas we were sitting at. I don't have time to think, and hurry between two sets of logs, daring to turn my phone's light on only long enough to search behind me for John-Paul. He hasn't appeared in the clearing yet, and it gives me grounds for hope. I shine the light around until I see the gravel path off to my left and then hurry towards it.

The stones crackle beneath my feet and I splash through newly formed puddles, but I keep telling myself I'm going to make it. I keep the light on this time, figuring it'll be safer than missing a step and falling again. I can hear John-Paul singing out my name, begging me to return, but I try to push it out of my head.

It's almost as if I can hear Faye cheering me on from the side, urging me not to give up. I always wanted justice for my sister, and I can't let this prick get away with what he did.

And then I spot the car ahead. The interior light a beacon of hope to strive for. I make it to the passenger side, and dive in, quickly pulling it closed behind me. I scan the dashboard for anything that resembles central locking, but none of the buttons or switches look obvious, so I slide over to the driver's seat, but when I try to insert the key, there is no ignition slot.

I can feel the panic rising in my neck, picturing John-Paul making it back to the car and dragging me out, but then I spot the Start-Stop button, and stab my thumb against it. The engine revs in an instant. The soles of my trainers are caked in mud, and slip off the pedals, but I adjust and reverse the car in an arc, searching for the roadway we must have come in on. I hear the car automatically engage the locks, and I put the car in park, reaching for my phone to try and call Sasha back, but my phone says it has no signal. I drop the phone onto the dashboard and drive forwards, but the tyres are slipping on the ground, and it takes all my effort to keep the car moving in a straight direction. There's no sign of John-Paul coming along the footpath, which is the only thing that's going my way. I keep glancing at the phone's screen, waiting for it to get at least one bar of signal.

This appears to be a private track of some sort, as there aren't any signs offering direction or distance. I look at the screen built into the dashboard panel, keeping one eye on the road, whilst the other looks for how to engage the navigation equipment. Just when I think I've found it, my phone pings, and I slam the brakes on. Another message has come through from Sasha, and I try to call her, but the phone beeps to declare the signal has gone again.

'Damn it!' I shout in tearful frustration.

The windscreen is starting to fog with condensation, and I have no idea how to switch on the car's heating system. Nothing is where it should be, and I don't have time to find the instruction booklet.

I put the headlights on full beam, but this track is twisty, and there's no sign of any passing traffic anywhere ahead. I'm sure those are tyre tracks I can see. The car jerks to the left and right, and it's almost impossible to maintain my grasp on the steering wheel. I need to get out of here, but if I go any faster I am going to lose control. I slow to barely five miles per hour, willing time to speed up.

There is a bend just up ahead, and I begin to turn the wheel when suddenly something heavy lands on the bonnet, frightening the life out of me, and I slam the brakes on, the car juddering before it stalls.

John-Paul's swollen and bloodshot eyes stare back at me through the windscreen, and I quickly try to restart the engine, but it screams out in resistance. John-Paul slams a large rock against the windscreen and it cracks, quickly spreading out like a spider's web. He doesn't hesitate, pulling the rock back over his head once more.

The engine starts, and I slam it into reverse, and John-Paul topples off, just as he's about to bring the rock down again. The car slams into a tree trunk and the airbag explodes out of the steering wheel and splats against my face. I'm dazed, but I don't have time to think about my options.

Quickly putting it back into first gear, I smack my muddy foot against the accelerator pedal. Up ahead, John-Paul has risen to his feet, and stretches out his legs and arms in an effort to block my path. I don't want to hit him but he leaves me little choice. He tries to dive out of the way last minute, but not before the front of the car catches his hip. I battle with the wheel as the car slips and slides, but I don't stop to check on him.

The driver's side of the car collides with a tree as I make the bend, and I'm sure that's a road up ahead, so I floor the accelerator, but the last crack must have done something to the axle, because the steering wheel is turning in my hands, but there's nothing I can do to prevent the head-on collision with the enormous trunk ahead of me.

39

I jerk awake, the taste of the wet mud still lingering in my nostrils. For the briefest moment I'm still in the car, hearing John-Paul's voice calling out after me, but then I blink and see that I'm lying in a bed, the smell of cleaning fluid heavy in the air.

I try to sit up, but my back feels as though I've been lying on a bed of nails for days. There is an oxygen mask over my mouth and nose, and a regular beeping sound somewhere nearby.

Either I'm in a hospital or I'm dead, though the former seems more likely.

How on earth did I make it to hospital?

I start at the sound of a chair scraping on the hard floor. I'm not alone. I momentarily dread the prospect that John-Paul is waiting to finish the job. But then I see Sasha's beautiful face and frizzy hair, and the relief brings me to tears. She won't let anything bad happen to me.

'Hey there, how are you feeling?' her sweet, angelic voice says.

'I've been better,' I croak, but the words are barely audible.

Sasha reaches to the side and a moment later presses a paper straw between my dry lips. I take a sip, but the water is warm and stale, and I grimace.

'I'll ask the nurse for a fresh jug when she returns,' Sasha says. 'The police are going to want to speak to you soon, so it would be a good idea to try and rest and recuperate.'

The police? They still think I killed Faye.

'Tell them to arrest John-Paul,' I say quickly.

She presses a cool hand against my chest, gently pushing me back down.

'You don't need to worry about that. They have him under observation in the room next door. When the two of you didn't show up at the office last night, I worried, and started tracking your phone through an app on mine. I couldn't understand why you were heading down the A40 and then onto the M25. I tried phoning several times, assuming the two of you must have uncovered a fresh lead. But when you didn't answer your phone, nor respond to my messages, I figured something bad must have happened.'

Bless her suspicious mind. I think that's why the two of us have always got on so well.

'Wait, John-Paul said he switched off my phone at some services. How did you figure out where I was?'

She pulls a face like a child about to admit they broke a parent's favourite antique.

'Don't be mad. I phoned that Detective Roach who you said interviewed you. I told him you and John-Paul were absconding to avoid further trouble. I didn't know what else to say. When I initially told him you were in trouble and in need of help, he was dismissive. I figured he'd have more resources to track you. They managed to get the car details from DVLA and used ANPR to track the car to Southampton, and I told him about your weekend trip to Ashford, and he said he would alert some colleagues to pick you up. When your phone pinged back on, they were able to narrow your location.'

'I need to speak to them,' I splutter. 'John-Paul, he... he admitted to killing Faye.'

'Oh my God, really? When the police found you both in the early hours, they could see there'd been an altercation between the two of you, but he's not regained consciousness yet. I over-heard two of the officers talking by the vending machines, saying they thought you'd found out that John-Paul had dropped you in it, and you attempted to run him over as revenge.'

The impact of the airbag bursting in my face floats into my mind's eye.

'I don't know if it was your intention, but his car's a write-off by all accounts.'

This brings momentary joy, but quickly evaporates, when I think about all that Faye missed out on because of John-Paul's panic and unforgiveable behaviour.

I press my left hand to my forehead, wincing as my thumb catches my cheek.

'Ooh, yeah, you want to be careful. They had to stitch a nasty cut on your cheek. The good news is there's nothing so serious that you won't recover from apparently. But you're going to need to take it easy for a few days. No work, just bed and lots of rest.'

I move my hand to my neck, and it feels swollen and sore.

'The police will want to take pictures of your injuries.'

'Is it bad?' I ask, barely able to control the emotion.

Sasha fishes a compact mirror from her bag and holds it out in front of me. There is banana-like colouring beneath both eyes, a purplish burn covering my left cheek stretching beneath my ear. And my neck and collarbone are red raw, but bruising in places too.

'H-he tried to strangle me,' I say, my voice breaking, and Sasha gently nods. 'The same way he did with Faye.'

Sasha rests a hand over mine.

'Do you want me to go and fetch one of the officers, so you can tell them everything?'

It sounds so absurd that I'm not sure they'll believe me, but I want to give a full account whilst it's still fresh in my mind. I want to see John-Paul prosecuted to the length of the law. I owe Faye that much.

'Please,' I say, but then see Sasha dab at her eyes with a tissue.

It's only now I notice how visibly upset she looks. She's always so full of energy that she's barely recognisable as a muted version of herself.

'I'll be fine,' I say, squeezing her hand. 'We'll be fine. I mean, the business will probably go up in flames when the truth about Faye's murder comes out, but I'm not going to run from account-ability any more. I'm going to make sure that the right man is punished for killing her.'

'I will support you in any way you need. *And*, if you're willing to consider the television production company's offer, they've said they're willing to offer a percentage of your payment upfront, and that should be enough to cover the rent for at least the next twelve months.'

I can see the enthusiasm back in her eyes, and as loath as I am to host a television show, it would serve as a good platform to bring justice for so many others. If I have my pick of the cases to be reviewed, it will be the job I still remember but with a far larger budget and support. Faye was always the one who craved the limelight and saw herself as a future actress. And maybe if I channel her energy, I can help make her dream come true vicariously.

The next few hours pass by in a blur, with nurses and doctors in white coats running various tests, and then Roach arrives with two uniformed officers and interrogates me for over an hour. I give him as much detail as I can recall about last night, and although I'm not totally sure I've convinced him, I will fight with every breath.

I'm exhausted by the time dinner arrives, and although the steamed vegetables and cottage pie look like they've come straight out of a microwave, I wolf it down. I'm just about dropping off when I receive another visitor that I'm not expecting.

Eddie Douglas enters, bringing a whiff of smoke with him.

'Mind if I sit down?' he asks, not waiting for a response, scraping a chair across the tiled floor, and dropping into it.

He reaches into his inner jacket pocket and passes me an open envelope.

'What's this?'

'Just read it.'

I lift the flap and extract a single sheet of paper. It's a hand-written letter addressed to me. I don't understand what I'm reading at first, but then I look at Eddie, and see he's ashen-faced.

'It's from Damian,' I say, and he simply nods.

I return to reading. It is a detailed confession to Rodrigo's murder, summarising everything he told me at the cemetery on Monday. He says he wants me to deliver it to Rodrigo's family and pass on his deepest regrets, but only once his mother has passed away.

'I don't understand,' I say. 'Why can't he tell them himself...?'

My words trail off as I see the grave look on Eddie's face. My hand shoots up to my mouth.

'Oh, God, no, tell me he didn't...'

'Damian's body was discovered at South Ealing Cemetery last night beside the grave of his husband. They tried to revive him, but he'd taken a cocktail of painkillers and vodka and passed away in his sleep. I found a note in my mailbox this morning, instructing me to deliver this letter to you at the earliest opportunity. I read the letter first, so I understand what he wants you to do. I guess it really wasn't your fault he withdrew from the civil case.'

He looks angry, but I sense it isn't because of the lack of a payday.

'I think you should do as he asks,' Eddie says, unable to make eye contact. 'Rodrigo's family deserve to know how their son died, but is it worth trampling on an ailing mother's memories when a short delay avoids that? Obviously, I won't mention this meeting to anyone else, I'm just a messenger.'

I don't know why, but I feel as though I owe Eddie an apology.

'Listen, I heard through the grapevine that you're having a bit of bother with the police. If you need any help, I'm happy to step in. No charge for friends.'

And then he stands and leaves the room without another word, and I bury my face in the bedsheet and let the tears flow.

EPILOGUE

I don't go home to change after Damian's cremation, instead returning to the office ahead of my final appointment of the day. I'm not surprised that none of Rodrigo's family were at the service, and it was a relief not having to hide the truth from them. I'm still wrestling with Damian's final request, but every time I think I should go and speak to them, I hear Eddie's words in my head, and resist. Mrs Johnson doesn't have long left and with the passing of her son, I sense her time on earth has shortened significantly. I remember how much my parents suffered after losing Faye and I'm convinced it robbed them of years. Rodrigo's family will demand answers and probably publicly seek restitution and that will almost certainly be the final nail in her coffin. For now, Damian's letter will remain locked in the office safe.

And that is where I'm returning now. Ten days have passed since John-Paul confessed to murdering Faye. He remained unconscious for three days, and it turned out my hitting him with the car resulted in a leg fractured in three places, which required pins to reset it. I don't want to admit how satisfying it was to learn that, even if it is less than he really deserves.

A lawful search of his house uncovered a small wooden chest in his loft, and when it was unlatched, they found the same yellow and navy Ben Sherman shirt he'd worn that day. It should be enough to prove he was the one who tried to strangle her when they match it to the fibres originally recovered from her neck. Roach has also confided droplets of blood have been recovered from the forensic check of the shirt, and if that's a match to Faye's DNA then the CPS will agree to prosecute.

They can't currently charge him with Faye's murder until Anderson is acquitted, and that could take several months, owing to the snail-like speed the justice system moves at. To my relief, John-Paul's request for bail was denied owing to the high possibility that he might try to flee the country.

His wife's picture has been on the front cover of every tabloid for the last week, but I refuse to read any of their conjecture. If she has any sense she'll apply for divorce and distance herself from him as much as she can.

I sit down in my chair, and Freud hops up onto my lap, and begins to lick at his paw. I ruffle the fur on the top of his head, grateful that I won't be alone for my next call.

I know Peter Graves has been trying to get hold of me since I was discharged from hospital, but I've kept him at arm's length until now. I've decided I will do what I can to support Anderson's appeal, so that John-Paul can be properly tried for what he did to Faye.

But that isn't what I want to talk to him about. I understand why he felt compelled to follow me and pressure me to reveal what really happened that day. I don't agree that he did it in the right way, but I believe his motivation was legitimate. It's his continued relationship with Terry Anderson that worries me. Like Faye, he has been the victim of a manipulative monster, and it doesn't sit well with me to not speak up for him.

I'm not convinced that he'll be prepared to listen to what I have to say, but I'm not going to give up on him. What he did to me was scary, and I worry that under Anderson's influence he could wind up crossing a line from which there is no way back. Sasha thinks I'm crazy for even wanting to try, but my desire to find justice for all means I have to try.

The line rings several times, before it connects.

* * *

MORE FROM M. A. HUNTER

The Teacher's Pet, another pulse-pounding psychological thriller from M. A. Hunter, is available to order now here:
    https://mybook.to/TeachersPetBackAd

ACKNOWLEDGEMENTS

Thank you so much for reading *The Confession*, and for sticking around to read this final word from me.

I always worry about what to write in my acknowledgements ahead of publication day, especially after nearly 30 published books. I never know how many people actually read this part of the book, or pay any attention to it, but I still want to keep it original and not just a copy and paste of every other acknowledgement I've ever written.

This time, it feels more poignant than usual, and that's because two weeks ago I had a heart attack, and for the first real time in my life, I'm conscious of my own mortality. The moment the doctors and nurses rushed me through to the resuscitation area of A&E at Southampton General Hospital, I can remember praying that this wasn't the end. For most of my life I've feared the idea of dying, but it wasn't the fear of no longer being around that was driving my prayers, it was the prospect that I wouldn't be around to watch my children growing; it was the thought of not being there to walk my daughter down the aisle one day; it was the fear of not being able to pass on parental advice to my son.

Spoiler alert: I survived the heart attack!

Thanks to the epic efforts of the myriad of doctors and nurses (too many faces and too much panic to actually recall any of their names) who worked on me that day, I had two stents fitted to widen one of my arteries. Two days later I had a further four stents fitted to widen my remaining arteries. If not for the quick-thinking and dedication of those doctors and nurses, I wouldn't be writing this today.

So, that is why this book is dedicated to all the staff who looked after me during my brief stay on the Coronary Care Unit at Southampton's General Hospital. The empathy and care shown by each of the doctors, nurses, catering staff, and cleaners is immeasurable. Thank you all from the bottom of my heart.

Sadly, recovery from a heart attack is not a quick journey. I am now in week two of a 6–8-week recovery period, and am dictating this acknowledgement using voice software. That means, I am not allowed to undertake any activities that might raise my heartrate. And as I'm sure you can imagine, the plots and twists that appear in my novels are not for the faint of heart. Please, rest assured that I will take my recovery seriously, so that I will bounce back stronger (and possibly darker) than ever.

Thank you for reading *The Confession*. Please do post a review to wherever you purchased the book from so that other readers can be encouraged to give it a try. It takes less than two minutes to share your opinion, and I ask you do me this small kindness. Please also tell all of your friends and family (and any other person who will listen) how great it is. And please do get in touch with me via the usual social channels to let me know what you thought about it (remember to be kind).

If this was your first read of one of my books (where the hell have you been?) then thank you for taking a chance. If you enjoyed it and want to read more, I have plenty of other, equally gripping books also available to buy online or from good bookshops.

I am fortunate enough to being taken care of by two power-house agents. While Emily Glenister is on maternity leave (and championing me from the sidelines), I'd like to say a huge thank you to Diana Beaumont for taking such great care of me this year.

They both work at the DHH Literary Agency, which is one of the best agencies in the land, and I feel honoured to be one of their clients.

Thank you also to my eagle-eyed editor, Victoria Britton, at Boldwood Books, and the whole creative team there who have treated me with compassion during my recovery, and have urged me to put my health ahead of any writing deadlines. It is such a relief to have such a talented team of editors, marketers, and publicists working with me to bring you these stories.

As always, thank you to my wife, Hannah and my children Emily and Ethan who make sure my feet remain firmly planted to the floor. It goes without saying that I wouldn't be the writer I am today without their loving support, even if I do bore the pants off them when I share the latest twist I've conjured and they have no idea who or what I'm talking about.

I remain active as time allows on the usual social media outlets (Facebook, Instagram, and TikTok), so please do stop by with any messages, observations, or questions. Hearing from readers of my books truly brightens my days and encourages me to keep writing, so don't be a stranger. I promise I *will* respond to every message and comment I receive.

Best wishes,

Stef (a.k.a. M.A. Hunter)

ABOUT THE AUTHOR

M. A. Hunter is the pen name of Stephen Edger, the bestselling author of psychological and crime thrillers, including the Kate Matthews series. Born in the north-east of England, he now lives in Southampton where many of his stories are set.

Download your exclusive bonus content from M. A. Hunter here:

Visit M. A. Hunter's website: www.anautieauthor.com

Follow M. A. Hunter on social media:

- facebook.com/anautieauthor
- x.com/anautieauthor
- instagram.com/anautieauthor
- tiktok.com/@anautieauthor
- bookbub.com/authors/stephen-edger
- goodreads.com/stephenedger

ALSO BY M. A. HUNTER

Boldwood

Boldwood Books is an award-winning fiction publishing company seeking out the best stories from around the world.

Find out more at www.boldwoodbooks.com

Join our reader community for brilliant books, competitions and offers!

Follow us
@BoldwoodBooks
@TheBoldBookClub

Sign up to our weekly deals newsletter

https://bit.ly/BoldwoodBNewsletter

www.ingramcontent.com/pod-product-compliance
Ingram Content Group UK Ltd.
Pitfield, Milton Keynes, MK11 3LW, UK
UKHW040622221225
9701UKWH00054B/1324

9 781835 617526